"Crisply written . . . this ..... debut novel ....
21st century motherhood . . . Erika Raskin captures . . . the
perils of making the private public, and the vulnerability
that comes with loving a child. Her ability to portray a
mother's love for three very different children is
uncanny."

— Alice Randall, *New York Times*
bestselling author, *The Wind Done Gone*

"Raskin's debut novel delivers witty, insightful prose, flesh
and blood characters and a compelling plot with a twist that
keeps you on the edge of your seat. A terrific read!"

— Deborah M. Prum, author, *Fatty in the
Back Seat*, a Shelf Unbound Annual Top
Twelve Notable Indie Book for Young
Adults

"…a poignant and edgy story of a divorced-family dynamic
through complex characters and the real life struggles of
parenting and adolescence…"

— *LitPick Student Book Reviews*
5 Star Rating
www.litpick.com

"Raskin's debut novel will keep you turning the pages in this turbulent family drama..."

— Jenny Gardiner, author of the Kindle #1 Bestseller, *Slim to None*

close

erika raskin

Harvard Square Editions
New York
2014

Published in the United States by
Harvard Square Editions

ISBN: 978-0-9895960-3-9

www.HarvardSquareEditions.org

Printed in the United States of America

Chapter One

Sometimes the dread was just a light tapping on the edge of awareness. Other times it was a howl in that dark space between anxiety and terror. Kik was lying in bed listening to the roar, waiting for her sixteen-year-old daughter to sneak in.

Again.

The strange maternal emotion of heartache-slash-outrage wasn't helping anything either.

Doone knows Thursday is my worst day at work!

Kik was looking at grueling back-to-back sections of Creative Writing. In the best of circumstances, teaching the class of fragile-shelled freshmen took lots of careful tiptoeing. Doing it on no sleep was going to be a crapshoot. There could be casualties all over the place.

A sudden scream pierced the quiet.

"Mother! Help me!" Tess wailed. "Hurry, hurry!"

Kik leapt up and ran into the hallway, heart charging her ribs. She almost plowed into fourteen-year-old Casey, who was also racing towards the kindergartner's room.

"What is it?" Kik panted, as she groped for the light. "What's wrong, Tess?"

"Someone is trying to get in the window!"

"Oh, honey, no, no!" Kik soothed, scooping the child into her arms. "It was only a bad dream. We're all the way up on the second floor! No one can reach up here!"

Right then there was an angry rap on the glass and the three of them jumped.

"See!" Tess cried, two parts misery, one part triumph.

"It's a branch, sweetie. It's really windy out."

"Well, I do not like it!" the five-year-old announced, pink-flannelled chest still heaving. "I would prefer if you could make the tree stop. Please and thank you."

Kik and Casey exchanged a bemused look over the little one's head. Tess's odd diction, including a staunch refusal to use contractions, cracked them up. With the exception of Doone, everyone found it endearing.

"Perhaps Sister might have a cozy in here?" Tess asked, already scooting towards the wall. "It will help me to understand that it was only the tree knocking. Not a very scary man like I was worrying."

Kik shuddered.

"I'll stay in here if you let me brush your hair tomorrow, Tessa-messa," Casey negotiated.

"We should discuss that in the morning," Tess demurred. "I am awfully tired."

"And on that note," their mother smiled, bending to kiss them. "Good night, my lovelies."

Kik's daughters were variations on the same doe-eyed, olive-skinned theme. But Tess had insane corkscrews that bounced from her head and Casey's mane fell straight down her shoulders like a satin scarf. While Doone was clearly related she'd modified her appearance with piercings and a chop-cut dyed a flat, mother-torturing black.

Kik returned to her room and glanced at her own reflection in the mirror. Her resemblance to the girls was evident.

In this light, the forty-three-year-old thought glumly.

She pushed Bean, the aging black Lab, over to his side of the mattress and got back under the quilt next to him. In the process, she accidentally allowed her gaze to settle on the family portrait Doone had done.

Back when she still sort of liked me.

The oil was a dead-on rendition of the four of them stretched across Kik's bed, hanging onto Bean like a pool raft. The painting's boundless artistic promise could induce hope or despair depending on how Doone was doing.

Kik quickly looked away, went back to waiting. Her frustration was intensified by the nowhere-to-be-found cordless phone, which emitted another strangled, too-brief warning from its undisclosed location. Missing for nearly a week, the battery was about to die altogether.

And then the stupid thing will be gone forever!

The concept of lost drove her crazy. Kik was pretty sure she could remember every item she'd misplaced since elementary school.

She checked the clock again and actually groaned. Not only was her first class looming, so was the compulsory dinner party at the new chairman's house, an event Kik had been dreading since the invitation popped up in her inbox like a suspicious skin mole.

She suddenly remembered she'd forgotten to ask Casey to babysit and felt a rush of guilt.

I wish I didn't have to rely on her so much. But who knows what would happen if I left Doone in charge?

The tears that had been threatening since her eldest's missed curfew suddenly spilled.

Why is everything so difficult now?

When Casey and Doone were small, the Marchesons' light and art-filled house vibrated with kids and classic rock and craft projects spread for days at a time over the dining room table. Kik threw elaborately themed slumber parties for the girls, baked bread and made pizza from scratch. She sewed matching doll dresses and nightgowns. Doone's storms blew over quickly. Life was messy and loud and full of laughter. Kik wrote and wrote. And though it didn't sell a lot of copies, her novel got good reviews. Which led to the great teaching gig. Everyone seemed happy then.

Even Owen.

The past was crammed with haphazard snapshots that Kik was sure could be separated into two albums: *When My Husband Loved Me* and *After He Stopped.* The first picture in the second volume would be the celebratory dinner she'd made in honor of Owen becoming the youngest full professor in the Biology Department. He'd come home from work that night and steadfastly plucked offending ingredients from a dish that she'd spent hours on.

"You eat raisins in restaurants, Owen!" Kik had complained, hurt. "You *like* curry!"

"Please don't tell me what I like," he'd said, continuing to Balkanize his plate. "I guarantee you have no idea."

From that night on his voice downshifted into the somnolent whisper of the Permanently Disappointed. Kik responded by dancing as hard as she could. She struggled to keep the house cleaner and the girls quieter when he was home. She stopped sleeping in sweatpants. She bought him the high-end road bike he'd bookmarked on the computer.

But her husband remained detached.

The solution came to her a few weeks later when she peeked into a stroller at the park and saw the balletic movements of a newborn. The sweet dance of the infant triggered contraction-strength longing and Kik had been shocked by the clarity of the answer. That very night after the two girls went to sleep, she propositioned her husband.

"Owen, let's have a dessert baby! Remember how much fun it was when Casey and Doone were teeny? How happy we were?"

(*How much you loved me in their glow?*)

"What do you think?" she'd pressed. "Wouldn't it be great?"

"No."

"No it wouldn't be great or no we can't?"

"Both. Either."

"Can we at least talk about it?" He just shook his head, went into the kitchen. Kik followed. "Owen, please. Let's talk about it."

"There's nothing to discuss. I said no."

In a culmination of unnamed fears and frustration, she picked up a dirty plate and pitched it towards the sink. A mound of spaghetti landed on the floor. When Bean ran in to lap it up, Owen tripped over him.

"Yeah," he hissed, limping back to the bedroom. "It'd be a great idea to bring another baby into this."

Her breath caught. "What's *this?*" she repeated, trailing him. "What do you mean?"

Owen dropped onto the edge of the bed. His eyes looked feverish.

"Kik," he whispered. Then he put his hand out. All of their worst news had been shared with their fingers laced. Owen's brother's death. Her father's.

Heart pounding, she refused the touch.

"Kik, we need to talk."

She shook her head.

"I didn't mean for it to happen."

Kik froze. Her throat felt tight. An unfamiliar voice finally came out. "You didn't mean for what to happen?"

"I've fallen in love with someone else."

She could hear her pulse beating in her ears but was unable to get her mouth to work.

"Say it again," she eventually whispered.

He did.

"Who is it?"

"Her name's Vivy. Vivy Karr."

"The one who wrote that article about your funding? *Last year?*"

The duration of the deception added to the injury. In a fleeting, piercing moment Kik imagined the unfolding of the whole relationship. She envisioned all of it. The first time Vivy went to Owen's lab to interview him about his big oxygen transport grant. The instant mutual attraction. The phone call for unnecessary follow-up questions and the easy decision to just finish the interview over a coffee. A long coffee. Leading to chatty emails and teasing texts. And then lunch. And then more lunches that could be written off as innocent since they took place in public settings. But private topics would have already been broached. Tentatively at first, eventually breached with abandon. The first time he put his hand on the small of her back. And then the inevitable admission of feelings and desire.

Kik began to sob so intensely she couldn't breathe. Owen tried to quell the volcanic spasms with a tight hug.

"You'll be okay, Kik. You will."

"But I love you, Owen! I love us," she begged into his chest. "What can I do?"

"Shhh," he whispered, holding soundly. He stroked the back of her neck and the unexpected tenderness became a kiss.

And then a forlorn passion overtook them both.

Afterwards, Owen began shoving things into a suitcase. He was frantic. Shirts unfolded between drawer and bag. Sock balls rolled under the bed.

"Is the embassy falling?" Kik asked, stunned by the frenzy to escape. "The rescue helicopter leaving?"

"What?"

"Are you afraid I'm going to keep you captive? Or are you feeling guilty for cheating on your girlfriend?"

He didn't respond and she went to splash cold water on her face. She felt drugged. The medicine cabinet was open, the blue case holding her diaphragm at eye level. She gasped. Owen came in and saw what she saw. His scientific brain did a quick calculation.

"Where's the spermicide?" He grabbed the tube and applicator from the cupboard and thrust them at her. "Here! Put some in!" Panic caused his voice to rise and crack. "Call your doctor! I'll run into town and get the emergency contraception. I can't believe this! It's the *exact* wrong time of the month for you to have unprotected sex."

His desperation woke up her fury. "You know what, Owen? I'm done trying to please you. It's my body. And you can just get out. *Now.*"

Disgust chased shock across his face.

It wasn't an end-run to trap him. It was just an attempt to control a little piece of her careening world. But Owen's ovulatory prediction was accurate, of course. Their third daughter was the product of his exit interview. Basically, Tess was conceived while her father finished packing.

Kik declined Owen's weak offer to reprise his role as labor coach. It was Kik's sister, Maddie, who eventually accompanied her to the hospital. And it was Maddie who asked the hospital chaplain to speak with Kik when she cried for two straight days following her C-section.

The newly-single working mother-of-three eventually reached equilibrium. What most hastened her journey back was the discovery that Vivy left town shortly after Tess was born. The departure of the Other Woman provided a liberation of sorts. Kik still got to hate her. But at a safe, non all-consuming distance. (Which isn't to say she didn't regularly search the web for the reporter's byline in order to chart her geographic and professional shifts.)

For a long time, Kik engaged in full-length reconciliation fantasies starring herself and an earlier, more relaxed Owen. And even though there was a conveyor belt of middle-aged women who appeared one after the other to wave from the car when the girls were being transported by their dad for weekend visitations, Kik's imaginings always ended with her magnanimously agreeing to let him come home.

Then last year she saw another one of Vivy Karr's bylines. In the Charlottesville paper. The Mistress was back in town. Owen reconciled all right.

With the woman who broke up our marriage!

Kik was looking at the clock again when the back door finally creaked open and Bean, who'd slept through the earlier crisis involving the knocking tree, suddenly jumped from a dead sleep to the floor. He never barked at Doone's stealth entrances because the pragmatic vegan carried sandwich meat in her backpack to keep him quiet.

Kik listened to the dog's nails make a happy clicking sound all the way to the kitchen below.

I should go down, too; have it out!

But her last conscious thought before slipping sideways into sleep was that of surrender.

I am lost. And, as Tess would say, getting loster.

The fading cries of the wayward phone entered Kik's dreams, a child gone astray calling for its mother. She awoke a few hours later, fractured and exhausted, to the radio announcer excitedly calling for afternoon snow.

Perfect.

The mere prediction of precipitation could wreak havoc, triggering a full-on child-care scramble. Kik was sure her sanctimonious new boss would be monitoring everyone to see which members of the faculty had things under control — and which poor planners had to cancel classes and scurry home.

Why can't Owen just pick Tess up if school gets out early? He's tenured — I'm tenuous!

But her ex wouldn't offer to leave his lab and Kik wouldn't ask. She knew the rules. Owen's graying ponytail of false advertisement disguised the rigidity that had come to characterize him. He took the girls on the agreed upon days.

Well, Casey and Tess, anyway, Kik thought. *Doone refuses more often than not.*

Kik steeled herself for the morning dance with her eldest. The last parenting manual she surreptitiously read, hunched over by the bathrooms at Barnes and Noble, recommended children deal with the results of their own behavior. Which made sense in theory only. Because the eventual outcome of Doone not getting up would be Doone flunking out. Which seemed pretty extreme.

"Rise and shine," Kik said, knocking first on Tess's door.

"We're downstairs," Casey called from the kitchen below.

" *We're downstairs!*" Doone mimicked snottily from across the hall.

Kik's shoulders crowded her ears in nervous anticipation of the impending struggle. She took a deep breath.

"Please get ready, Doonie. Dress warmly, though! It's supposed to be really cold."

"Thank you, Weather Channel chick."

A myriad of responses flashed. Many included storming the room and snatching the teen out of bed by her hair. Before she became a parent, Kik never would have guessed that boundless love plus fathomless worry added up to deeply pissed.

Doone's behavior had nose-dived after the divorce. Not that she had ever been easy. Her school struggles began before she even lost her first tooth. Mysterious challenges that defied labels — and therefore treatment.

"Unspecified learning disability," according to the ridiculously expensive school-recommended psychologist. "Low tolerance for frustration."

Very helpful.

Kik received countless calls 'inviting' her to come in and meet with the pre-school team. The teachers were concerned about Doone's tantrums when paper would rip instead of cut. Or when regular milk was provided instead of chocolate. But what most troubled them was her flitting from one learning station to the next, never alighting anywhere for very long.

Not me, Kik had wanted to say. *Give me a short attention span over hysterics any day.*

She went to dress, choosing a blue sweater and gray pants with an elastic waistband. Comfort clothes that didn't cut into her softening midsection or self-esteem. Then she brushed concealer on the bags under her eyes and wondered why puffiness didn't smooth out laugh lines. Kik didn't really mind those, though. She thought they made her look kind.

The two younger girls were down in the kitchen, Tess mid-monologue.

"And not only that! I shall also be asking Santa for jewelry. Pierced earrings. And a locket. But he knows that because I asked last year. He just forgot. And some more movies from before my time. Black and white ones, too. And perhaps a hamster. Did you know soon it will be my turn to bring Pinky home on the weekend? We used to have two hamsters at my school but one of them dieded."

"I think I heard about that," Casey responded.

"That is the problem with hamsters, you know. They die."

Kik smiled as her middle daughter changed the dicey subject. "You look pretty, Mom."

"Not haggard and peri-menopausal?"

"Ew," Casey laughed.

"Oh, Mother!" Tess said, eyes wide. "I forgot to tell you that I discovered the phone. It was in my doll bed all along! Underneath all sorts of items. I think, perhaps, Harperly put it there. She can be quite naughty at times."

"I've noticed."

Harperly was Tess's imaginary friend who had recently taken up residence. Kik played along but found something slightly off-putting about her baby suddenly having long conversations with, and about, thin air.

Because, basically, the idea of invisible playmates is creepy!

"I'm just relieved you found it. I thought we'd have to have another search party. Did you put it in the charger?"

"No, but Casey did."

Which reminded Kik to ask about babysitting.

"No problemo," the teen answered. "I'm just going to be doing homework."

"Thank you, sweetie." Kik put a mug of water in the microwave, then noticed Tess had on her snow boots, apparel she generally refused. "Look at you! I'm so glad you're wearing those, babiest-girl! Otherwise I'd be worried all day about your piggies being cold!"

"Casey said she would give me a dollar for each one if I did not cry."

"Thank you," Kik smiled at her middle daughter. "I know that was no mean feat."

"They are not mean," Tess shouted. "They just do not like to be sweaty!"

When Doone finally turned on the shower upstairs, Kik put her cell phone in her bag and kissed the younger girls goodbye. Little by little her shoulders unbunched as she passed the sprawling horse farms on the winding back roads into Charlottesville. The rolling hills, even in their denuded condition, were her own private tranquilizers, and by the time she turned towards campus she felt calmer.

Kik decided to spring for parking rather than getting amped up again racing from her appointed space in Siberia. She pulled into a close-in lot and hustled over to the little kiosk graffitied with the esoteric musings of uber-educated attendants, handed the cute kid her keys, and ran across the street. Although rushing, Kik still noticed the elegance of the postcard-pretty college grounds, replete with red brick buildings and balconies held up by smooth white columns. The school's beauty always left her cold, though.

It had been built on the backs of slaves.

The classroom had a frat party vibe when Kik arrived. She smiled at the sudden quiet and carefully examined the reading glasses hanging on her chest. She'd learned from an unfortunate encounter with a sesame noodle that accessorizing with eyewear was tantamount to strapping on a highchair tray.

She smiled again at the group.

"Okay. So, a) I apologize for being late and b) I really enjoyed your essays about character identification. I was impressed by how many of you independently chose biblical figures as literary corollaries."

Luke, an adorable lacrosse player who probably got young teachers in trouble back when he was in high school, raised his hand. "What about you? Would you say you're most like the protagonist in *Heading South*?"

Kik actually felt herself blush.

Did he read my book?

"I'm sure we share some characteristics."

"Such as?" Luke pressed.

"Let's see. We both worry about things like how many participants a prayer chain actually needs. We're both seriously steadfast. Think *Horton Hatches the Egg*. And our hair color is the same. Though I'm not crazy about her cut."

Everyone laughed.

She kept glancing out the window throughout the day, praying for the forecasted snow to start falling.

Mandatory attendance at Martin's party will surely be waived for inclement weather!

But the temperature aggressively stayed in the high forties all afternoon and Kik raced home after her last class. Casey and Tess were sitting at the kitchen table in the glow of the TV that lived on the counter. It was tuned to *The Dr. Price Show.*

"Who's on, Case?" Kik asked.

"This woman who's addicted to plastic surgery. She's had like forty operations."

"Yikes," Kik leaned towards the small screen, squinted. "She does look good, though."

"*Mom!*" the teen laughed.

"Kidding. What's Price say?"

"That this kind of thing makes him sad."

Out of all the therapy shows that Casey had a baffling affinity for, Kik kind of liked the British import. While the other TV shrinks reminded her of medicine men pitching product from the back of their horse-drawn buggies, Price didn't go in for the self-aggrandizing hype. He seemed more interested in helping his guests. More than once she'd gotten sucked into watching an intervention done by the stoop-shouldered shrink with the nice eyes, and ended up in tears.

She bent over Tess, busy lining up a battalion of crayons in front of a coloring book, and kissed her head.

"Where's Doone, Case?"

"Um, she texted. She's studying with a friend." The obvious lie was repeated without commentary.

Furious, Kik grabbed the landline and tried to call Doone but went to voicemail. "It's me. You do *not* have permission to be out tonight! Especially after last night! I want you home now."

For icing, when Kik went to change she discovered her strappy stiletto had been shoved inside a stretchy sock. Probably thinking it was some kind of new toy, Bean had chewed a good quarter inch off the shoe's heel. She hobbled downstairs and asked Tess if she'd been playing in her closet.

"I might have done," the little girl said earnestly. "It is just that I do not want your things to think I have forgotten about them! I have not visited in quite some time."

"Casey, is it noticeable?"

"Don't worry about it, Mom. No one's going to look at

your feet. Just try and enjoy yourself, for once!"

"I did mention where I was going, didn't I?" But she was taken aback. "You're my rock, Case. Thank you."

"Am I a rock?" Tess asked. "Or am I still a gravel?"

"You are my helium balloon," Kik said.

The temperature outside had dropped and a noisy funnel cloud of papery leaves danced across the unpaved driveway. Kik shivered. She just wanted to cozy up on the couch, be close with the girls.

All three of them!

Dread tapped her on the shoulder and she took a deep breath to try and shrug it off.

She steered the car onto the curiously named Dick Woods Road, then into the dark template of a heavily wooded, half-built community. It was clear that like Charlottesville proper, nothing made sense layout-wise. Street names changed willy-nilly. The bumper scraped ominously and Kik suddenly feared becoming seriously lost, her body not discovered until spring by heavy equipment drivers.

If the party wasn't at Martin's, I'd just bag it.

Her phone rang.

"Mommy!"

"What, sweetie?" Kik smiled in the dark. Tess had learned everyone's numbers while she was still in nursery school. And used them freely.

"Casey says we cannot make brownies and I have a very large yen for them!"

"Did she say why not?"

"Because she has to work on a Spanish paper. Even though she could do that after my retirement at eight o'clock!"

"Let me talk to her."

"Arghhhh," Casey groaned in Kik's ear.

"Hi baby. Listen, it's probably in your best interest to go ahead and just let her make them. The mix I got the other day, all you have to do is add water."

"All right," Casey sighed. "Are you at the party?"

"No! I can't find the freaking house. I'm beginning to feel like Meriwether Lewis out here. I'm pretty sure I've crossed parts of the county no one else has."

"Oh, Mom. Poor you."

Suddenly a parade of parked cars leading up to a McMonticello petulantly facing the woods instead of the street, appeared. "Wait a minute — I'm here!"

"Good luck," Casey giggled.

Mindful of her fragile heel, she stepped carefully along the Shuster's candle-lined path. As far as she was concerned the homey touch with the luminaries was akin to a well-decorated waiting room outside an oncology office.

The lead-up might be nice. But for the most part you're hosed as soon as you cross the threshold.

When Martin joined the faculty just two months before he said his tenure would be characterized by camaraderie and gentle stewardship.

An enormous, big, fat, mean lie.

He'd been making a concerted effort to distinguish instructors from the real professors, dropping in on so many of Kik's classes "to observe" that the last time he slithered into a seat she had a nearly insurmountable urge to peg him between the eyes with an eraser.

The rumor was that Martin planned to bring in more degreed faculty, ratchet up the qualifications of the department as a whole. Perhaps even phase out instructor-level teachers altogether.

Which would be just perfect. Then what will we do?

A sleek sports car with the vanity plate BSTSLR was parked near the top of the drive.

This just keeps getting better.

Though not an actual member of the department, Dorian True, the polka-meister of prose, the walking embodiment of self-promotion, and the reigning Southern champion of shiv insertion, had apparently wormed her way onto the guest list. Kik hated everything about the self-appointed doyenne of the Charlottesville writing community: her gaudy sentences, the plots she recycled from one book to the next, and the bizarre braid that sat on top of her head like a basket lid.

Kik tried to do that deep breathing thing from yoga but couldn't remember if it was inhale through the nose and exhale through the mouth, or the other way around. She'd had to flee class when she got intractable giggles after the guy on the adjoining mat let one rip during downward dog. She never went back.

The door swung open before she knocked.

"Klara! I'm delighted you could make it!" the mini-man pronounced.

"Sorry I'm late, Martin," she lied. Behind him a hideous copper contraption poured water down the wall like a plumbing emergency. "Nice fountain."

"Thank you, my dear. We had it custom made by one of Japan's most renowned water sculptors."

"Lovely."

Not.

An awkward silence grew.

"Can I offer you a rum toddy?"

"Please!" she said a little too desperately. A table set with a crystal punchbowl sat right inside the foyer. Little glass cups hung from it like shrimp hors d'oeuvres. "What a great idea, Martin! Entryway cocktails! I should try it at home — steel myself for what lies ahead."

The compact little man stared at her appraisingly and Kik put the drink to her mouth to prevent further logorrhea. Ever since his appointment she'd been plagued by her landlord dreams. She hadn't had them for a couple of years. The recurrent nightmare was an actual replay of the security deposit walk-through of her first apartment. The landlord had opened the oven and gasped as if he'd just discovered the remains of a voodoo sacrifice.

The dreams first started right after Owen left, stealing sleep night after night. It took therapy to understand they were about inadequacy. And humiliation. It wouldn't require a return to the couch to uncover the reason for their comeback.

Martin Shuster had arrived like some academic avenger after the laid-back former Chair had had a debilitating stroke. It was a widely known secret that Martin had been the search committee's second choice. The first had withdrawn his name at the last minute after being accused of taking credit for intellectual property not his own.

Kik had been amazed by how much a new manager could screw things up. She used to love going to work. It was like summer camp for artsy adults. Now there was backbiting and paranoia and serious job insecurity.

On Monday, Martin stopped her in the hall and casually mentioned that he was going to assign a *full professor* to help her edit the students' award-winning literary journal. Kik had been speechless. She'd been the faculty advisor since the inception of

Or Perish. Her eye twitched just thinking about it again. Behind her the doorbell rang. She turned.

"Hi you," she grinned.

Parrish Boudreaux beamed back.

"Go join the party, you two," Martin commanded. "There's just one more tardy guest."

"*Micro*-manager taking attendance?" Parrish muttered when they were out of earshot.

Kik giggled.

"Hey, girl, I heard you won again. Congrats!"

"Thanks. It's been the bright spot of my week. Oh, who am I kidding? Year. The bright spot of my year." She took a sip of her drink. "Martin's probably trying to think of a way to rescind it. Decree that the students can only vote for their favorite *tenured* faculty."

"You know if you sat your little butt down and finished your novel it'd be a non-issue. Your stock would soar. You'd get a promotion."

"Are you *trying* to push me deeper into the abyss?"

"Why don't you get in touch with your agent over Christmas?"

"Because I haven't written anything!"

Suddenly Dorian waved grandly from the sunroom off the kitchen. "Mr. Boudreaux!"

"The *barnacle's* here?" he whispered, jovially waving back.

"I'll protect you."

"She can rub up against me all she wants — just don't let her talk."

"I don't know," Kik said innocently. "I'm kinda interested in what she's working on these days."

"I'll kill you dead, woman. Do. Not. Get. Her. Started."

One of their favorite games was Six Degrees of Dorian True, throwing out topics ranging from spontaneous combustion to gastric bypass, just to watch her divert conversational traffic back to herself. Dorian had even commandeered a recent article on a poet's death. Kik and Parrish had taken turns reading it aloud. Dorian talked to the reporter about how she and the departed came up together, describing the literary salon for the 'myriad of successful writers in Charlottesville' that they had co-hosted for years (first Kik had ever heard of it), finally segueing into how she'd be dedicating her next novel, *Country Roads, Shining Stars,* to the deceased. Parrish said all the obit needed was an order form and Kik had almost wet her pants in the faculty lounge.

"How long do we have to stay?"

"Just stick with me, young lady. And seriously, podna. You'd better pace yourself in the drink department. Office parties are factored into job evaluations."

Her anxiety shot up but bumped against Parrish's wandering attention.

"Hey, is that Cisco's wife over there?" he asked.

"Yeah."

"Packed some pounds on, huh?"

"She had *twins,* Parrish."

"Did they leave one in?"

She shook her head and in return he did his slow grin thing. Which didn't generally work on her. But she looked away just in case. Women tended to pulse around him. He was tall and lanky with a Cajun accent and dark brows that arched high over dancing brown eyes, making him seem perpetually bemused.

"Forty-nine more minutes," he said.

"Until what?

"I blow this pop stand. I'm catching an obscenely early flight to New Orleans."

"You're leaving me here? What time is your flight?"

"Seven."

Kik snorted. "Want a wake up call?"

"Couldn't you just nudge me?"

"Aren't you ever afraid it's going to snap off?"

His hands flew to his crotch in the universal male sign for the world coming to an end.

Kik laughed. "Anyway, as you never tire of mentioning, I'm a day older than you. Which means I'm about two decades past my prime."

"No such thing, darlin'. Hey, you wouldn't be able to take care of Orbison for a few days, would you? He hates the kennel."

"Uh, no? That's all I need. Your flamboyant mutt harassing Bean all weekend. How's Colette?"

"Good. *I* won't be, though. Patsy awaits."

"What's going on?"

"Just the usual." His struggles with his ex had been percolating for years, ever since Patsy took their little girl back to visit family in Louisiana — and stayed. Parrish not only learned about the marital dissolution long distance, his wife also *came out* to him during the same conversation. In one of life's little ironies, the world's biggest heterosexual flirt had inadvertently married a lesbian. "How's Doone?"

Kik shrugged her pain.

"Oh well. We're a pair. Let's go mingle. Consider it a wise career move. None of your usual marginalia. Laissez les bons temps rouler!"

"Whoa. What do you mean *wise career move?*"

"Come along." He led her towards a resolutely middle-aged woman in a red and orange quilted jacket who was sauntering around like she owned the place. He introduced himself.

"I'm delighted that you were able to come tonight, Parrish!" the woman in the tea-cozy barked. "Martin was telling me you're going to teach song writing when your sabbatical is over?"

"Yes. And the Build-a-Novel course," he smiled. "Allow me to introduce Kik, which is acronym-ious for Klara Isabella Kaufman."

"Marcheson," Kik added, "is my last name."

"She's one of the stars of the Mixed Arts Department," Parrish went on. "Just won the Faculty Prize in fact!"

"Pleased to meet you," the woman pinched out.

The insincerity was so unmistakable Kik felt hot shame. She mumbled appreciation for the dinner invitation and could have cried with relief when her cell phone began ringing in her purse.

Kik excused herself and walked back towards the quieter kitchen. "Hello?"

"Mom, I'm sorry to bother you again but — "

"Is something wrong, Case? Is it Doone? Did she get home?"

"No. But, um, Dad just called and, um, Vivy just got asked to be on *The Suzanna Show* tomorrow about an article she wrote and Dad wants to know if I can go, too. He said it could be an early birthday present."

"You want to go on a trip with your father's girlfriend?"

"Dad's going, too." The three words contained a world of hurt.

"Casey. I'm sorry. You should definitely go. Really."

"Are you sure? Because I won't if you don't want me to."

"Honey, I do. I want you to go."

Please let me have sounded more sincere than Mrs. Shuster.

"Thank you, Mom!"

Kik immediately began worrying about how this would play out with Doone. Tess's exclusion could be chalked up to age — but what about Doone's?

Oh, who am I kidding? I can barely get her to go out for dinner with him. He hasn't even seen her since she began stretching her earring holes to National Geographic dimensions!

Martin tapped a spoon on a wineglass to announce dinner. The guests were ushered into a huge dining room where beskirted chairs brushed the floor with mauve hems and candle centerpieces sprouted from rings of gold-tipped pinecones.

"It's like walking into one of Dorian's paragraphs," Kik whispered to Parrish, a tad too robustly. Their assigned seats bookended the woman.

Martin asked the room to bow heads for prayer. Beneath the heavy tablecloth Parrish's fingers began doing itsy-bitsy spider up Kik's thighs.

"Cut it out," she hissed.

His face remained in placid contemplation until Martin finally sat and waiters appeared with salad plates.

"Are those *anchovies?*" Kik whispered.

"Stop pouting. It's unbecoming." He turned to the woman on his right, abandoning her to Dorian.

"So, Kik, how are you?"

Here we go.

"Fine, thanks. How are you, Dorian?"

"Very well. You'll appreciate this — I just had the most

interesting discussion with my editor. Oh! That reminds me! I saw a copy of your little novel — ”

Little novel!

“— at the library sale. I picked it up for you since it's out of print. It was on the last day so it was 75% off. You owe me a quarter,” she laughed merrily. “I'll put it in your faculty box next time I'm there.”

Kik's face smoldered as Dorian plowed on.

“Anyhoo, what I was going to tell you was that some of the mid-list authors are throwing absolute hissies about not getting enough post-pub support. They're all over. Tweeting and posting, *complaining* — ”

“Why shouldn't they complain? The whole system is rigged, Dorian. Do you really think you and Nina What's-Her-Name are the only novelists in the country?”

“I don't understand what you're getting at.”

Right.

“It's just that there are all sorts of really great writers out there who either can't get published or who are buried by marketing for better-known authors.”

“Careful, dear,” Dorian patted Kik's arm, all Southern comfort and false concern. “Someone could get the idea the dinner wine came from sour grapes.”

That's it. Game on.

“Any*hoo*, Dorian, I'm really glad we're sitting together because one of my students asked a publishing question and I was totally stumped.”

“Fire away.”

“She wanted to know the ethics behind a writer having the same friends she thanks in the foreword provide the blurbs on the back cover. She mentioned the objectivity factor. And the thing is, she brought in one of your books! As an example," Kik said, lying through her teeth. "How should I have answered?"

"You could have just explained that the more successful an author is, the smaller the peer group."

Ok, that's a wash.

"Hey, I enjoyed that article about you, Dorian."

In spite of the flying knives, the woman's cheeks pinked up. "Which one?"

Parrish squeezed Kik's knee before she could answer, choking off what he knew was coming.

(Your friend's obituary!)

Then he and Dorian started talking about the Charlottesville Book Festival and Kik checked out. She suspected the annual literary event had been designed to make her feel like a failure in her own backyard. Successful authors, agents and publishers made a pilgrimage to town putting on panel discussions about all things writerly. It generally set off a career-related depression.

Perfect.

She excused herself and walked quickly down the hall in search of a bathroom. Her unsteady gait pushed the weakened stiletto to its limit and the thing snapped off altogether. She sat on the toilet lid awash in apocalyptic sadness, and unstrapped both shoes.

What is wrong with me? Why would I take on Dorian True?

Kik closed her eyes. Eventually a knock startled her from her stupor.

"Just freshening my make-up," she announced, lest anyone think she was in there so long for some bodily function. At least she didn't have to flush. When she opened the door Parrish was waiting with her purse and both of their coats. While he helped her into hers, he nodded towards the vanity where a bonsai tree, pebbles and a miniature rake sat in a tiny jade saucer.

"Small man, small garden?" he asked.

That got a smile.

"You okay, Klara?"

"More or less. Mostly less."

"C'mon beautiful. Let's go."

"Do you really think I'm still pretty, Parrish?"

"You're kidding, right? You know I've always held a candle for you." He helped her into her coat. "Now quit fishing. I told the petite chairman you were needed at home. You're going to drive slow and I'm fixin' to follow you. Hey, little girl, where are your shoes? It's snowing."

She showed him the problem, which he fixed by snapping off the remaining heel. They were awkward to walk in but at least her feet weren't getting wet. He put his arm around her shoulders and guided her to the car. She unlocked the door and looked up at him.

"Thanks, Parrish. Thanks for being my friend." Which broke the dam. "I'm sorry," she cried.

He held her to him until she stopped crying then took her face in his hands, bent down and kissed the tears and snowflakes from her cheeks. Then he put his lips on hers. Her mouth opened. His tongue was soft and insistent.

And then it was over.

He stood straight. "Come on. Let's get you home."

"Parrish?"

"That's me," he acknowledged, offering nothing else before he closed her door.

His headlights shined in her mirror the whole way home,

illuminating the hope and longing that flooded the car.

Did that really happen?

Chapter Two

Casey finished packing and glanced at her sister who was tunneled deep under the blankets. *Tunneled*, Casey thought. *Burrowed, channeled...*Her muscles tightened as she tried to come up with another synonym. *Burrowed, channeled...drilled!*

Her three-synonym superstition had arrived one day without warning, compelling her to think of parallel words in triplicate in order to ward off bad things. She knew it was ridiculous, but couldn't stop. Her only consolation was that the urgency was literary, probably inherited from her mom, and not something sciencey from her dad. That would have been tragic. Still, though, the whole exercise got pretty dire for a while — in eighth grade she was constantly running to *Thesaurus.com*, which in itself made her tense because she wasn't sure if that was cheating. When she got to high school Casey forced herself to confine her word regimen to her morning routine.

She quietly opened the door and put her purple and pink quilted overnight bag in the hall. Then she went back and gently squeezed her sister's foot. "Time to get up, Doone."

Her sister punted her off. "Hands to yourself, Kappa Kappa!"

"Ouch!" Casey rubbed her jarred shoulder. "I just thought you might want to have one morning this month that didn't suck. That really hurt!"

"Yeah. Sorry about that," was the muffled response.

Casey's AP English class had recently discussed Orwell's *1984.* One of her classmates kept saying he didn't get the whole festering war thing. *Come on over to my house,* Casey had thought.

"Maybe you should go live with Dad if it's so bad here," Doone sneered, as if she'd read her sister's mind.

I wish.

"Hello, beautiful daughters!" Kik said, coming in behind her. Casey did a quick trio of toe clenches for luck that Doone wouldn't be able to reel their mother into anything, and smiled.

Doone let out a ferocious howl from her blanket cocoon.

"You little women up?" Kik asked, ignoring the bellow.

Casey asked her mom to call the attendance secretary, instantly regretting it.

So much for my clean getaway.

"Are you going to be staying up there for the whole weekend?" Kik asked.

"Yeah."

A loud braying erupted from beneath the covers.

"Stop that, please, Doone," Kik said, her body stiffening visibly. "I'll see you guys downstairs."

Clearly, it's every man for himself around here. Thanks, Mom.

Casey had a sudden image of the two of them attempting an escape, getting stuck like cartoon characters trying to squeeze out of the door at the same time. She almost laughed.

"You going somewhere?" Doone demanded from beneath the blanket.

Uh oh.

"Um, Dad invited me to go with him and Vivy to *The Suzanna Show.* Vivy's going to be a guest on it!"

"UmDad invited you?"

"Yeah. Because I'm interested in journalism. Writing."

"Yeah, that's probably why," Doone stage-whispered into

her pillow. "Ass-kiss. Sorority girl."

Nice.

"Well. See you Sunday."

"SeeyouSunday," Doone mimicked. Casey made it as far as the stairs and remembered her book bag so she could do homework on the plane. She ran back to the room and saw Doone sitting up. With a new safety pin through her eyebrow. The skin around it was volcanic.

"Oh," Casey whispered. "What'd you do that for?"

"Spare me the fake concern, Kappa Kappa."

Stung, Casey grabbed her backpack and went downstairs.

Over the summer she'd seen a scary-looking guy on the Downtown Mall with tattoos all over his cheeks. Casey couldn't see the face of the girl he was talking to but the way she was standing with one hip jutting forward was classic Doone — confrontational and provocative. Casey didn't wait for her to turn around. She didn't want to know.

In the den, Tess was having an intense conversation with Bean. He was staring at her as if she were making a great deal of sense.

"When did you get up?" Casey asked.

"While the night animals were still at play."

"Tess, you are a weirdo. I like your outfit, though. Denim on denim is very bold. Did you eat yet?"

"Yes. Thank you for asking. Oh, and I think you are in trouble."

"For what?"

"That boy coming over last night."

"Are you still planning a career in law enforcement?"

"Perhaps."

Casey tickled her little sister. "Find me a brush and I'll

braid your hair."

"Fine."

Casey started through the hallway of the old Arts and Crafts style cottage. The passageway, painted a sort of burnt pumpkin, was lined with built-in shelves and books. Some stood soldier-straight. Others lay in piles to hold up their friends.

At the kitchen's threshold Casey watched her mother. Kik was holding her favorite mug; the one with blue hydrangeas and a silver rim, playing with the arc of light it threw on the walls. She directed it up and down, experimenting. All of Casey's friends talked about how pretty her mom was. But to Casey, more and more Kik just looked dazed. Like she'd gotten on the wrong train.

"Hi, Mom."

"Case, did you have company while I was out?"

"Just Henry. He stopped by to get the Spanish book I borrowed. He didn't even come in. His dad was waiting in the car." She opened the refrigerator and grabbed the juice, angry. Blanket house rules were yet another way Doone's recklessness affected Casey's life. Her hand lifted stupidly because the carton was totally empty. She imagined Doone dumping it out in the sink, putting it back.

Casey once wrote a list of things her sister had done. Stole babysitting money. Pitched phone messages. Pretended she was deaf. Made a show about not sitting next to her in the cafeteria. When Kik found the paper and asked about it Casey played it off as homework. "We're doing character sketches. We were supposed to think of things that would be consistent with who they are. Idiosyncrasies and stuff."

"Yikes! This one's scary. Great assignment, though. I'll probably steal it."

How could she be so clueless? Casey wondered. *How will things ever get better?*

"Case?"

"Hm?"

"I said there's some iced tea. Would you like some? Or one of Tess's juice boxes? There may even be a bottle of cider in the pantry."

"Thanks. I'll just have some milk."

"Smell it first."

"Okay. How was the party?"

"Hm..." Kik tilted her head in contemplation, giving the question her full attention.

She's always been good about that, Casey thought. *It's just the things that go unsaid that aren't heard. Which probably isn't fair.*

"Let's see. It was an all fish menu, the house looked like the oriental furniture section in a department store, and I had to sit next to Dorian True."

"So it was a good time?"

Kik laughed. "Actually, it ended up being...nice. Surprisingly nice."

"I'm glad."

Casey went in the bathroom to put on make-up in the well-lit mirror. Right before ninth grade she'd gotten really pretty. Her cheeks had thinned out and her braces came off, leaving her with a wide smile of even, white teeth. She wore her dark hair long in a loose clip just off to the side. Considered one of the hot girls, guys wrote about her all the time on *Shh*, Ivy High's underground blog.

But her popularity was in stark contrast to Doone's outsider status and that made Casey really uncomfortable. When a secret admirer sent her flowers she was flattered but put them on the kitchen table and pretended she'd bought the bouquet herself. She didn't want her sister to feel bad. That was just who she was. Even when Casey was Tess's age she forced herself to play with the red-haired doll Uncle Terry had given her — despite the buck teeth and weird lobster hands that flipped her out — so it wouldn't feel badly.

That wasn't the only toy that haunted Casey's childhood. Doone used to torture her with a femme action figure that could morph from placid to mean biker chick with a twist of the head. Casey hated not knowing which face was going to be showing. Unpredictability terrified her.

Which was exactly why she was dragging out her time in the bathroom. If she had her choice she'd wait for her father out on the porch. *Of course if I really had my choice,* she thought sadly, *he'd still be living with us.*

Since that wasn't in the realm of possibility, she just wished her mother would chill about Owen. Or be constantly unpleasant. One or the other. It was the changeability that was so hard. Casey stuck her head into the hall. "If you come quick, Tess, I'll do your hair."

Just as she finished the braid there was a knock at the back door. Casey clenched her toes three times for luck and braced herself for the parental exchange.

"Hello, Owen," Kik said coolly.

Casey rushed out to compensate. "Hi!"

"Daddy, Daddy!" Tess shouted.

"Come here, little bear!" Owen scooped her up and initiated a tickle fest; peals of laughter filled the kitchen. "Where's the eldest?"

"Getting ready," Casey answered.

"Doone?" he shouted up the stairs.

The strangeness of the invisible barricades felt like something sitting on Casey's chest. She could totally remember when her father lived there — when he walked through any room he wanted. Now, the kitchen and den and bathroom were all right (although the latter was a little awkward — somehow hinting at sex), but upstairs was strictly off-limits.

It reminded Casey of a story he told her once about when he was a kid. He had to give his dog to a neighbor because Uncle Terry turned out to be allergic. Afterwards whenever her dad saw Fang he felt uncomfortable because what he wanted to do was just throw his arms around the shepherd and tell him how sorry he was. But Fang no longer belonged to him. And after a while it seemed that the dog, too, was embarrassed about the change in circumstances. Owen said they both eventually looked the other way if they bumped into each other outside. Casey always thought it was one of the saddest things she ever heard.

"We've got to get moving. Tess, tell number one daughter that I love her. Okay?" Owen asked, putting her in a chair.

"How come she always gets to be number one and I always have to be number three — no matter what?" Tess pouted, crossing her arms.

"Well...three can be one if you go backwards," Owen responded.

Tess thought this over. "But number two is always stuck in the middle!"

"Thanks, my friend," Casey responded.

"Absolument, chérie!"

"We watched a movie about a cabaret singer," Casey explained, picking up her bags. "Tess practiced her French accent all night."

"I guess there's no question she's going to end up in Hollywood," Owen laughed. "Support us all."

Casey noticed Kik's tight smile and her own agitation spiked. *Let's just go!*

"C'mon, kiddo," Owen said, opening the door.

Finally!

"Your baby sister's a character, isn't she?" he asked, popping the trunk of his old wagon. Next to his suitcase was a jumbo pack of toilet paper and an old umbrella that used to attach to his brother's wheelchair.

"What kind of storm are you expecting?" Casey queried.

"Good one," he laughed, giving her a hug. "You have your mother's sense of humor."

Although this was supposed to be a compliment it made Casey tense. She wished there could be some sort of law that when people divorced they were not allowed to mention their former spouses.

Ever.

Upstairs, Doone was studying the bathroom mirror. Her eyebrow definitely looked terrible. She'd wait a while to see if it improved before doing anything. It would suck to have to take the pin out. It seriously hurt going in. She turned towards the tub and glanced out the window. Her father was hugging Casey, who was cheesing it with her trademark homecoming smile. There was no denying it. Doone felt all kinds of bad.

Nice of you to ask me to go to New York, Owen! Nothing like playing favorites. Ass-hat.

She stripped and climbed into the shower.

Downstairs, Tess was already bundled in her puffy coat and complaining. "I'm hot!"

Kik swung open the back door for a blast of winter air, then grabbed a chunk of brownie.

"Why will Casey not take me to the bus stop?" Tess whined.

Because she's on her way to New York with your father and the woman who destroyed our family.

Kik sometimes worried that her bitterness might actually outlast her. "You know why, silly. Doone will be down in a minute."

"Will she hold my hand?"

"Yes, of course."

I hope.

When her eldest finally appeared, Kik gasped. "Oh Doone! What's next? Foot binding? Plates in your lower lip?"

"Alrighty then, Klara. And anyway, don't you think that's a little hypocritical considering the fact that you do things like bleach your teeth?"

"Wait! What?"

"We all want to look our best, Moth-*er*."

Is this my fault? Some sort of distorted modeling? Comeuppance for my vanity? "Doone, why do you hate me so much?"

"What makes you think everything is about you? Why can't you just support who I am?"

Which did give Kik pause. Could this all just be an artistic child's plea for space and encouragement?

But don't I do that?

Doone opened the fridge then slammed it again. "So how come the little suck-up got to go to New York and I have to go to school?"

Thanks, Owen.

"Would you have wanted to go, sweetie?"

"Moot point, don't you think?" Doone grabbed her backpack. "But thanks for sticking up for me. Hurry up, Tess. I'm leaving."

Miserable, Kik watched them go up the driveway. *At least they're holding hands,* she thought, making her way back to the brownie pan. She would never cut a piece as big as what she'd just eaten on the installment plan. She wasn't even that crazy about chocolate — it could just as easily have been a sleeve of crackers or a bag of stale chips. The protagonist in Kik's book —

little novel!

— had proposed a caloric discount on foods people weren't fond of, arguing that it didn't seem right to gain weight off something unenjoyable.

A wave of regret hit when the previous evening's confrontation with Dorian began to replay. She had no idea she was going to say what she did about the incestuousness of marketing in the book world. *You blurb mine, I'll blurb yours.* It just slipped out.

For years, Kik had studied forewords and book jackets for literary gossip. Who knows who, who owes who, names of children, names of agents, current marriages.

She'd been particularly fascinated by the demise of a novelist's marriage that played out in a succession of dedications. It began with the faint praising of his wife in the first novel. The second book was dedicated to his superlative-laden researcher (who also had a character named after her). The third novel in the series also commemorated his wife — the former researcher.

Fridays were Kik's late day and she decided to sit for a little while, catch up on email. While she waited for the laptop to wake, the dishwasher downshifted and the tortured ticking of the homemade clock became audible. She looked up at the once

playfully decorated timepiece. It had long been reduced to a pair
of reluctant hands traveling around a circle of smudges. Doone
had saved up to buy the kit in third grade, working on it for
weeks before its Mother's Day reveal. She'd sat on Kik's lap,
pointing out each of the twelve fauna she'd drawn, providing little
histories of the bunnies in tuxes and the squirrels in evening
gowns, introducing them by their surnames. Other than Mr.
Bunion and Mrs. Schoolstinks — a pair of woodchucks wearing
cummerbunds and pumps — Kik was unable to remember who
they were. She wished she'd had the foresight to write it all down.
It never occurred to her that she wouldn't be able to remember.

Or that I'd be too afraid of Doone to ask for a recap.

Still staring at the clock she wondered if Parrish made it to
the airport okay. Which, of course, brought her to The Kiss.
And to the way her insides felt even before it happened, when all
he'd done was just take her face in his hands.

For the blink of an eye, for the first time ever, she allowed
herself to wonder. But almost immediately her romantic
imaginings took a dire turn.

*What if, at this very moment, he's contorted with such gut-
wrenching regret over what went down that he finally decides to
just pack it in and move back to Louisiana?*

Kik, who'd been waiting for that particular shoe to drop for
years, felt a wave of anticipatory grief at the thought of losing her
best friend.

Even my fantasy life is a minefield.

She sighed and turned to her laptop, absently picking at a
food stain on the space bar. Her mailbox was stuffed. There
were virtual reams of papers waiting to be graded. And the Little
Dictator had sent another reminder to submit an annotated
syllabus for her spring classes.

What'd he do? Send it out in the middle of last night's party?

Then, without meaning to, she saw the letter that she'd been saving-as-new for weeks. It had been thrumming in her inbox since she first opened it.

Another roll in my dread basket!

The $25,000 dollar advance she'd received —

seven years ago!

— for her still-unwritten second novel was suddenly back in play. Up until October she'd thought she was safe, that her contract had fallen through the cracks of two consecutive publishing house mergers. But then she got the note from an unfamiliar editor "hoping" to set up a phone meeting to talk about delivery of her "eagerly anticipated" manuscript.

The book had never developed past an elevator pitch. And the money was long gone. There had been all sorts of big expenses beyond the quotidian ones. The roof, the transmission and even Bean, who needed emergency surgery after eating a sock. Kik had no reserves to repay the publisher.

And there's no way in hell I can write a novel now. I can barely read one.

The dishwasher revved and Kik felt herself inching toward familiar surrender. The gentle tug of melancholy was incredibly seductive, tenderly pulling her with promises of isolation and days and days of dreamless sleep. But checking out was an indulgence that she knew she couldn't afford.

Pull it together, she told herself, firmly. *Call someone if you need to. But who?* Her roster had shrunk after Owen split. *Substantially.* Back then Kik's sadness had not been of the suffer-in-silence-deep-slumber variety. Despite a daily goal of classy reserve she couldn't pull it off and often found herself regaling virtual strangers with Owen's shortcomings.

While her invitations didn't dry up completely, it was pretty obvious she'd been relegated to payback events — the B-list affairs where everyone looked around the table and recognized their own loserdom. Eventually her therapist got her to see cause and effect and wrested a promise that she'd restrict detonating her verbal IEDs to his office.

Of course he had to go and get Alzheimer's, Kik thought despondently. Initially Dr. Freed's condition mostly escaped her attention, but by the time he closed up shop it was clear what was going on. He even fell asleep at his desk once. When he woke, lost and confused, Kik had taken his hand until he remembered. She'd loved him. But he was gone.

Too.

Defeat was metastasizing.

She blew her nose on a piece of rough paper towel and decided to call her sister. *Family,* she reflected, picking up the phone, *the place where burnt bridges grow back.*

Madeline was, and always had been, everything Kik wasn't. Organized. Sweet. Calm.

Christian!

Whenever Kik visited the rambling farmhouse, she purposely avoided looking at the chalkboard calendar in the immaculate mudroom. Between the boys' glut of athletic events, Maddie volunteered with the Junior League, wrote a gardening column for *Albemarle Monthly,* played on a tennis team, and attended Bible Study. She and Drew were also part of the Charlottesville Dazzle, the A-List flock of actors, writers, and random millionaires who swooped from cocktail party to fundraiser en masse. Dorian True was a fellow traveler.

"Hello?"

"Hi, Aunt Madomine," she employed Tess's pronunciation.

"Kik! It's so nice to hear your voice! Can you hang on just a sec?"

Take your time. I'm just dying over here.

"Sure."

Kik listened to Maddie chat up some guy who'd just finished removing branches from the yard. The audience appreciation came through the receiver. While the Kauffman girls were afflicted with polar characteristics of their mother's far-flung traits, they both shared her let-me-entertain-you-gene, the one that required a full court press for anybody in range.

Shelby Kauffman had swung between Southern Repression and Party-Girl With Her Dress On Fire. When she was taking some sort of mood enhancing substance — bottled or inhaled (a predilection her daughters discovered as they got ready for the estate sale), she warmed right up. Big time. Effusive to near-sycophancy, she could make anyone feel as if the sun hadn't shone until they showed up on the scene. Mechanics, gardeners, and saleswomen adored her.

Well, some of them did.

Those who saw Shelby's alter ego played rock, paper, scissors to determine who had to wait on her. She could be blistering, scorching souls with inflection, a look, or even plain carelessness. Kik spent her childhood waiting for the next catastrophe. The Pool Incident was fairly representative. Shelby had been sunning near the shallow end, drinking a succession of martinis with her tennis partner, when she said that for a plastic surgeon Dr. Jonston sure had ugly children. "You'd think he'd be able to fix that," she drawled.

Kik and Analisa Jonston had just popped up from an

underwater tea party at that very moment. Analisa's tears were immediate. Kik would never forget the burn of her reflected shame.

More insidious than the chronic potential for sudden disgrace was Shelby's shifting favoritism. *A monumentally horrible thing to do!* Kik thought, remembering the guilty pleasure that accompanied superior daughter status.

"Sorry," Maddie smiled in Kik's ear. "How are you, big sister?"

"Terrible! Doone has a new piece of hardware sticking out of her eyebrow."

"Another piercing? Oh, I'm so sorry!"

The depth of the sympathy felt extravagant. "What the hell, Maddie? She didn't kill anyone!"

"Of course she didn't. I was just responding to how upset you sounded. I didn't mean to overreact."

"Never mind. Let's not talk about it. What's going on with you?"

"Not much. That last storm brought down a ton of trees."

Kik was actively regretting her decision to call. "Yeah. I heard a lot of them came down your way."

"It's just an annoyance. How are my other nieces doing?"

"Fine. Well, actually Casey is with Owen in New York. They're watching Viv-eee tape *The Suzanna Show.*"

A wary silence followed. Then Maddie found some natural segue into the impending visit of her in-laws and began detailing the bizarre eating requirements of her husband's family. Kik marveled at her sister's ability to choreograph conversations, sidestepping ruts and danger spots with uncommon grace.

Whereas I inevitably manage to step knee-deep in the only pile of dog crap on the dance floor.

"Hey, Kik, I'm trying to get all my shopping done early. Do you have any Christmas suggestions for me?"

Remember we're half Jewish?

Kik recognized that this response was a little disingenuous as she herself inevitably ran out of Hanukah steam after the third night.

But at least I'm Jewish enough to feel guilty about it!

"Doone always needs sketch pads. And you can't go wrong with accessories for Case."

"And Tess wants old movies, right?" Maddie laughed.

"Yeah."

"I feel lazy giving them the same things year after year."

"Don't. How about the boys, Maddie? I can't ever figure out what to get them."

"Books. And don't worry about them having read anything before because that won't be a problem."

"Maddie, do you think it's possible that Doone is just going through a phase?"

"Absolutely! You remember how wild we were!"

"That's a joke," Kik said. "The wildest thing you ever did was smoke that time in the basement — and I made you!"

"Wow. I forgot about that. Well, the only reason I wasn't wilder was because I was scared to death of turning into Mother."

Intriguing, Kik thought. *Maddie's constipated by choice?*

Which precipitated a startling realization. This was the very first time they'd ever broached the subject of their childhood.

How is that possible?

"Mads, do you know that Philip Larkin poem, *This Be The Verse?*"

"No."

"It's pretty apropos."

"How's it go?"

Kik started to recite it and then quickly changed her mind. It had the f-word in it and her sister didn't curse.

"It's just about how parents screw up their kids. Mads, how do you know what's a phase and what's permanent? With your boys, I mean."

"You just have to go with your gut. And if things get too bad you can always get help."

Kik was so startled she forgot to speak. Had she neglected to mention to her sister that she'd financially supported the whole mental health community of the Blue Ridge at one time or another? That Doone had seen a long line-up of shrinks since forever?

"Klarabelle?"

"Yeah?"

"This is a hard time to be a parent. Let alone a single one. The girls are lucky to have you."

Flimsy as it was, the reassurance was a straw Kik decided to reach for. Sometimes simple encouragement was all it took to be pulled out of the ditch. She had an urge to tell Maddie about the publisher and her financial problems, but it passed. She already owed her sister thousands and couldn't bear to add to the never-mentioned debt.

They chatted about a slew of inconsequential topics and Kik felt her shoulders return to their rightful position. By the time they hung up the cloud of agitation had truly lifted.

In fact, Kik decided she actually felt strong enough to give her daughter's latest therapist a call, to provide an update on Doone. Although Dr. West relied on a "confidential voice-messaging system," Kik's second favorite manner of communication following e-mail, she inevitably broke into a sweat when dealing with Devrah West. The psychiatrist was judgmental and condescending, a noxious cocktail that gave Kik the vapors. Which she figured was precisely why Doone never complained about her.

During their in-person sessions, Kik paddled hard to connect, woman-to-woman, mother-to-mother. But the doctor consistently withheld, sitting prim and silent in her high-backed chair. On more than one occasion, Kik had envisioned herself casually picking up the shrink's ridiculous brass letter opener and stabbing the stupid owl sculpture that sat on the desk. Just to get her attention.

Even the office building was irritating with an interminable elevator and insufficient parking spaces.

"Does she think her patients carpool?" Kik once complained to Doone, a question that actually earned a smile.

Wondering why it wasn't in her speed-dial, Kik looked up the number while composing the message she'd leave.

"This is Dr. West."

"What? Oh!" *Dammit!* "Sorry! Hi! Dr. West, hi — it's Kik Marcheson. Doone's mom?"

"This is a coincidence, Kik. I have you on my list of people to call today."

"Really? Doone's been bringing in the co-pays hasn't she?" Kik nervously fake-laughed.

"Actually, I wanted to speak with you about her progress."

Kik swallowed. "Is, uh, something wrong?"

"I'm afraid so. Doone is both hostile and resistant."

"But isn't that what you're helping her with?"

"I understand this is disturbing, Kik," the woman said coolly. "But sarcasm is rarely productive."

Kik felt like driving down and slapping her.

If parking wasn't an issue!

"I actually wasn't being sarcastic, Devrah." (A first name first.)

Long pause.

"My practice has a waiting list, Mrs. Marcheson."

"Congratulations."

Now I'm being sarcastic.

"I would like to offer Doone's weekly slot to a young person who demonstrates motivation to change."

"And what are we supposed to do, Devrah?"

Devrah, Devrah!

"I'd like to send you a list of other therapists who may have better luck overcoming her resistance. Hopefully she'll be more amenable to buying into therapy with one of them."

"So you're firing us? Just like that?"

"No. As I said, I'm going to give you some names. And I'll devote the next sessions to termination. In the meantime, I wanted to give you a heads up. Unfortunately, my next appointment is here. Can I get an email address to send the list to?"

"I don't understand! Is this even ethical?"

"Mrs. Marcheson — I don't have time now but I'm quite troubled about your daughter."

"Well, I am, too! That's why I called! She pierced her eyebrow with a safety pin!"

"Which is why I strongly recommend you interview some other doctors. I'm thinking two, maybe three more sessions together. All right?"

Kik recited her email address and slammed down the phone. Then burst into tears. So much for the fleeting sensation of well-being she'd achieved with Maddie.

A thought fluttered by.

How big of a deal would a little vodka in OJ be?

For a moment she seriously weighed the slippery slope of solitary drinking, then squelched the notion. Unscrewing the cap would be as dicey as crawling back into bed. Klara Isabella Kauffman Marcheson knew there was no such thing as moderation. In anything. Craft projects. Smoking. Searching for Lost Objects.

A few miles west, the bus was pulling into Post Elementary to let the little kids out. Tess surprised Doone by grabbing hold of her arm and hugging it goodbye when she got up from their shared seat.

"Bye, junior," Doone said. "Have a good day. Or whatever." While she watched her little sister skip into the old brick building she decided to make an impromptu detour by Dust's, smoke a little weed before going to school herself.

I have got to chill.

Doone had spent her whole life feeling like a caged animal lived just under her skin. Rocking used to soothe the agitation. Apparently, even when she was a baby in the crib she'd rock so hard the headboard would bang against the wall. The noise once caused a panicked babysitter to call the police from the living room below.

But not being able to mellow on command didn't go over well with teachers. Even at her hippie nursery school Doone probably broke some kind of a record for time spent in the Quiet Corner.

And things were worse in public school.

A lot worse.

She constantly got in trouble for being disruptive. Not working to potential was another popular complaint. (Doone believed for a long time that there was a chart for potential like the one for weight tacked above the infirmary scale.) In third grade she was put on a bobbing carousel of stimulants. And while the moving target of meds and dosages did keep her from jumping up every five minutes, nothing touched the restlessness that caused her knees to jiggle back and forth and her fingers to tap-dance on tabletops.

Until middle school when she discovered track.

Then weed.

Which was even better. And what was the big deal? It wasn't like she hadn't already been popping pills for years by then. One time when Kik went ballistic after finding a nickel bag in Doone's drawer, she retorted, "You're such a hypocrite! You and Daddy were the ones who put me on drugs in the first place." Her mom had looked confused, then burst into tears and gone to bed.

Doone was pretty sure it was a genetic thing, though.

Because if I do have a hyped rodent inside, I inherited it from her. One body part or another's always moving. Not to mention the meltdowns. Klara'll be fine, fine, fine and then just lose it. That's always fun.

Doone imagined Casey-O-Perfect-Child sitting on the plane in her designer jeans and cashmere sweater, being fawned over by the stewardesses. It was always like that. People were just attracted to Casey. She'd been a homecoming princess two years in a row and was president of Ivy's service club, which got her special recognition at the school award ceremony in October.

Little Amish barn-raising girl, star of the show, with the principal putting her hand up to keep her from leaving the stage so she could get four prizes in a row while me and Tess got to sit between the beaming parents!

Everything was like that for Casey.

It wasn't long after the award night that Doone got her tongue pierced. She knew it was pretty predictable; if Casey was going to be the good girl, she'd be the bad.

But so what?

The thing was, rolling the silver ball inside her teeth and against the roof of her mouth gave her something to do. It was a little like rocking but not as noticeable. Of course her mom went and ruined it when she said the way Doone moved her tongue reminded her of a side effect from medicine for schizos. Doone blew that off until her social studies class watched a documentary about mental hospitals. All these old people sat around rolling and flicking like lizards. She removed the ball that night. She still missed it, though.

The bus slowed to take the turn into the high school parking lot, passing the small house that reminded Doone of an over-decorated aquarium. Concrete lions flanked a stump of a driveway and a cluster of black metal silhouettes of children grew from the ground like creepy mushrooms.

Yard art gone seriously wrong.

There was a sudden lurch and she stood. The hardest part was slipping away undetected. Ironically her camouflage jacket would hamper her escape.

Real camouflage at Ivy, she thought with disgust, *would be a $300.00 ski coat.*

When the back door folded open Doone climbed down and casually crept behind a parked car. Then she bent and pretended to tie her shoe while her schoolmates strolled inside. The bus took off to wherever buses go during the day.

She considered stashing her backpack to avoid lugging it all the way into town but quickly vetoed that plan. If somebody were to turn it into the office she'd get nailed.

Big time.

She checked to be sure nobody was watching and headed down the wooded path next to the lacrosse field. Then she crossed the street and walked towards the cemetery where the headstones were so close to the road that whenever her mother drove past she always pointed out the final resting place of a man named Toom.

Funny like maybe the first five hundred times.

A wicked wind blew and the sun disappeared. Doone looked up. Gray clouds were gathering, leaning thuggishly against the mountain range. She had forgotten her hat on the bus the week before, right after she'd lost one of her sketchpads. She wondered if bad luck held the door open for its friends. Her ears were so cold they felt hot and she tried to arrange her hair over them but the wind kept rearranging it.

A split second before it happened she felt an awareness that made her skin crawl. She whipped around. The street was deserted except for a station wagon quietly trailing her. Her heart began to skip.

Maybe it's somebody going to lay flowers in the cemetery?

But it wasn't, of course. The car was following her, moving slowly, the way the driver would have done on foot. It kept a steady pace. There was no other traffic. No other walkers. Doone glanced over her shoulder again. Three guys were hanging out of the windows.

"What else you got pierced, honey?"

"Want to play hooky with us?"

"I'll stick somethin' in your face!"

Their throaty laughter rose above the engine.

She gave them the finger and immediately regretted it because they all hooted as if it was a come-on. Fear made her pant, her pulse do wind sprints. She had no idea which way to run — the road was wide enough for them to do a U-turn. They could also jump out of the car at any moment.

Doone realized no one would have a clue where to look for her.

Why do I do stuff like this?

She could throw up from fear. Her heart was beating in her ears.

Then a slow-moving trash truck pulled up behind the wagon and honked. One of the rednecks pegged something that clattered to the curb.

"Pass if you're in such a hurry, old man!"

The truck driver leaned on the horn. The car honked back. There were more shouts and then the wagon peeled off, passing Doone as she ran. She could hear the truck chugging along, lagging behind her like a big suitcase on wheels.

Is he following me now? Tag-team molesters?

She refused to turn around again. She just ran. Under the railroad bridge with the graffiti inside, past the restaurant that changed hands more often than a blunt, and beyond the tiny train station that once housed the library. Doone ran until she thought her lungs might explode and all the while the truck followed until she finally got to the plumbing shop beneath Dust's apartment. She turned.

"You going to be okay now?" the ancient truck driver asked. His skin was the color of a shriveled, peeled apple. "I don't reckon those fellas will be back."

Doone grabbed onto the banister that was fitted to the side of the building. "What?"

"You got somebody waiting on you?"

Doone nodded. Her throat felt like it was bleeding.

"Good. Okay, then. Have a good day."

"Thank you. A lot," Doone smiled tentatively and waved, then climbed the slippery outdoor steps. She wiped her cheeks where tears had been streaming without announcing themselves.

Screeching sound effects from some game vibrated off the porch. It was cranked so loud she had to take off her glove and smack the freezing window to get Dust's attention.

"Hey," he said, finally swinging open the door. "You okay?"

"Yeah."

"You look funny."

"Thanks. Dust? You ever notice how just when you think the world is totally broken somebody does something that makes you think it might not be?"

"Not really."

She followed him in. His jeans were hanging off and his hair was greasy. From the back he looked like a middle school kid who'd refused to shower. Rubbing the spot above her kidney where the backpack had pummeled her, she looked around the skanky apartment. It smelled worse than the last time she visited and she wondered if there was another dead bird in the bathtub, like the one she discovered over the summer.

"Now I got a question for you," he said. "Do you ever feel like you got bugs walking across your skin? I'm 'bout ready to tear myself up. I ain't never felt nothing like this," he said, thrusting his bare arm out for inspection.

"I don't see anything. We all had head lice once but that just itched our heads. I wonder if they ever, you know, migrate?" She laughed a little too hard and realized her adrenalin was still revved from the trip over. "You should probably go to the doctor, though. It could be bedbugs. Or scabies." She decided not to sit on the possibly infested couch and perched on the edge of the coffee table. "You working this afternoon?"

"Nah. The foreman sucked. I quit."

She glanced at her watch. She didn't want to miss art.

"So to what do I owe the pleasure of your company? Come by to get happy per chance?"

Doone tried not to blush. She didn't want to be that obvious. Asking to dip into his stash ran the danger of owing him something.

Tit for tat, so to speak. An offer, though, that's on him.

But the way he brought it up left it confused.

Crap.

The option of being friends-with-benefits was always there, hanging in the air like one of those pine-scented room fresheners. They'd done it a couple times. It sucked. But so did doing it with every other guy she'd been with. It wasn't anything personal against Dust.

Doone always separated from herself right in the middle, hovering above in a hook-up fly-over. It never felt good and the attention the guy poured on at first only lasted long enough for him to roll off.

Doone figured the way she felt about sex had to do with the suspicion that maybe her parents were right about her and her friends being screw-ups. Which was really unfair since the popular kids at school — the jocks and Ivy League legacies and country club members — did the same things. They hooked-up, dropped E, used fake I.D.'s. Only they did it in better clothes. So somehow that was different.

You'd think the fact the principal had to send out an alert after the lacrosse team came down with herpes might have given everybody a clue!

"Doonernooner? Do you want to smoke some herb or not?"

"Sure."

He reached under the couch for the bong, in the process sweeping out an empty twist-cap wine bottle and some flattened boxes of cold medicine.

"You sick?" she asked.

"Been fighting somethin'."

"Maybe your skin itches because you're allergic to the medicine. That happened to me when I was on an antibiotic for an ear infection. I got a really bad rash."

"Yeah. Maybe."

She started to take her jacket off, and then remembered he might have scabies and just unbuttoned it. Dust tapped some weed into the pipe, struck a match and sucked in a mongo cloud of smoke through the glass tube before passing it over. Doone tried to nonchalantly wipe it off in case whatever he had was contagious. Sucking up the bittersweet smoke, she wondered which would piss her parents off more: the weed or the confederate flag sticker slapped on the bong.

"Man," Doone said after they passed it back and forth a few times. "I am seriously baked."

"Right? I don't know if it's laced with anything or not. But it sure does the trick."

That didn't seem to require an answer so Doone just sat quietly, semi-dozing.

"You checking out my new kicks?" Dust asked, pointing down.

She wasn't but said they were nice.

"Yep, one Benjamin twenty-five."

"You spent that much on *shoes*, Dust? You're as bad as my sister."

"How is the little hottie?"

"The same."

"How do you know which one I'm talking about?"

"That's disgusting." She reached for the bong. "What is that smell? It's like a litter box."

"I don't smell anything."

"It's coming from the kitchen. Probably a dead something. My mother calls the place behind the refrigerator mouse Florida."

"Why?"

"Because it's where they all go to die. If I wasn't afraid of what I'd find, I'd go investigate."

"Straight up, Dooner, I wouldn't go sleuthing if I was you."

Sleuthing, she thought.

Looking at him you'd never guess he got the second highest score on the English PSAT's — especially since they'd been in remedial reading together back in ninth grade. The whole school had been shocked when the principal announced it over the PA.

"Want a little more?"

"I better not. Thanks, though. I feel a gazillion times better than I did when I got here. I was pretty extreme. Hey, Dust? You ever wonder where school buses go during the day?"

"I know where they go. At least the one Mr. Wing drives. He parks it behind his trailer up on 710."

"Oh. I kinda thought maybe they all went and partied somewhere together."

"You are definitely high."

"Yeah." She looked at her watch. "I gotta bounce."

"Want a ride? We can grab some grubbage first," he said,

as he pulled his hoodie on. "My treat."

"Nah. They'll call my mom if I have any more absences. And if the drama queen has one more fit, I'm going to shoot myself. Thanks, though."

"Ok."

He looked genuinely disappointed which made Doone feel bad. She followed him down to the pick-up truck. "Aren't you afraid Aaron's going to be pissed you've been using this so much?"

"I'll get the odometer rolled before he gets out. He'll never know."

"I hope you're right. No offense, but your brother's scary. A serious douche."

"That's not really a news flash."

The last time Doone saw the thirty-year-old addict he hinted around about how much she could make just by doing a few dates on the weekends. She sat there with this smile frozen on her face until Dust threatened to knock him all the way back to Afghanistan. She'd stayed away from their place until she heard he'd been busted for robbing his own grandmother.

Dust pulled up in front of the entrance to the office.

"Thanks, pal."

"Aiight," he smiled. "Hit me up later."

She got out and he raced the engine the way he usually did on school property, his way of saying hi to the principal who had personally pointed his locker out to the DARE officer sophomore year.

Doone was late enough to require a trip to guidance so she slouched over to Mrs. Branch's desk hoping she didn't smell like weed. She waited her turn while one of the blond pre-fratboy friends of Casey's signed the late log. He turned, looked at Doone, then shook his head. "Nice eyebrow, freak."

"Nice personality, brohan," she shot back.

When she got up to the window Mrs. Branch announced in the heavy drawl of Southwest Virginia, "Goodness gracious, Miss Marcheson! You seem to have slept in a sewing basket!"

"Ha-ha."

"Seriously, doesn't it hurt? I can barely pluck my eyebrows."

"Thanks for sharing."

"Mind your manners, Doone Marcheson. You're at school."

"Sorry." And she was. Except for art class, Mrs. Branch was the best thing about Ivy.

"Is your sister sick?" the secretary asked, filling out the tardy slip.

"No. She's in New York. Didn't my mother call?"

"Not yet. No."

"Why doesn't that surprise me?"

"I'm sure something just came up, Miss-Perfect-And-Getting-Better. Now off to class, young lady. Third period started a few minutes ago." Doone started walking and the secretary called, "Watch out for magnets!"

A smile pulled at the corners of Doone's mouth, but she didn't turn. The band teacher and his seeing-eye dog were coming out of the bathroom. "Hi, Mr. M.," she said, feeling like she should announce herself in case he thought he was alone and did something embarrassing.

"Who's that?" he turned, his eyes going their own ways. She was used to it now, but it used to flip her out. They were like marbles in a cup. Could he feel the way they spun? The good thing was that he couldn't see her looking away.

"It's Doone Marcheson." She patted the lab's big head quietly.

"Haven't seen much of you this year," Mr. M. said.

His choice of words made Doone tense.

Of course, what else could he say? I haven't heard you much?

"Yeah, I've been kind of busy."

"Staying out of trouble?"

"Sure."

"Good. Stop petting Bob. He's on the clock."

Doone went into the studio where a still life had been set up beneath the large window. A wine bottle with wax stalactites held a sunflower whose lolling head leaned into an ornate gold mirror like it was studying its reflection. It reminded her of 90 percent of the chicks she knew.

"Doone," said Ms. Lonnie. "Come join us."

"Hey. Sorry I'm late."

"I was just pointing out the way the sun is hitting everything outside. See the way it's skipping off the snowy branches? That's called lambent lighting. Since we don't get a whole lot, take a picture with your eyes. And you can focus your work on that as either a backdrop to the composition on the table or as the main subject. If anybody thinks they'd like to work on this as a long-range project, I'm happy to take a real picture of it."

Doone raised her hand and Ms. Lonnie nodded and went to get the digital camera, turning up the Bach on her way. Classical music didn't bother Doone in the studio. Sometimes it seemed to make the pencil dance while the rest of her chilled.

She bent down to take out her sketchpad and realized she'd left her bag at Dust's. She thought about the irony of not ditching the bag on campus in the first place.

More Doone Marcheson luck.

She walked over to the metal cabinet where Ms. Lonnie

kept extra supplies, grabbed a charcoal stick, a loose sheet of paper, went to her usual spot, and pushed the stool under the table. She liked to sketch standing. Within seconds she gave over to the bond between her eyes and hand. It was magic the way everything else vanished. Drawing was what she loved most in the world. It was better than eating. Or getting high.

And definitely way, way better than sex.

The still life appeared like a photograph on the heavy white paper. What she wanted to concentrate on, though, was the snowy light behind it. *Lambent.* She quickly outlined the tree on the other side of the glass, shaded the branch.

Ms. Lonnie explained the difference between skill and talent to Doone back when she was a freshman. "You can have either," she said. "But if you don't have talent your work is mechanical. Like when people sing together. Everyone can know the words and the tune but the person with the gift will naturally outshine the others. That's you," she said to the fourteen-year-old. "The question is what are you going to do with it?"

Doone had been asking herself that a lot lately.

Only one more year of school and then what?

"That's off the hook," Hank Carlisle said from behind, startling her so much that she jumped back.

"Whoa! Easy on the toes," he said pointing at his sandal.

"Sorry! Aren't your feet cold?"

"Not since October. Seriously, Doone, that picture is tight."

"Thanks."

Unlike the other creeps in their grade he was a nice guy. And so hot Doone could barely look him straight in the face. People were always posting Hank things on the school blog. All the girls were after him. Some of the boys, too, for that matter. One guy wrote that Hank was the gateway crush for guys on the fence. He was sort of famous because the Charlottesville paper ran a big piece on him about going from homeschooling to public school. They also did an article when his rockabilly group won a band competition down in Richmond.

Ms. Lonnie walked behind Doone and studied her work. "Have you given any thought to the camp?"

"Hm?"

"Come on, Doone! The art camp I told you about. I really think you should go. But you can't drag your feet any more. I need to give my recommendations next week. And I don't want to waste time writing one for you if you're not interested."

"Okay."

"You're going to need to talk to your parents about it, too. It costs, but there are scholarships if you hurry."

"Yeah. Okay."

"I need to know by Monday." Ms. Lonnie paused and tucked some of her gray fluffy hair back under the blue bandana. "Hank will be going."

Which is totally bogus since he's standing right here. Now if I go they'll think it's because of that!

"You should really come," Hank said. "I didn't have to get asked twice."

"Why?"

"Two weeks without llamas? I signed up on the spot." Hank's parents had a big farm. Doone heard they were retired hippies who got rich off tech stock or something.

"Let me know Monday," Ms. Lonnie said again and continued her survey around the room.

"You don't like llamas?" Doone asked.

"Only for lunch."

"You eat them?"

"No. I'm just kidding. They're all right. Some of them are kind of like big poodles. Course, a couple are just hoodlums. Head butting and spitting all over the place. And their pen gets pretty egregious in the summer."

"Wait — you can tell them apart?"

"Well, yeah? I mean they all look different. Haven't you ever seen one?"

"No. I guess I thought they were like deer or something."

"Seen one, seen them all? You should come over. I'll school you in the ancient art of llama farming. You can meet Felix and Chopper, my favorites. My brother and I used to race them around the pen."

"Fun times," she smiled. Her face felt like it was on fire.

Is he asking me out?

"Here — give me your number and I'll call you. To see the farm. We can do some chillaxin' afterwards." He grinned like he was being purposefully goofy. She wrote on a corner of sketch paper, ripped it off, and handed it to him.

Clapping broke out.

Hank bowed from the waist. "How'd I do?"

Someone whistled. Doone felt a wave of paranoia. Was he playing a trick on her? Was this some kind of mean joke? Like that *Carrie* movie? She felt an invisible drawstring tightening the skin across her cheeks.

"That'll be enough, people," Ms. Lonnie said, turning the music up even more. "Let's concentrate on art, shall we?"

Doone watched Hank to see what he did with her number, her heart doing an Eminem thump.

If he pitches it, I'll just leave.

But Hank took his wallet out of his back pocket and slipped the paper in.

Chapter Three

Casey and Owen were seated in the green room waiting for the taping to begin. The intense lights, the guys running around with headphones, the woman writing fat words on cue cards — everything gave off a pre-prom energy that Casey was drawn to.

She was excited and she felt good.

Being away from Doone was a relief, like the end of a longstanding sore throat. The morning had been yet another soul sucking. Casey wished she could go to boarding school. It was selfish, but she couldn't help it. She knew she'd never really go. Her mother needed her too much. Tess, too. But it was definitely an excellent fantasy. Maybe there was some summer camp like the one she saw on the news for siblings of kids with cancer.

Sleep Away For Sisters of Stoners.

Guilt immediately roiled inside her gut. She leaned back for a minute, closed her eyes, and squeezed her toes. Once, twice, three times.

"You okay, kiddo?" her father asked, slipping his hand between the couch and her neck, massaging.

"Just tired. I had two papers due."

"I'm really glad your mother said you could come. I know Vivy is too. It means a lot to both of us that you're here."

Yeah, I'm sure that's why Mom gave me permission, Casey thought, treachery flying in all directions.

She hadn't wanted to like Vivy. It made her feel disloyal.

Intensely disloyal.

Casey wouldn't be able to ever really relax about her dad's

relationship until her mom found one, too.

Although a couple of the other women her dad brought around were okay (*now you see her, now you don't*), Casey liked Vivy the most. Over the summer she got sick at their apartment and spent the whole night throwing up and having diarrhea. Vivy sat with her in the bathroom for hours, rubbing her back, holding cool washcloths to her forehead while Casey's body made heinous noises and Owen stood outside the door asking if he could do anything. Over and over. Eventually Vivy whispered, "If I throw water on him, do you think he'll go away?"

Despite everything, Casey had laughed.

The other thing that she found really appealing about Vivy was she said no, which Casey knew sounded weird. But her mother never said no, which meant truckloads of resentment for a good twenty percent of all yeses.

Maybe thirty percent.

Just a few weeks earlier Casey asked for a ride out to a ski party when she was staying at her dad's. Vivy said she couldn't take her because she was on deadline. Kik would have gotten in the car and been tense all the way. Then Casey would have felt guilty the whole night, worrying that maybe her mother would get in an accident on the way home and that it would be her fault.

One time she heard Vivy on the phone saying she didn't "do" guilt, like it was a conscious choice instead of something uncontrollable like hunger or fear.

A few more people arrived in the green room. Everybody introduced themselves. They were all family members of the show's guests. A woman asked how Owen was connected and he explained that his girlfriend had written an article about a group of kids who lived in a squat. A thin guy in a poorly fitting, shiny suit said, "You're lucky, man. You ain't coming from the same vantage point we all are. There ain't nothing worse than having outta control kids."

Owen nodded.

Does he really not know?

Casey's toes clenched on their own. She wondered if she'd ever be able to tame this habit like she did the synonyms.

The monitor showed the guests being seated.

"Where's Vivy?" her dad asked.

"Sometimes they have the experts sit in the audience," Casey answered, watching the screen where Suzanna was making her way through the auditorium being cheered like a rock star. Casey felt bad for Vivy because when the guests didn't get to sit on stage they only got to speak for like a minute. She always felt a little embarrassed for the ones demoted to the front row.

Authority Lite, she thought. *Audience Plus.*

Suzanna appeared on the screen. "Today we're going to be talking about a social movement that some of America's youth are joining. These kids are dropping out of society and banding together. Many are undertaking body modifications. Vivianne Karr, who is with us today, wrote a very interesting article about the subject."

There was clapping and a monitor showed a close-up of Vivy. Usually she just wore lip-gloss but the show's make-up people had obviously convinced her to bump it up some. With the addition of amber liner, her blue eyes were sparkling violet and the old chicken pox scar on the side of her nose had been expertly hidden. Vivy's thick blonde hair had been pulled into a loose chignon.

"She looks great," Casey whispered. The extra weight Vivy unapologetically carried did not detract from her natural beauty.

"She does," Owen said. He was tense and concentrating.

"So tell us a little about your investigating, Vivianne," Suzanna prompted. "Who are these kids? And, forgive me, but what the hell are they doing?"

The audience laughter turned to gasps as pictures of young people with bifurcated tongues and ocular jewelry flashed on the screen behind the stage.

"Ew," Casey whispered. She felt woozy.

"They call themselves modern primitives," Vivy said, after being handed a mic by a guy standing in the aisle. "They're doing their best to retreat from society. Some say that they have to go to extremes to differentiate themselves from their peers."

"What do you mean?"

"In order to make their personal and political statements they have to be even more extreme than before. Think about how common tattoos are now. A huge percentage of people have them. So these other kids are using their bodies to broadcast — "

"What?" Suzanna interrupted, unnecessarily. "What are they broadcasting?"

"They would say their life-style choice. Their philosophy. I'd argue social estrangement. But one girl swore the reason she put huge spools in her ears was to select her own peers. To weed out superficial people."

"What do you mean?"

"She said she wouldn't want to be friends with anyone who'd make a value judgment based on appearance."

"So you're saying she uses her body as a litmus test?"

"Pretty much. And as piercings have become more mainstream some of these other kids have gone so far as to have fingers or toes removed. Horns implanted, lizard scales tattooed over their whole bodies."

"Tell me you're kidding!" Suzanna exclaimed.

Casey thought she might vomit. *What if Doone decides piercing isn't enough? What if she thinks she needs to go farther?*

"How about their families, Vivianne?"

"A lot of them are from broken, dysfunctional homes. They're unhappy, disillusioned kids who are using their bodies to scream it."

One of the women on stage interrupted, her angry face filling the screen. "I'm sorry but I'm just going to have to disagree with you. I am sick to death of being blamed for my son's choices. My marriage is intact and he was given every opportunity. We had family dinners and family meetings. I read your article Ms. Karr and I have a question for you. When you wrote about the kids who were living in that squat, did you call their parents? Or even the police?"

"As a reporter, that's not my role."

Casey composed a quick character sketch of the mother: *Country club membership committee. She manages to work into random conversations her vacation home and charitable givings. A grownup show-off. Insecure?* Casey asked herself. *Immaterial.*

The camera had swung back to Vivy. She was smiling her patient smile. "The young people I wrote about were not juveniles."

"Says you. As far as I'm concerned you reporters are despicable. What would you have done if one of them OD'd while you were with them? What's your responsibility then? Stand by and take notes?"

"You bring up some interesting points," Suzanna said, reclaiming control.

Casey tuned out. She felt dangerously close to hyperventilating. She got to her feet, muttered something to her dad about finding a bathroom, and went in the hallway. She wasn't sure which way to go and stood still trying to collect herself.

What if Doone starts doing that stuff? What's my responsibility?

An English accent startled her. "Hullo, little lady. Where are you scarpering off? You're not a runaway guest are you?"

Casey looked up and recognized the gangly man asking the question. It was Dr. Price, the TV therapist.

No way!

He was her favorite.

"Hi!" she said, blushing, feeling simultaneously stupid around his celebrity and surprised by how tall and thin he was. "No. I was looking for the restroom."

"I'm heading in that direction. I'll take you. So what brings you to the show? You're not one of those punk girls Suzanna's talking to, are you?"

"My dad's girlfriend is a guest. She wrote about them."

"Didn't think so," he said, running a hand through his snowy hair. "You're far too cute to be mixed up with that."

"Thanks," she smiled. Price said things like that to girls who were on his program. Well, to *some* of them. Actually, Casey was acutely aware when he didn't comment about a girl's looks. It was obvious.

"There you go. Second door on your right."

He started to walk away and something ruptured inside Casey. Her heart was slamming. She felt the way she did in a jumped up game of tag she used to play. Like if she didn't get to home base something bad — not just being tagged but something *really* bad — was going to happen.

Casey was dazed. Could this be God telling her to flag

down help? Maybe bringing her to this very point was why Vivy did the article in the first place; and why Casey came on the trip; and then decided to go to the bathroom at the same moment when Dr. Price was walking down the hall.

She burst into hard tears.

"Goodness, young lady! What's going on? Let's nip in here for a minute," he said, guiding her to a small room. "What's wrong?"

"My sister."

"What about her?"

"She's doing drugs. I found a pacifier under her bed. People use those when they're doing ecstasy! She's never home when she's supposed to be and she keeps getting piercings, too. *She* could be one of the guests!"

"Is that how your dad's girlfriend came to write the article?"

"No. They don't even know, really."

"Do you live with them?"

"My mom. She doesn't know either. I mean she does sort of. But not really. She and Doone — my sister — fight all the time. She's always angry."

"Your mom?"

"My sister."

"What's she mad at?"

"Everything. Me."

"Why is she mad at you?"

"I don't know!" Casey practically wailed.

"Are you scared of her?"

"Not really. I'm more scared for her."

"Do your parents know how you feel?"

"No."

"Would you like for me to speak with them?"

"Could you?"

"Listen, I just had a thought. We're looking for a new family to work with. Maybe you would want to come on my show and talk about what's going on? You'd be doing a service, you know, for the legions of other people going through the same thing. You'd be helping a lot of viewers."

"Really?" she whispered.

There had been times Casey had watched the guests on his program with stark envy. One girl he had on was just like Doone, hooking up with random guys, getting high. But by the end of her time on the show she was a lot better, getting ready to go to college even. And Dr. Price had arranged for her to have a nose job, which sounded kind of weird but that was one of the things that made her depressed. He said since she'd done the work on the inside, he'd see to the outside.

"What do you think?" the doctor asked. "Should I broach the subject with your parents?"

Broach, she thought, breaking her rule about the synonym superstition outside of the bedroom. *Mention, approach, raise.* "Yes. Please."

He asked her for the phone numbers. "You all sure have some unusual names."

"Doone was named after a great aunt. And my real name is Carson. But when I was little I thought that sounded too much like car seat. So I started calling myself Casey. And Tess was just one of my mom's favorites. She says she likes how it sits in the front of your mouth."

"You're a gust of fresh air!"

Casey's face heated up. "Sorry, I don't mean to be so chatty."

"I love someone with so much spunk. I'll give your parents

a call."

She looked him directly in the eye. "Thank you, Dr. Price. Thank you so, so much."

"We'll see if we can't take that burden off your shoulders. Here's my card. If something comes up in the meantime. I'm going to write my home phone down too. That's how special you are. You can catch me anytime. Stick with me, duck. We'll get things straightened out." He stood. "Keep your pretty little head up. Things'll start looking better soon."

Please. Please. Please.

After using the bathroom Casey went back to the green room in a heightened state. She kept caressing Dr. Price's business card in her pocket, the paper promise of a fix.

After the show was over there was a little reception for the guests. Suzanna made the rounds, meeting everybody. She looked decades older in person with deep lines going from pinched nostrils down to her mouth and smudgy half moons under her eyes. Casey was kind of shocked by the difference.

When Suzanna shook her hand, Casey asked if she'd autograph two guest badges for her sisters.

"Aren't you a nice girl? I don't normally do that but since you asked for your sisters instead of yourself, find me a pen!"

Doone probably wouldn't appreciate it, Casey knew. But after Dr. Price worked with them, she might. And Tess would definitely be psyched. She already had an autograph collection that started a couple of years back, when they all went to the circus. By the time the performance was over Kik had a crushing headache, Doone was in a funk, and Casey was left to stand with Tess in a long line of kids waiting to get their programs signed by an aging trapeze artist in too much make-up. The nursery-schooler had been star-struck, though, and kept looking at the letters as though they might disappear from the page. Afterwards she'd ask random people for their autographs.

Casey noticed Vivy stiffen and saw the guest who called reporters despicable heading towards them.

"Uh-oh," Vivy said. "Let's get out of here."

The high from Casey's contact with Dr. Price began to dissipate in the taxi. In fact, Casey found herself feeling increasingly anxious. The long, jerky ride provided a lot of time to think. Too much time. Dread was gaining on her. She cracked the window but the cold blast of exhaust fumes didn't help.

What if instead of being happy about my reaching-out, Mom and Dad get really mad? What if Dr. Price calls before I warn them? Then a salvation thought, followed immediately by three tight toe clenches, provided relief. *If I tell them first, then all they have to do is say no!*

At the hotel, after the bellboy made an embarrassing show of pointing out light switches and extra pillows, and her father finally handed over two crisp dollars, Casey could no longer hold back.

"Um, Dad?"

UmDad. UmDad. Doone's mocking tone repeated in her ears like a football chant. For the second time in as many hours, Casey Marcheson burst into tears.

"Casey!" Vivy and Owen rushed towards her. "What's the matter? What happened?"

"When we were at the show — "

"What! What happened?" Her father's words were shot through with paternal fear. Casey could tell it was laced with sexual trepidation.

"No — nothing bad! It's just I met Dr. Price."

"Who?"

"He's a TV therapist," Vivy explained.

"A what?"

"Daddy — I told him about Doone."

"What did you tell him about her, Casey?" Owen sat down on the bed, looking completely confused.

"That she's in trouble."

"What kind of trouble? What are you saying? Is she pregnant?"

"No! But she hangs out with really sketchy people. And she's awful most of the time at home. Awful! She treats me with . . . contempt!" Casey's voice cracked and her throat grew sore. "And she's really mean to Mom. And she's even not nice to *Tess* sometimes! I'm pretty sure she's doing drugs." Fat dollops of tears dropped from the corners of her eyes.

"I don't — I'm stunned," Owen said.

Casey noticed that he didn't bother to look at Vivy for confirmation. Doone refused to meet their dad's girlfriend. Casey had tried to apologize about it once but Vivy told her to stop feeling responsible for things that were outside of her control — like other people's behavior.

"It's hard work being the good sister, isn't it?" Vivy asked, stroking Casey's back. "You're always on call."

"I can't take it anymore!" Casey sobbed. "I feel like I'm being crushed."

"Hush," Vivy soothed. "We'll get her help."

"I don't understand," Owen protested. "She *is* getting help!"

"Well, it's not working, Dad!" Casey exploded. "Sorry. Dr. Price said that he could help her. Us."

"How could that happen? Does he have a practice in Charlottesville?"

"I think he flies people to be with him," Vivy offered. "Like Suzanna did today. But on a regular basis."

"You're not saying he does therapy on television? Who is this guy? How do you know him, Viv?"

She rolled her eyes. "Sometimes, Casey, I worry your father is culturally challenged. Would you really want to work with him, honey?"

"I don't — I mean he really seems to help," Casey whispered.

"Though for a while, people were saying his brand of therapy was as transformative as putting a bowtie on a Hollywood hunk," Vivy said.

"What does that mean?" Owen asked.

"That his patients weren't bad off to begin with," she answered, rolling her eyes again.

"But I don't think that's true!" Casey argued. "Like there was this one family where the boys were beating each other up all the time. Seriously beating up. With stitches and the police coming over and everything. Dr. Price got them to stop."

"And it was all on television? These families didn't mind having their privacy invaded? Exploited?"

"It's not like that, Dad. He helps people!" Casey spilled tears again.

"Owen," Vivy warned, narrowing her eyes. "*Listen* to your daughter."

Casey watched as her dad walked towards the window and pushed the heavy drapes apart. His sunken shoulders reminded her of how he used to look when his brother was dying. Owen's anguish was what Casey remembered most about Uncle Terry and his Lou Gehrig's disease. She felt terrible. This was supposed to be a special day and she'd ruined it.

Sorry, sorry, sorry.

Clench, clench, clench.

The dreary winter light from outside seeped in and eventually Casey lay back on the bed and curled up in the gloom. Vivy rubbed her shoulder and Owen covered her with the bedspread from the other mattress. The tickets to *The Book of Mormon* and the after-theater dinner reservations went unused. In the morning Owen asked if Casey wanted to go home instead of waiting until Sunday.

"It's not that I don't want to stay, Daddy. It's just — I don't know."

She felt like she might cry again and Vivy said, "You just want the adults in your life to start taking care of business? And you don't feel like sightseeing?"

Casey blushed.

"Well, we're on the same page about that," Owen smiled.

They went stand-by, so none of them sat together, which was a relief. The closer they got to Charlottesville the more she worried about what she'd say to Doone. Then she realized it didn't really matter; her sister was going to kill her no matter how she presented the story.

Owen pulled up in front of Vivy's and his place. Before she got out, Vivy turned around and said, "Call me if you need anything, Casey. I'm a good listener."

Owen tried to echo the sentiment a few minutes later, but failed. "Everything's going to work out. I promise."

"You don't know that, Dad," Casey said from the backseat.

He swung around and looked at her, surprised. "I retract the guarantee. How about if I promise that we'll be on the same team?"

"Okay."

They turned onto her street. Casey wondered what it was like for him. Did he miss his old life at all? How things used to be? Right after he moved out she asked him why. In a particularly lame response he said her mom was an artist and he was a scientist. So for the whole summer before fifth grade Casey thought there was some kind of rule about different professions getting married, one her parents hadn't known about beforehand, like the old laws prohibiting blacks and whites from dating.

If Casey had been an experienced interviewer she would have insisted on follow-up questions. Then she'd have learned that what her mother accepted as normal family life — the noise and mess and neighborhood children in and out — was unadulterated torture for her father. She'd have learned that Owen had been sinking beneath the increasing weight of Uncle Terry's shrinking body. That her dad was left without the wherewithal to deal with the minutia of daily life — let alone Doone's school troubles. Or Kik's birthday party persona. Or the writer's block and self-doubt that were never far behind. Casey would have learned that when the Lou Gehrig's disease finished turning Terry into a living mummy the serene and put-together Vivy walked into Owen's life and all he had to do was close the door after himself.

By the time Casey finally did pose a follow-up question about the separation, it was to ask if he switched from his scientist job, could he move back home. Owen didn't know what she was talking about and she let it go.

Tess was born soon after and she was so much fun that Casey stopped waiting for reconciliation. It was as if the baby took their dad's place in a weird way. Not just because his study was made over into a nursery and unruly stuffed animals replaced the alphabetized texts, but because Tess took up a different kind of space, a needful one.

Casey loved being the big sister, loved pretending she was the mother. Sometimes, when Kik seemed particularly tired, Casey would get up in the middle of the night and make the bottle and rock the baby until she fell back to sleep. Casey wouldn't even tell Kik about those midnight ministrations. She just let her think Tess slept all the way through. Her mother had been delicate back then and ten-year-old Casey understood that quiet help was the best kind.

The house came into view and she studied the yard. It would be better in the spring. Or with more snow. Kik had once likened the autumnal condition of the garden to a debutante stripping off her party dress in a drunken frenzy. The planters of brash geraniums sat empty and all that was left of the climbing pink roses were spindly brown twigs and yellowed petals that had forgotten to fall. The willow swept its leafless branches across the car roof, cicadas on the march. The tires crunched the gravel.

"I didn't think it was possible but I think the driveway is worse. Does your Mom ever talk about having it paved?" Owen asked.

"Nah. She says it's better than an alarm the way the stones get spewed all over the place. Like a monster blender. Like the minute a burglar turned onto it he'd know he was in trouble and back out."

"Did you know we used to call it the missionary trap?"

Casey shook her head.

"Yeah, a long time ago I came home from work — "

(an allusion that sent a nervous jolt through Casey)

"— and found your mother sitting at the table with a group of clean-cut religious recruiters. They'd just come over for a quick conversion but their van got stuck in the driveway. They were waiting for a tow truck, fingers drumming on their Bibles. Your mom looked like she was being eaten by fire ants. But the visitors were having a crisis of faith."

The heaviness lifted for a moment.

"Here we are," Owen said. Forgetting, he reached up to the visor for the garage door opener that had been surrendered years before.

Casey pretended she didn't notice.

"Daddy. Um, if Doone is here — could you and Mom maybe talk about this later? Or go out for a coffee or something? I don't want Doone to know that I told you..."

"Promise."

Tess was out front wearing a tutu on top of her overalls, playing in the shallow snow on the lawn. "Hi Daddy! Hi Casey! I am practicing snow ballet. Watch!"

She executed a clumsy twirl. Owen picked her up and swung her around. "You smell like pancake syrup and cinnamon, little bear."

"Yes, thank you. I do. Did you perhaps bring me a keepsake?"

Casey rolled her eyes at her dad.

"It's possible that a keepsake or two made it into your sister's suitcase," Owen answered.

"Two, really? Is one for Harperly?"

"Who?" Owen asked.

"Tell him," she instructed Casey, with a quick stamp of her tennis shoe.

"Don't boss. It's her imaginary friend. Harper Lee. She must have heard me and Mom talking about this paper I had to write. Tess thinks it's one name, with the emphasis on the wrong syllable. Anyway, she's moved in big time. I've got to run to the bathroom," Casey said. "I'll bring your souvenirs out in a minute, Tessa-messa."

Owen put Tess down and followed a few steps behind into the kitchen.

"Mom?" Casey said, picking up a piece of paper from the table and heading into the den. "Mom?" Kik was asleep on the couch, which was startling. Naps had never really been part of her repertoire. "Mom?"

"Casey?" Kik sat up, disoriented. "Wow, I must have just passed out. I haven't been sleeping well. I fall asleep, wake up, fall asleep — wait a minute! It's Saturday, isn't it? Why did you guys come back so early? Is everything all right? Wasn't it fun?"

"Um. Dad wanted to talk with you about something."

"Where is he?" Her mom's voice tilted into full-scale panic.

"Outside with Tess."

"Tess is outside? With Doone?"

"No."

"She was outside by herself?" Kik threw her head back in a violent up-nod to get her bangs off her face and yelled, "Doone!"

"I don't think she's here," Casey said, handing her the note she'd just found on the table. All it said was, 'Back later.'

"That's it. I am officially at the end of my rope."

"I think that's what Dad wants to talk to you about."

"What do you mean?"

"He wants to talk about Doone."

"Oh, he's ready to plug in?"

Casey felt herself contract.

"Hi," Owen interjected, coming in the den right at that moment, getting Casey off the hook. She went up the stairs, maneuvering around the envelopes, shoes and magazines that poked through the banister posts like hanging files.

"You okay, Kik?"

His concern was disarming.

"I don't know. Sometimes I wonder if I'm going through the change."

"That would be premature, wouldn't it?"

A self-conscious silence ensued while they simultaneously concluded that this might not be an appropriate conversation topic for former spouses. She regrouped first.

"Why did you cut your trip, Owen?"

"We need to talk, Kik. About Doone."

Instead of turning on him she offered tea.

"Sure. That'd be great."

She went to the backdoor and opened it. "Tess! I'll make you and Harperly some hot chocolate. You can watch a movie in a few minutes. White marshmallows or rainbow?"

"Rainbow please, Mother. With extras in a sandwich bag."

"Of course."

Tess always insisted that her snacks be served like that. She even unwrapped gum and put those in bags, too. She claimed they made everything taste better.

"Tess must be freezing," Kik said. "In those shoes."

"She'll be okay."

Kik lit the burner beneath the ancient kettle. "What's going on, Owen?"

"Casey told me about Doone."

Kik was sure that he could see her heart pounding through her thin sweater and moved her left arm forward to cover her chest. "What about her?"

"That she's in trouble. Out of control."

"Out of control? Really, Owen, I wouldn't go that far!"

"Calm down, Kik. I'm not assigning blame. I'm just telling you that Casey is terribly upset. Sad. She even spoke to some guy up in New York about it."

"What guy? Who?"

"A Dr. Price? Some TV shrink?"

"What!"

"Yeah. Case approached him. He offered to do an intervention with Doone. Or all of us, I suppose. On television. Do you know who he is?"

"Of course I know who he is. The whole country knows who he is." She took a deep breath. "Out of all those TV shrinks, I like him the most. He seems decent. And he's not out their pimping his own brand all the time."

"What do you mean?"

"A lot of them use their shows to sell things."

"What kind of things?"

"Their books, their spouses' books, their kids' books. Diet products. Or they do those rating grab things like paternity tests and lie detectors. Price doesn't do any of that. He just tries to help."

"You have got to be kidding. That happens on TV?"

"Yeah. The other thing Price doesn't do is any of the psychoanalytic crap that *Doctor* Devrah West does." Kik paused, wiped her bangs out of her eyes and looked into Owen's. "Who, by the way, informed me yesterday, that she's dumping Doone."

"What?"

"Yep."

"I didn't know they could do that."

"Me either. I guess nobody likes failure."

"Well, according to Casey, that Dr. Price was serious about working with us."

Utterly taken aback, Kik got out two mugs, poured from the kettle. Her hands were shaking. "What exactly did Casey say about Doone?"

"That she thinks she's doing drugs. That she can't stand being home with her. That she's scared."

Kik jerked and the hot water jumped the rim, splashing onto her. "Ouch!"

Owen jumped up. "Are you alright? Can I get you some ice?"

"No, I'm okay. Are you sure she said she's *afraid?*"

He nodded.

Kik slumped into the ladder-back chair. "I had no idea."

"Apparently she's been trying to suck it up for a while. I think her defenses just got swamped. I guess there was something about that guy that induced her to reach out."

"He seems to have that effect. People you'd never expect go on his show. Professionals, celebrities. Politicians. He offers really clear suggestions. With a minimum of hoopla. Which is probably why his ratings never touch the other guys'."

"Well, Casey practically begged me to consider it. She feels like she's carrying the rest of us. And she's exhausted from being so responsible. It was heart-breaking, Kik."

"What am I supposed to do? Encourage her to act out, too? Oh, it's Wednesday, sweetie. Your turn to go out and pierce your eyebrow!"

He ignored the bait. "It's not something we ever talked about in counseling, is it? How Doone's issues affect Casey?"

"You'd think one of them might have wanted to meet with the other girls. Spare me the bloody experts."

They were both quiet. She looked at him. "Owen, you wouldn't seriously consider doing the show, would you?"

The back door flung open before he could answer. Tess, all pink cheeks and wild ringlets, flew in. "Is it prepared?"

"Just about, sweetness." Kik reached into the cupboard and was momentarily startled by how prominent the veins in her hand had become. They rose above the surface like suspension bridges.

When did that happen?

She pulled out a plastic elephant mug from the tipsy stack of mismatched china and poured the boiling water, added the instant hot cocoa mix and marshmallows, dropped an ice cube through them, then dumped some extras into a snack bag.

"I am ready to watch a Shirley Temple movie now," Tess announced, satisfied with her mother's performance. "She was just so adorable!"

The phone rang.

"Here, let me carry this into the den for her," Owen said, taking the mug and following Tess into the other room. "Come on, little bear."

"Hello?" Kik said.

"Mrs. Marcheson?"

"Yes?"

"This is Officer Woody Tiper. Are you Doone's mother?"

"What? Why?" Kik's pulse began pounding so loud in her ear she unconsciously moved the receiver to hear better.

"Is she home, ma'am?"

"Why? What's going on? Is she okay?"

"As far as we know she is. But her backpack was discovered at a Kyle Cousin's apartment which was being used as a meth lab."

" *Who?* What?"

"We'd like to come and ask her some questions."

Kik immediately entered the zone of maternal defensiveness. "Maybe the bag was stolen!"

"The young man who is being detained said it belongs to his friend. Is she home, ma'am?"

"No!"

"Well, we'll want to talk to her. I'll check back."

When Owen reentered the kitchen Kik's head was in her arms on the table. "What is it? What's happened?"

"What are we going to do, Owen?"

"Who was on the phone? Kik, what's going on?"

"Doone's stuff was found in a meth lab."

"Where is she?"

"I don't know. I just can't take any more of this, Owen. I really can't."

"Mother! Daddy!" Tess yelled, distraught. "Come quick! Casey is crying very hard! And even though it is not allowed, I saw her listening on the phone!"

After that, everything happened fast.

Chapter Four

Doone's parents tracked her down at Felicity's where she was smoking a little weed in the pool house, *Poison the Well* cranked up loud. They showed up —

together!

— and practically kidnapped her. Owen, wearing one of his stupid sweatshirts (r u solution or precipitate?) reminded her of a storm trooper straight off the History Channel, telling Doone to hurry up, hurry up, grabbing her elbow, pulling her out of there. Felicity, who always had some smartass thing or other to say, even to other peoples' parents, just sat there with her mouth open.

If Doone hadn't been worried that something had happened to one of her sisters she would have just refused. Instead, terrified, she followed them to the car. Three times she asked what was wrong, but all her dad would say was they were going to have a face-to-face discussion. Then he ignored her, acting as if she were a little kid wanting to know how much longer 'til they got there. If it had just been Kik, Doone knew she would have been able to find out what was going on.

And probably could have gotten a ride back to Felicity's!

She sat behind her mother and watched the familiar landmarks go by. When they didn't turn off at the hospital she figured that no one had been in an accident. But then she worried about cancer. Or her father having Lou Gehrig's like Uncle Terry.

Owen's an ass. But still.

They went past the newest shopping center, and the rip-off

store where she went with Dust to rent a TV, and past Bean's vet all the way out by the airport. And by then, in spite of the pot, Doone's heart was ecstasy-stoked. She wondered if she was being kidnapped and flown to one of those boot camp places. But her father turned into some Edward Hopper-looking diner and Doone was practically overcome with relief. Nobody said anything.

A cashier with hand-drawn mountain peak eyebrows and a pink uniform creased into rolls of back fat seated them at a booth. The tabletop was sticky.

"Awesome place, Owen. How'd you hear about it? *Charlottesville for Tightwads?*" Doone asked.

"I am not in the mood for any of your crap," her father said, low and dangerous. "I'm going to warn you only once to watch yourself."

When her father held up a finger she wanted to thank him for the visual but there was something about the harsh line of his narrow mouth that told her to keep hers shut. Owen was seriously pissed.

And there's nothing like a faux hippie getting mad. They hold back for years, but when they blow, all sorts of toxic pours out!

Doone looked down sullenly and found herself temporarily distracted by the Virginia fun facts on the placemat. Pretty much all of fourth grade Commonwealth History was shouted from the rough paper. *Mountainous and sandy coastal plain! Birthplace of eight presidents! State flower: Dogwood TREE! Dulles airport — one of the busiest in the world!*

In a Casey-move, she half-felt like folding it up and taking the thing home for Tess in case she needed it in a couple of years.

"Do you want a hamburger, Doone?" her father asked.

"Owen!" Kik said, shocked.

"Yeah, thanks, Dad."

"What?"

"I've been a vegetarian since I was twelve."

Dumbass. If Casey didn't eat meat you'd probably wear a shirt advertising the fact.

"I'm sorry. I'm a little distracted. Do you want something else then? A chicken sandwich?"

Tears stung Doone's eyes. She had to stop herself from lashing back. "I'm not hungry."

He shrugged. Kik looked concerned. "Are you sure you don't want to eat, honey? A grilled cheese, maybe?"

"I'm sure! Are you going to tell me why we're here?"

No one said anything and Doone grunted, turned her attention to an old man sitting at the counter, methodically working through his meal. Finished with his eggs, he steered the dish a quarter-turn and went for a sausage. Doone thought of Tess and how she didn't like different foods to touch each other.

Owen finally broke the silence. "Your friend, Kyle Cousins, was arrested."

"Who?" Then Doone realized. "*That's* why we're here? What does that have to do with me?"

"Your stuff was found there."

She challenged her father. "And?"

"The police found meth, Doone. He had a lab set up in his apartment."

"So what! I wasn't doing it."

Tears rolled down Kik's face, washing twin mascara paths through her make-up.

Owen repositioned himself on the bench seat. "We are

terribly concerned about this. You're obviously spending time with troubled kids. And more to the point, *you're* making dangerous choices. And that's going to stop."

"Honey, we just want to see you happier!" Kik sobbed.

Doone looked away from her so she wouldn't begin crying, too.

Kik went on. "We want you to talk with someone — find out why you're doing such self-destructive things."

"What do you mean? You already make me go see that West loser!"

"What?" Kik responded, confused. "I thought you liked her!"

"I *hate* her."

"Wow, I wish I knew that — I hate her, too!" Kik laughed, using the napkin to dab at her face.

"Let's not get sidetracked," Owen said impatiently, hardwired to just march forward.

"The thing is," Kik hurriedly added, softening the facts. "Dr. West is scaling back on her practice. And one of the things we wanted to discuss is this opportunity that seems to have opened up for us."

"What kind of opportunity?"

"When Daddy and Casey were in New York apparently Dr. Price offered to do some therapy with us."

Doone practically snorted. "From TV? What do you mean he offered? How? You can't make me do that!"

"You're right," Owen agreed. "But things aren't going to stay the way they are, Doone. Too much is at stake. There are other options."

"Like?"

"You come live with Vivy and me. Transfer out of Ivy. Start

fresh."

Doone noticed her mother flinch.

Owen plowed on. "Adjusting a variable can completely change an outcome. I can tutor you. Or arrange to have someone come — "

"No freaking way," Doone said savagely.

His eye twitched but her father kept his cool. "Boarding school is another option. Although, frankly, they're wildly expensive. Your mother and I discussed it and the tuition will have to come from your college fund, which means you'll have to take out loans later. But if you don't graduate, you're not going to college anyway, so that's neither here nor there."

He stopped talking, leaned forward. "Something's going to give, Doone. We are not going to continue to tolerate your behavior."

She thought of all the snotty kids she knew who went to boarding school. "I'd run away before doing either of those!"

"That's an option, of course. But then you wouldn't be living at home anyway. So you might as well get a diploma at the same time."

Her father's logic had always driven her insane. Delivered in mono-speak, she imagined the color of his words as slate, their texture granite. Just like him. "There's no way I'm switching schools. Owe-en." Her pronunciation alluded to obligations and things withheld.

Kik squeezed her daughter's wrist. "The goal is for things to just improve, sweetie. Get your grades up. College is right around the corner."

Doone pulled her arm back so quickly Kik's palm thudded onto the table. "Who said I was going to college?"

"Well, how are you planning to support yourself then?"

Owen pressed. "You're just a couple years from being on your own, an adult."

"Off your payroll you mean? Yeah. I was thinking of hooking for a while. You know, between high school and whatever. An opportunity actually presented itself."

Her mother looked like she'd been smashed in the nose.

"I'm just kidding! Thanks for the vote of confidence, though." Doone's bottom lip suddenly began quivering and she said to her own surprise, "I got nominated to go to a special art camp."

"You did, sweetie?" Kik grasped at the straw. "When? Where? That's wonderful!"

"This summer. Ms. Lonnie asked me. Look, I'll stop hanging out with Dust. But can we just stop talking about this, please? I promise to stop messing up."

"Do you think you can?" Kik asked, putting her hand back on Doone's, her eyes red and swimming. Doone fought the impulse to pull back again.

"I'm sorry," her father announced. "But we've outlined your choices. And they are non-negotiable. Summer camp is irrelevant at this point."

"You know what, Owen? I'd go on that freak's show before living with you," she erupted. Then she grabbed her coat and stormed outside to wait in the car

They drove back to the house in a silence so heavy Doone was sure she could see it. Owen dropped them off and she went up to her room and slammed the door. She didn't speak to anyone for the rest of the night.

Which was a relief to her mother.

Early the next morning the phone rang and a familiar British accent came over the line. "David Price here. Is this Mrs.

Marcheson?"

"Yes. Hi — it's Kik."

"Hullo there! I don't know whether or not your delightful daughter had a chance to tell you about our discussion — "

"She did. It was very kind of you to talk to her. I just really don't — "

"I was hoping you and I could spend a few minutes conversing about what's been going on. Your girl seemed terrifically sad to me. I was awfully concerned about her."

His words echoed Dr. West's.

About Doone!

"I know I lean on Casey too much. I didn't realize it was so hard on her, though. The thing is, I walk around all the time just waiting for the sky to fall. For the emergency room to call about Doone." Her voice dropped, as she said aloud what she'd never admitted before. "Or worse. Nothing we've done has helped." Then she told Price about the meth lab.

"So things certainly do seem to be at a crisis point. I've taken the liberty of doing research on counselors in your region in the event you choose not to come on the show. Though I would really encour — "

"Oh, thank you. *Thank you!* That's such a relief. Because honestly, Dr. Price, I've been panicking about this all night. If I could tell Casey that *you're* given us the name of a family therapist that may be almost as good. We're not really the kind of people — "

"The kind that need help?"

"Sorry. That came out wrong. I mean obviously we need help," Kik started to feel a little disoriented. "I meant on tel — " she interrupted herself again, not wanting to sound rude; changed tacks in a confused rush. "On top of everything my new boss hates me. And I may be sued by my old publisher for breach of contract because I never delivered the novel I was supposed to. So finances are an issue and committing us to trips to New York — "

"Well, as long as we're on that topic, I can tell you that while we obviously don't pay guests for appearing on the show — that would be highly unethical — we do compensate for licensing fees."

"I'm sorry?"

"The production company can reimburse for rights to pictures and home movies. I believe the last family was provided upwards of $50,000 for access to their photo albums."

Kik had an image of the man hurling a stone towards the muddied waters where she was flailing. The commotion roused her generally dormant intuition.

Don't! Stop all this now! Hang up! Find other help! This isn't about money!

"While the decision is yours, of course, Kik, I do hope you consider the fact that Casey reached out to *me*. It couldn't have been easy. My sense is she could use some validation from you. Proof that you're listening."

Guilt trumped Kik's resolve. She heard herself agreeing.

And then the train left the station.

Chapter Five

In far less time than it took to schedule a hair appointment, the production staff had set everything up. Less than a week after Casey's abbreviated trip to New York, Kik was waiting for the camera crew to arrive.

"It's something brand new the doctor is trying!" Price's producer had gushed. "Cinéma vérité in the service of change! It's just for a couple days so the doc can get a taste of how things happen in the home. He's thrilled to be able to offer this incredible tool, now."

(Which was when Kik began feeling like she was in a plunging aircraft.)

Wandering nervously around the house, she spied a rhinestone barrette that had been the subject of a desperate search a few weeks before. Tess had inherited her mother's deep panic over losing things and had been inconsolable over misplacing her dimont barrettes.

"They were a very special present from Mr. John Bride for me inviting him to Grandparents' Day even though he is really just our neighbor," she cried.

Kik had commiserated, offered to get replacements.

"No, Mother! That would not be right. I would always know they were not the true ones."

Kik wondered if finding only half of the pair would be worse than finding neither. *Definitely could go either way.* Just as she started to slide the clip into her pants' pocket, Bean raced into the kitchen with Orbison in hot pursuit. They almost knocked her over. Kik's poor dog had spent the past couple of days fending off his houseguest's advances.

Parrish had called and pleaded with Kik to get his dog from the kennel. He and Colette had decided to do an impromptu college tour and he couldn't stand Orbison being boarded for that long. So, despite the fact that her whole world was spinning out (and despite her brackish envy over a parent-child campus junket while she was getting ready for a televised family intervention), Kik had driven almost to Staunton to retrieve the retriever.

To be fair, Parrish has no idea what's going on.

Both dogs began barking like lunatics. An enormous trailer was trying to reverse down the gravel driveway. Kik had forgotten to warn them about its hazards. She ran outside, waved them back towards the street. A young woman with headphones around her neck hopped out of the cab and made her way to the porch.

"Hi there!" the young woman said, putting her hand out. She had a beakish nose and a receding chin, an unfortunate combination that gave her an uncanny resemblance to a box turtle.

Kik was horrified by the size of the truck and blurted, "Dr. Price's producer promised it was just going to be a couple of cameras!" She'd pictured little ones, like the unobtrusive orbs over the toppings at the frozen yogurt place.

"There's less equipment than it looks. Really! It won't take us too long to get set up. I promise! Then we'll be out of your hair. It really does look worse than it is. But do you mind if we get started? We're a little behind schedule." The young woman leaned in conspiratorially. "Those slackers decided to take a two-hour lunch. Great house by the way! I've never been down here before. This neighborhood is amazing. Country and city at the same time! It's just beautiful. *Cold* — but beautiful."

And so, guilted, Kik opened the door. When the guys started carrying the equipment to the porch, the dogs grew increasingly apoplectic and she closed them in the kitchen to muffle the barking. By the time the younger girls got home, cameras had been hung throughout the first floor, industrial cords were tunneling under rugs and winding out again, and Kik had a raging headache. There was every bit as much equipment as she had feared when she first saw the truck.

"Mother? Tell me again why these people are here!" Tess commanded when she dropped her backpack and lunch box in the hallway.

"They're from Dr. Price, remember? They're going to put our house on TV."

"Why does our house want to be on TV?"

Tess ducked away when one of the men tousled her hair. "I would prefer you not touch my head, please. It is quite a bother to fix."

"Sorry, ma'am."

"You may pat Bean. Or Orbison. But he has bad manners. He is always trying to make our dog give him piggyback rides." She turned back to Kik. "Mother? All day I was thinking about how much I would like an orange supper. Macaroni. With the cheese from the packet. Not the kind you try and make. And chips and nacho sauce. And candy orange slices for dessert."

"Normally, I just serve organic," Kik said, and everyone laughed.

"In a plastic bag," Tess added.

Doone called right after the crew left.

"Where are you?" Kik asked.

"I had some stuff to do. I'll be back in a little while," she said before hanging up.

Kik's eye started to twitch.

Any minute I'm going to succumb to a stampede of tics.

She complied with Tess's color coordinated menu request, microwaving some carrots to go with it. At the table, Casey was uncharacteristically subdued.

"You okay, honey?" Kik asked. "You look a little pale. Are you getting your period?"

"Mom!"

"What?"

Casey pointed at the camera on top of the refrigerator.

"Oh! Sorry!"

"Excuse me," Casey said. "I think I'm going to go up. I'll give Tess her bath."

By the time Doone got home, angry, high, and hungry, Kik didn't have the energy for a confrontation.

Particularly a televised one!

Instead she took Dr. Price's just released parenting manual ("hot off the press!") and went to bed herself. The book was hard going. There always seemed to be at least two dueling aphorisms to choose between. Kik decided that if it had been sent to her to review during the brief gig she had following the publication of her own novel —

when I obviously accrued enough negative publishing karma to tank any future writing career of my own

— she'd have said the manual was rife with stupid inconsistencies.

The chapter devoted to grooming children's inner beauty flew in the face of the section dedicated to healthy competition — which included coaching tips from The Tiny Priss Pageant. The unit urging parental flexibility immediately followed pages dedicated to the importance of immutable rules. And Price's bold-print exhortation to **never** accept responsibility for teenagers' bad choices was undermined by the subsequent listing of consequences for parental blunders.

So we are to blame?

By the time Kik drifted off, she was more confused than ever and the low buzz of unease became a loud drone that interfered with sleep. She spent the whole night dreaming that she was actually awake.

The next morning, Tess appeared in the kitchen and announced she was ready for school. She was wearing shoes, socks, and her pink flannel pajamas.

Kik felt her face freeze in the camera over the sink. "Sweetie. You can't wear those to school."

"Of course I can," Tess said reasonably. "They are quite warm. And everyone will be very excited to see them. And then tonight I will call Aunt Madomine and tell her I showed the ones she gave me to sharing circle."

"Honey, you can *describe* the jammies to your friends."

"No, I want them to see me *wearing* them. And also Mr. John Bride. I am going to knock on his door when I go to the bus stop. He likes it when I bring my sharing circle things over to his house."

"I know! How about I send a picture to your teacher and she can pass her phone around?"

"Nope."

"Tess. You are not wearing pajamas to kindergarten."

"Yes, I am."

"No, you're not. There's a dress code."

"*What?*" Tess's voice rose dangerously. A herd of leaves rustled across her face. A tantrum was definitely blowing in.

Perfect.

Kik could practically hear Martin-the-Time-Keeper tapping his little foot at the Mixed Arts Department door. She was on the verge of being late. Again.

What the hell — I'll just go for parental flexibility this morning. The world won't stop because Tess Marcheson wears PJs to school!

Almost immediately after the girls left for the bus stop, Parrish knocked on the back door. Kik grabbed her purse and coat, called for Orbison, snapped his leash on and went outside. There was no way she was going to admit everything in front of the camera.

"Were you a good boy?" Parrish asked his dog who was going nuts.

"Other than molesting poor Bean for hours on end?"

"Darlin', you okay? You don't look right."

"I have to tell you something. And I only have a minute."

His twinkling expression turned serious. "What's going on?"

Her mouth opened but nothing came out.

"Hey! Talk to me. *Please.* What is going on? Come on, let's go inside."

"We can't," she said miserably. "While you and Colette were looking at schools I was getting phone calls from the cops."

"What? Why?"

"Doone's been involved with some meth producer."

"Slow up a minute. Tell me what happened."

The story came out in cold, gray bursts. "She says she didn't know her friend was into that and I think I believe her. The cop who brought back her bag back from the drug house seemed to, too. He even made some joke about how the bologna she keeps in her backpack for Bean drove the drug dog wild. But the thing is — Doone keeps skirting closer and closer to the flame. I'm scared, Parrish. I'm finally ready to admit that I'm really, really scared."

"Oh, honey."

She took a deep breath and plowed on. "And that's only part of it. When Casey was up in New York with Owen — right after Martin's stupid party — she met Dr. Price from TV. And now we're all going to be going on his show to do family therapy."

Parrish laughed.

She leaned against the icy porch railing for support. "I'm serious."

"Please tell me you're not."

She didn't say anything. She couldn't.

"All this happened in the past five days? Why the hell didn't you call me? Shoot me a text even?"

"Oh," a rush of tears threatened to spill over. "Oh. Please don't. Everything is so bad. I'm so scared for Doone. And Casey, too. She's the one who asked for it. How could I say no?"

"Um, how 'bout, Casey, I love you but that just won't work for me, sweetheart."

"I better go, Parrish. I can't afford to be late."

He took hold of her arm. "I'm back."

"What?"

"Please let me help you."

Eyes clouding, she made her way to the car.

Chapter Six

Doone actually felt dizzy.

How did this happen?

Everything had gone down at lightning speed. The cameras got taken out of the house just two days before and now they were up in New York getting ready to go on TV. All five of them.

The pre-nuclear nuclear family.

She was pretending to study the huge headshots of Dr. Price that hung on the walls of the green room. But mostly she was trying not to puke. Images of maggots twisting in her stomach kept flashing in her mind. As soon as they made their debut, Hank would see what a loser she was and would join the rest of the school in thinking she was a freak.

He probably won't even go to art camp now. Now that I've signed up! Not that he ever even followed up on the whole visiting the llama farm thing. But still.

She went back to studying the photos. Price's batwing ears looked Picasso-ish, disjointed handles with little white hairs on them in the backlight. She wondered why he didn't have them pinned when he was a kid. It was probably too late now. Everyone would remember what they looked like before.

"I would like a cruller," Tess said. "If you please? I cannot reach."

Doone snatched a garden variety glazed from the snack table. "Here! When are you going to start speaking like a normal person? Aren't you worried that people are going to think you're a freak? Do you even know what a contraction is?"

Tess studied the wrong pastry, her nose crinkling in pre-
tears warning.

"In a perfect world," Kik offered, getting up, "I'd start on
the chocolate croissants, move east through the jelly rolls and
finish with three of those dainty little bran muffins for dessert.
Did you say you wanted a cruller, Tess?"

Doone turned up the heat. "In a perfect world, Mother, we
wouldn't be here."

"There is that!" Kik said, way too brightly.

Take a pill, Klara, her eldest daughter wanted to scream.
We're not at one of your stupid cocktail parties!

"Do you want some coffee, Mom? Dad?" Casey asked
from the other side of the buffet.

"Give it a rest, Kappa Kappa," Doone said. "They're able
to get their own beverages."

"That's enough, Doone," Owen said sharply, cutting the
thunderstorm tension in the room with a lightning strike. Then
he walked over to Kik and said in a low voice, "I'm having
serious second thoughts about this."

Tell it, Papa-san, Doone cheered silently. *I'd high five you
if you weren't such an ass-hat.*

"What!" Kik jumped as if he'd just dumped scalding oil on
her thighs. "You were the one who suggested this, Owen! Casey
met Price on your watch! What are you talking about — *second
thoughts?*"

Doone spun around and glared at Casey. Her sister's face,
already pale, was turning translucent with a tinge of blue beneath,
a milky glaze over cerulean.

"I'm not owning this one, Owen!" Kik's voice rose shrilly.
"This one's on you!"

"Calm down. I wasn't blaming — "

Right then the door pushed open and Dr. Price entered, walking around shaking everybody's hands. "Welcome, Team Marcheson! I am just so delighted to meet you in person. Has my crew been treating you well?"

"Fine," Kik and Owen said together.

"I assume you've signed the legal mumbo jumbo," the rangy man chuckled. "Do you know what they call a hundred lawyers under a rock pile? A good start! All right, I'll see you on stage. Don't forget to make a stop in the loo, if you need to."

A couple minutes later a production assistant came in. "Hi! I'm Liza?"

Are you or aren't you?

Doone hated it when chicks put question marks at the end of every sentence. She studied the girl who was flapping all over the place, carrying an assortment of blue shirts.

"Are you guys excited? You must be so excited! And look at you!" she said to Tess. "I love your hair! Isn't she cute? She is so cute!"

Doone rolled her eyes at the way the girl's words chased each other uphill.

She ought to consider taking something. Too bad Dust's in jail or I could hook her up.

"Anyway! Mr. Marcheson?" Liza said, tentatively. "Dr. Price thought you might be more comfortable in one of these shirts?"

"Why?" Owen asked.

"Um?" the girl looked over at Kik, pleading silently.

"She's too polite to tell you the one you're wearing looks like a garrote. Honestly, Owen I'm surprised you can breathe."

"And blue shows up better on TV? White looks dingy?"

Liza added.

At first it seemed like Owen might say no, but he took off his tie, and then turned away, stripping modestly. Doone caught her mother glancing at her father's naked back and felt surprise sadness for her.

Once, when looking for money in Kik's desk, Doone had discovered a single typed sentence on an otherwise empty sheet. "Regret, insistent as a stray cat, keeps coming back." Doone was sure it was about the end of her parents' marriage. Kik had pretty much been destroyed.

"This an improvement?" Owen asked Liza when he finished buttoning and turned back around.

A surge of hatred shuddered through Doone and she jumped in. "Yeah. You look like the stud you are, Father. Freakin' amazing."

The production assistant began blinking nervously. "Dr. Price said for you to go on and take it with you? It's from his own personal closet! He's like the most generous guy I know? I can't even count how many times he's let our families in on tapings! You guys are just going to love working with him. So anyway, I'm supposed to tell you this first segment is the get-to-know-you session. It'll be edited down later and put with some of the footage that they got down in Virginia? Now don't worry about holding back. It's not a tightly scripted format until the editing. That's when what gets left in is decided. And this is going to be quick turn-around so you'll be able to see yourself on TV, Miss Tess, in a couple a days!"

Her walkie-talkie cackled and she told them to follow her.

On the way out of the room Doone realized her father's second thoughts had been lost in the flurry of activity.

"I kind of feel like I did on that whitewater rafting trip," her mother said in a strangled voice. "Right after the guide pushed us off and I realized there was no turning back."

In an awkward gesture Owen put his hand on Kik's shoulder.

"How excellent is my ensemble?" Tess asked. She pulled at the long sleeved periwinkle turtleneck she was wearing outside her overalls for some reason. "Post Elementary" was spelled out in Keith Haring-ish stick figures.

"At least it's not pajamas," Doone said.

"Come on, Tessa-messa," Casey interjected, taking her hand. "You're ready for a fashion shoot."

The audience was actually smaller than Doone imagined, tiny compared to a full auditorium at Ivy. She watched a couple of people hurry into seats in the front row, excitement all over their stupid faces. One obese woman, with a chin that faded right into her neck like a smile, was scowling at Doone's eyebrow.

Check a mirror!

What are we doing here? Why didn't I just tell them no when they brought up the idea? Agreed to boarding school?

She was sitting next to Price, her ankles hooked around the chair legs and her toes tapping a rhythmic march against the wood.

"You'll want to stop that before we start taping," Price said, leaning towards Doone. "The microphones will pick up the noise."

Don't boss.

She stopped though. Then a sloppy looking guy in a maroon sweatshirt began counting backwards, motioning the audience to quiet down. Dr. Price started speaking directly into one of the cameras.

"I'd like to introduce you to some special people who are

here to learn new ways of coping with problems shared by many families on both sides of the pond. Now, as I do at the top of every show I want to remind everyone that this program is for entertainment purposes only."

Entertainment?

"And I also want to tell you that I've just met most of them for the first time a few minutes before airtime. Casey and I are old friends though. We met last week when she was in town to watch Suzanna do a taping."

Doone saw her sister cringe.

Did the dumbass think I wouldn't find out?

Price was still talking. "I learned she was fairly distraught about things on the home front. We're going to take a brief commercial pause so that we can pay our bills," Price said. "Then we'll see what brings them here."

During the break a woman in the front row pulled out a phone to snap some pictures of the Marchesons.

"What is she doing?" Tess demanded, her face poppy red. The whole studio laughed.

Dr. Price leaned in. "That nice lady just wants your picture because you're so cute!"

"Yes. But it is very rude. People should not just take your picture without permission, you know." She leaned back into the oversized chair and started biting a fingernail, pulling at the little crescent until it came off, catching on her chapped lip. Doone saw Casey reach over and wipe it away.

The director, counting down, pointed at Dr. Price. "Here we are. So we're going to be addressing some common family problems with these fine folks. And hopefully I'll be able to contain the issues. If you know what I mean."

The audience laughed and clapped at the inside joke. None

of the Marchesons were in on it. Price was acknowledging the arrest of a former guest who'd been on the show for a shopping addiction. And just recently been busted in a call-girl ring. The late-night comedians had had a field day. They mocked Price's hair, posture, and the quality of therapy training programs in England. One of them Tweeted:

Help from Doc Price=going for manicure, coming out with stumps #quack.

The show's already lackluster ratings took another hit.

"Anyway," Price cleared his throat. "I met Casey when she was in New York watching her dad's girlfriend do a taping with Suzanna. She was utterly distraught about things at home and asked if I'd help. So here we are."

Doone glanced at Casey again. She looked like she was trying to hold in diarrhea.

"Kik and Owen are divorced," Price went on. "But they've come together to rally around their girls. Doone here — like many teenagers — is heading down the wrong path. And we're going to see if we can help turn her around. Again, this is my old friend Casey and five-year-old Tess."

"Five and a quarter," Tess corrected.

"Pardon me! This one's full of beans! So, Doone, let's start with you. Why don't you tell us a little about yourself?"

"What do you want to know?"

"How about telling us what you really like doing?"

"Art."

"Really? Any medium in particular?"

She shrugged.

"Doone's going to a special art camp this summer that she needed to be nominated for!" Kik interjected. "She's incredibly talented."

"I guess Mum's a wee bit proud, eh? Maybe at some point you'll share some of it with us?"

Doone shrugged again.

"Well, let's get to the task at hand. People are pretty worried about you. Can you think of why that might be?"

Doone remained aggressively silent; making Casey so tense she could barely keep track of her toe clenches. The agitation pumping from her sister was seriously triggering the thesaurus urge and she had to stop herself from doing her deflection dance: *Look over here! I'll say something entertaining!*

Casey'd been struggling since early that morning back in Charlottesville. The horror music (short-hand for the boogieman's under the bed) that often played low had been cranked up.

Way up.

Casey and her best friend, Caroline, had coined the term one afternoon in middle school. Lying together in the hammock, taking turns pushing off with their feet, they freaked each other out for hours.

"What's scarier," Caroline asked. "Being stalked — or some man just getting the rape-urge while jogging behind you in the park?"

Casey thought being watched was worse but Caroline had argued if convenience was all it took to turn somebody into a rapist then that was scarier. "Think of all the times you end up alone with strangers," she insisted. "Taxi drivers, repair guys, deliverymen! And any one of them could get the urge."

Casey wasn't sure that was how it worked, but the thing she and Caroline did agree on was the moment of realization. When if it were a movie, the soundtrack would switch to horror music.

Which was now blaring in Casey's head.

On top of everything, Dr. Price kept calling Kik, "Mum." She hated when random adults, like pediatricians and teachers, called her 'Mother.'

"Why don't you fill us in a little on your take on the situation, Mum?" Price prompted. "You've been divorced how long?"

"Separated for about six years. Divorced for around four."

He was obviously doing the math. "And Tess is — "

"My dessert baby!"

"I'm sorry did you call her your desertion baby?" Price asked.

"No-no! Dessert! Like an after-dinner mint?"

"Oh! I get it. The older daughters are your main course and Tess here is the bread pudding!" He nodded appreciation; the audience gave an indulgent laugh.

Casey thought it was weird how the spectators mimicked his expressions. It reminded her of a game she used to play with Tess, getting her to mirror different faces. Be so happy! Now be sad!

"From what I've read, you and Owen both spend time with the girls? Would you say it was team work?"

"For the most part, I guess."

Price looked at Owen. "You help with the financial support?"

"Of course."

"Spend time with the three girls?"

"Doone hasn't been that interested recently."

"How long has that been going on?" Price reached over and tapped Doone's knee. She pulled back like she could catch something through her jeans, setting off an uncomfortable stirring.

Casey saw two women look at each other in overdone shock and she wanted to defend her sister.

She just doesn't like to be touched!

"It's been going on a while," Owen admitted.

"Are we talking hours? Weeks? *Years?*"

"A long time."

"Gee, I wonder why," Doone mumbled.

"How about telling us why?" Price said turning back to her. "What's happened between you and your father?"

"Well, for starters he walked out on us. That might call for a pout. Don't you think?"

Casey recoiled into the chair. She hadn't seen that one coming. She didn't think Doone even liked their father. She glanced at him. He looked so sad.

What have I done?

Her right foot was practically in spasm from squeezing so much.

Spasm, she thought. *Seizure. Contraction. Fit.*

"I assume from your contorted body language, sir," Dr. Price said. "That your daughter has hit the nail on the head. Before you left the marriage did you give any thought to couple's counseling, Owen?"

"No."

"Why is that, Professor?"

Owen shifted in his seat and crossed his arms. Casey almost counted to sixty before her father responded. "You know, as it turns out, Dr. Price, I'm not comfortable discussing that in this forum."

"All right. We'll come back to it later. What do you think is going on with Doone?"

"Doone's behavior has always been slightly enigmatic," Owen said carefully.

"Gordon Bennett, there's a Ph.D. word," Price said, getting a big laugh from the crowd.

"Who's Gordon Bennett?" asked Tess.

"It's just an English saying like good grief," explained Price.

"Good what?" Tess pressed.

"Right now, I'm talking to your daddy. You and I can talk in a bit, okay?"

Tess did not look pleased but sat back.

"So Professor, would you say things were going along fairly well with the girls — in terms of them being happy, until the separation and the arrival of the cute caboose over here? Was that when things went off the rails?"

"Let's not overstate things," Owen answered tightly.

"I see. Well, how would you characterize a sixteen-year-old who is at serious risk for serious trouble? A girl who's been left to simmer for far too long?"

"Hang on just a minute here," Owen said.

"No, you *hang on*, Professor. I didn't bring you up to New York to muck about. You've got a chance here for some real help in taking the helm."

A few of the women in the audience started nodding, catching the spirit, which seemed to encourage Price. "Owen, you and Kik have got to right your craft before *all* of your girls end up in the drink!" His voice rose above the clapping that began like static and grew to concussive thunder in seconds. "Your middle child approached me because of what's going on in your family!"

"I'm well aware of how we ended up here," Owen said.

"Well, that's something." The audience continued to clap.

Price turned. "Now. Casey. Can you tell us what's weighing so heavily on you?"

She glanced up and saw Price was waiting for a response.

I want to go home, she telegraphed. But to whom? Price? Her mother?

God?

"Casey?"

Cringing, she tried to decide which would be worse to bring up, the drugs or the anger.

"I ... I don't know. I worry because Doone seems so mad."

"Do you think Doone might benefit from anger management training?"

"I don't know."

"Give me a freakin' break!" Doone erupted. "All sisters fight, Little Miss Perfect!"

Casey succumbed to the tears she'd been battling. "I'm not trying to be perfect!" she sobbed. "I just don't want to make more problems for Mom and Dad!"

The doctor handed her the tissue box. Out of the corner of her eye Casey could see Kik using her hand as a visor, trying to block the light from one of the huge bulbs hanging from the rafters. Her mother must be getting a migraine.

A memory Casey tried to keep buried broke through the surface. Over the summer a man selling mulch had knocked while she was babysitting. She'd opened the door, smiled apologetically, and said he'd have to come back. Instead of leaving he asked if he could use the bathroom. She knew she should say no. She *wanted* to say no. But she didn't want to hurt his feelings. So she let him in and she stood in the hallway, her heart pounding above the violent splash of his urine, terrified he was going to stay in the house, go upstairs and hurt Tess. And it would be her fault.

He didn't. He just thanked her and left. Casey'd locked the door after him and gone in the bathroom and thrown up from guilt and terror both.

The same toxins were surging through her again.

"Let's turn back down the path a ways," the doctor was saying to Doone. "We need to address what's going on with you. Can you fill us in on what's happening?"

"Nothing is happening."

"Well, according to my sources, you've been using drugs."

Sources? Casey thought desperately. *She's going to kill me!*

Doone sat up tall in her seat. "I'd prefer to think of it as experimenting. Which most teenagers do." She opened her hand, Vanna-style, towards Casey. "Exhibit A. Oh-Perfect-Child herself has partaken."

Casey's face burned with hypocrisy. Doone must have heard about her trying weed at the lacrosse party.

"Well," Price said. "We'll revisit that later. Right now we're talking about you and your risky behavior."

Casey jumped when the audience erupted again. *What makes them do that?*

"Time is of the essence, Doone. Are you familiar with the phrase 'self-medicate'?"

She shook her head.

"That's what people do who are hurting. They anesthetize themselves with things like drugs, alcohol, and food. Even sex. I'm going to assume that you've been doing some of that. To block out pain." He leaned in towards her, dropping his voice confidentially. "I grew up in care back in England. Had a run of horrid experiences straight out of *Oliver Twist*. Began drinking like a champ when I was younger than you. Self-medicated for years."

Doone, not a Price devotee, was hearing this oft-repeated biographical note for the first time and found herself really listening.

The doctor continued as if they were having a private conversation. "If I can, I want to help save you in the grief department by sharing some of my own experiences." He turned to the audience, a smile deepening the creases around his hooded eyes. "My friends, how do you climb Kilimanjaro?"

"One foot at a time!" they answered back infomercial style. He addressed the Marchesons. "The next time you come, we're going to get down to some serious work. This was only our get-acquainted session. We're going to take it step-by-step, using the outline in my new workbook you were given last week. Which, by the way, has already hit six different bestsellers lists!"

Clapclapclap.

"And every member of the studio audience will also be taking home an autographed copy."

After the revved up applause peaked again, he went on. "Journaling with the writing prompts included in the workbook is mandatory. The *price*, if you will — " he paused again for audience acknowledgement of his impending *bon mot* "— of admission. Even you, little one," he reached over to squeeze Tess's knee, making her giggle. "You can draw pictures about your feelings and you can talk into a fancy tape recorder that will type out your words! Is that a deal?"

"Perhaps. Should Harperly do it, too?"

"Who?"

Nobody said anything so Casey answered. "Tess's imaginary friend."

"Not imaginary, Sister. Invisible!" Tess corrected.

"Sorry."

Some of the viewers clapped until Price started speaking again. "So, now, little Tess, do you have any questions for me?"

"Um. Yes. How do snakes run so fast without feets?"

The spectators roared.

After the taping, which Casey had been stunned to realize had gone on for almost three hours, Dr. Price stood and led the way backstage, going over to Owen.

"I understand this probably isn't anything you ever thought you'd be doing, Professor Marcheson. But you'll be glad when things begin to change. Of course, next time we're all together we're going to have to do some delving."

Casey watched the exchange between the two men nervously. It was obvious her father was not a fan. The last time she'd seen such dislike on his face was when they were eating lunch at The C'ville and this student with one of those affected, premature beards came to their table, intent on talking about his grade right there. That time was about a ten on the discomfort scale.

And this is like a hundred times worse, Casey thought, her tension rising as Price moved on to Doone.

"You don't have to lose the plot here, young lady. You can get back on track. I promise. Okay? I did it."

"I guess."

"The happiest people I know are the ones who don't have regrets about their actions and that includes the way they treat others." He put his hand on her shoulder and squeezed. "Will you try and think about all this?"

Casey steeled herself for her sister's sarcasm. It didn't come.

"Yeah, I'll try," Doone said.

Liza entered carrying five green canvas bags. "Who wants some swag?"

"What?" Owen looked at her impatiently.

"Souvenirs from the show?" the young woman explained, nervously withdrawing and displaying a sweatshirt, mug, and keychain from one of the totes.

"I do, I do!" Tess jumped up and down.

Owen muttered something about not being a corporate shill.

"Oh, just take the stupid thing," Kik said, and he did.

Liza ushered them out into the waiting limo. "See you next week?"

"I'm cold!" Tess complained.

"You'll warm up in a second," Kik promised, hugging the child to her in the rear seat. "The heater is on. Look out the window at all the interesting things on the way to the airport!"

"Do you think the people will think we are princesses?"

Owen actually laughed. "The people? Where does she get this stuff?"

A few minutes into the ride Doone announced to no one in particular that she liked Price.

"What?" the rest of them said in unison, like some sitcom family.

Kik's reaction was the most extreme. She jerked against her seatbelt. "Really, Doonie? Really? That's great! What did you like about him?"

"I just did."

"He was funny!" Tess offered.

"So, Owen. We're going to keep doing this, right?" Doone demanded confrontationally.

"We'll see. Your mom and I are going to discuss it back in

Charlottesville."

"What's to discuss?" Doone pressed.

"That's enough," he said, before turning to Kik. "I thought Price wasn't a huckster? Did you hear him talk about his bestseller? He probably bought a couple thousand himself to scam the lists. It's not like he doesn't have a ton of people to foist them on."

"Wouldn't be the first time."

He laughed, remembering. "Do you and Parrish still think Dorian's got a basement full of her hardbacks?"

"Absolutely."

"Well," Tess interrupted again. "I think it is great fun to get all these presents. I will be bringing them in for sharing circle. I cannot wait to see what they give us next time!"

Casey shuddered, plugged in her earbuds and cranked Pharrell Williams up high, drowning out the horror music in her head.

Almost.

Chapter Seven

The yard glistened in the bright light like frosting spread over too-warm cake. Kik sat on the couch next to the window, listening to music, letting the early sun heat her face. It was beautiful outside and she was trying to take in the sight, to see the pristine landscape the way Doone might, as something to be stored and recreated later. Desolation would arrive soon enough. Charlottesville winters were mostly drab, pointless affairs, and Kik knew by February she'd feel terminal.

Bean was snuggled next to her, dreaming of things that made his feet run in place. She hoped it wasn't a nightmare of being chased by Orbison. Giving wide berth to the icky cyst by his shoulder, she rubbed his fur and was suddenly struck by an unfamiliar sensation. It was a blend of coziness and something else. A long moment passed before she could name it.

Calm! she thought. *I feel calm!*

Casey and Doone were still upstairs and Tess had allowed herself to be coaxed back to bed after a bowl of Lucky Charms. Everyone was where they were supposed to be and there were no immediate crises to obsess over. Doone had been less edgy in the days since they'd come back from New York and Kik's chronic siege mentality had perceptibly abated. The unremitting irritations that usually instigated huge blow-ups had somehow been defused. And once or twice, Kik's shoulders had actually unbunched when she was around her eldest.

Kik sighed and returned to the Price manual abandoned the evening before. She was having a hard time completing individual sections and kept skipping around the workbook as if it were a crossword puzzle. All she wrote in the page-long space for her approach to discipline was: *Does run-the-gamut count?* Then she moved on to Chapter Seven's PROUDER challenge.

Positive? *For the most part.*

Responsible? *Definitely!*

Organized? She left that one blank.

Uncritical? She scrawled *I try to be.*

Decisive? She left that one blank, too.

Emotionally intelligent? *I guess so.*

Relationship crafter? She answered in the affirmative but wasn't entirely sure what it referred to.

In the space left for additional comments, Kik wrote: *I love my girls more than life itself. I want more than anything to be a good mother.*

She tapped the pen against her cheek and wondered again what she was doing.

It was practically impossible to reconcile herself to the fact that they were involved in this. On the one hand it was so unbearably tacky she was beyond mortified. On the other, Casey was the one who suggested it and Doone seemed to be responding to the help.

How can I deprive them of it?

Particularly — God forbid — if something were to happen if we didn't do it!

"But can't we get the help somewhere else?" Owen had asked over the phone the day before. "Without cameras? Some place closer to home?"

"We got fired, remember?" Even to her the words sounded dumb.

"Oh, come on, Kik! There are boatloads of shrinks in town."

"But what if this is our one shot for Doone? He's the first one she's responded to!" Kik discovered herself arguing vigorously even though she agreed with him. It was one of those stand-by behaviors. "And don't forget that they bought rights to those old pictures. I've already used most of mine to pay off debts."

"What does that have to do with anything? I need to think about this."

"We're supposed to go back up in a few days."

"I'm well aware of that," he'd said before hanging up.

Kik tried to return her attention to the workbook but there was a sudden flash of crimson in the corner of her eye. A cardinal had landed on an alabaster branch right outside the window. She watched him bend forward to peck under his wing. Then wind lashed the tree and the bird stuttered off. Snow began rushing sideways past the glass. Kik imagined the individual flakes grabbing onto their hats, running for shelter.

She snuggled her feet deeper under the throw and flipped through the pages, stopping at a section that called for a description of her own mother. When she'd tried to tackle it earlier she ended up interrupting herself with a host of manufactured chores, including a clean sweep of the refrigerator and penning responses to holiday cards from annual friends.

She picked up the pen.

My mother was EXTREMELY difficult. I loved her. But I frequently felt like a foreign exchange student placed with some family at the last minute because the original match backed out. My childhood was spent in a state of hyper-alert. I was always worried, always on the verge of screwing up in some way.

Most of the time, Shelby (my mother) was the picture of Southern decorum. But problems always lurked. She reneged on commitments more than she kept them. Her temper was everywhere. Behind spilt juice, and interrupted naps, and once when she found out I told a friend's father how old she was when he asked. My sister and I both grew up fearful of volatility, afraid of setting her off. Our mother was happiest right before going out at night, when her perfume filled the house and the evening to come lay out before her like a room full of unopened gifts. Her mood was expansive then. And we would bask in the spillover.

Of course, the post-party hangover would meet us whenever she'd totter down the next day.

Without really thinking Kik wrote: *Also, I've always had a sneaking suspicion that my mother was a touch anti-Semitic. Problematic in that she married my father. She never said anything overt but*

Right then someone knocked on the window. The pen jumped out of Kik's hand and skittered across the floor. She looked up slowly, afraid of who might be standing there, observing her private moment. It was Parrish. He was bobbing a large white sack of Bodo's bagels in the air.

"Let me in," he mouthed. "I'm freezing!"

Kik was very aware she was wearing her bathrobe over nothing. And more importantly, she had no make-up on. Normally, her uneven dermatological terrain was camouflaged with problem-specific foundations.

Perfect.

Kik pulled the drapes to block the ruthless light before opening the door, wondered if she might ask Parrish to keep his eyes closed. "Hi!"

"Good morning, beautiful," he smiled. Orbison, dancing at the end of his leash, barked. "We bring meals on heels!"

"You walked over here?"

"It seemed like a good idea at the time. Now I'm thinking I may have to run over to the ER for a quick minute." He bent and gave her a kiss on the forehead. "How you doing, sugah?"

"Not too bad."

"Good. Want an everything with cream cheese?"

"Sure."

"Unchain the stud and follow me to the toaster. I'll hook you up."

She complied, freeing Orbison to assault poor Bean, then trailed Parrish into the kitchen, noticing how his jeans hung.

"Are you watching my rear end?"

"Don't flatter yourself."

While they had always laughed at sex stuff before, after what happened at Martin's party, this seemed different. She felt disoriented. She'd been working hard to only allow her mind to wander into The Kiss's terrain for quick peeks to make sure it was still there. She'd promised herself that when things calmed, and before Parrish could douse it with a cold splash of gentle letdown, she would allow herself one full-length feature fantasy about what had transpired.

At this point, though, she was hoarding it in the closet.

"I brought some real coffee, too. None of that instant crap today, Klara," he announced.

"Yum," Kik breathed in the cozy smell of garlic and onions.

"I got a couple of cinnamons for Tess and Doone. And a sesame for Casey," Parrish said.

"Perfect."

He scooped up a handful of empty sweetener packets from the counter and shook his head. "You go through this stuff like a junkie on a day pass."

"I know, I know. And it's expensive! I need a fake-sugar

daddy."

"Cute."

"Any*hoo*," she said, in a Dorian True trill. "This is really nice. Thank you."

She nuked their coffee and they went into the living room and sat next to each other on the couch. She had meant for him to sit across from her in the brown leather armchair, but he'd followed her to the sofa, making her feel particularly naked again.

"So what're the headlines, Klara? Fill me in."

She thought about running upstairs to change, but there was no natural break for her to do it without broadcasting her unease. There was something about being practically undressed so close to him that was throwing her libido into high gear. She watched his lips as he spoke and imagined him leaning forward, kissing her mouth, her neck. Untying the belt.

Get a grip! What are you doing?

Kik tried to arrange her expression so it wouldn't betray her roiling interior world. Then, prudishly overcompensating by clutching her robe closed, she bent to retrieve her coffee from the table.

"So what are you up to?" he asked.

"I've been trying to do the Dr. Price homework."

He lifted a dark eyebrow so she rushed on, describing the assignment rather than addressing the underlying issue of participation. "I'm trying to write about my mom."

"You're going there?"

"I know, right? Once I started writing though — "

He picked up the manual. "Can I?"

She hesitated. "You might as well, I guess."

He smiled at the irony of privacy and started reading.

"Whoa! Do you really think she was anti-Semitic?"

Flashes of old loyalty sparked, but she ignored them. "It's not anything I've ever actually said before. But yeah. There was always this weird undercurrent."

"Funny how we've never talked about this."

"I've never even talked to *Maddie* about it! It's just too awful, I guess."

"So what's the story?"

"Mom's family went from riches to rags. Granddad was always buying things. Land. Cars. Businesses. He had a sweater drawer full of gold watches! Anyway, he blew through the family money and by the time Miss Peachtree Parade went off to college she was on a mission. She looked around, set her sights on my poor father and reeled him in. He was the perfect payback. Granddad apparently went apoplectic when she brought home her Jewish boyfriend. So she married him."

"Wow."

"I don't know. Maybe I'm wrong. There were some good times, too. At least at one point. She did love her nightlife, though. Married or not."

"So a feral streak runs in the family?"

Kik smiled and thought back to high school when her teacher gave out a questionnaire about risky behavior. Numerical weights were assigned to positive responses. She was so distracted trying to tally her answers (Ever lied to your parents? Snuck out? Had sex? Gotten high?) that she missed the discussion of the point scale. When Kik raised her hand to ask the significance of her score the class laughed uproariously and the teacher, himself a bad boy, looked at her with newfound interest. (Which culminated in a mutual grope outside the auditorium, senior year.)

"Thing was, Parrish, even though I was on the wild side, I was on student council, in A.P. classes — except for math, of course. And I was a candy-striper." She looked into his kind eyes. "Doing all this has made me think about something, though."

"What, sugah?"

"That maybe I was too much like Shelby for Owen. Too excessive. You know when I used to tell him I loved him, he'd always say that he loved me more. And I was always so reassured by that. But it turns out what he really meant was that it *took* more to love me."

"You mean a degree of difficulty factor? Like in the Olympics?"

Her self-consciousness finally caught up and quieted her. She was suddenly excruciatingly embarrassed — Eve simultaneously discovering nakedness and cellulite.

Fortunately, Bean came bounding into the room, agitated about something.

"Where's Orbison?" she asked Parrish.

"Probably having a cigarette."

"I think not."

Bean began barking maniacally at the glass door. The squirrel that devoted its life to tormenting him had appeared on the porch railing, inciting a canine frenzy.

"What's happening?" Parish asked.

"The stupid rodent is waving at poor Bean."

"That's still going on?"

"It'll probably continue in the after-life." She got up to let the dog out. He skidded across the icy deck and into the porch swing.

"Ouch!" Parrish laughed.

Kik stayed at the window. "Do you think dogs experience disappointment?"

When she turned around she almost bumped into Parrish. And again that vast unknown territory within became molten. He smelled like coffee and sweat and sexual promise. Afraid her attraction was so intense he might see it; she ducked her face in a Princess Di pose. "Whoa, sorry. I didn't know you were there."

"Oh, Klara. What are we going to do with you?" He paused a beat. "So, a candy-striper, eh?"

A toilet flushed above them.

And the heat began dissipating. "I'm going to get some of those bagels toasted for the girls," she said.

Tess appeared. "Hello, Uncle Parrish. Did you have a sleepover?"

"I wish."

Upstairs, Casey retrieved *The Price Workbook* from beside the bed where it had slipped during the night. She decided to free write the section on her mother, try not to obsess, just get it over with. An earlier attempt had left her questioning the English prize she'd won the year before.

Klara Isabella Kaufman Marcheson. Sunshine and light and birthday parties and Easter egg hunts and paper dolls and hand decorated band-aids and brownies and color coordinated dinners. Laughter and electricity. The sound of a frustrated hand slapping down on the table. Her husky laugh floats. Funny like no other, she spills over the lines. When she listens to people, they're the only ones in the whole world.

Casey reread her words, panicked and considered ripping the page out. But the producer guy had warned them not to edit. "We'll be able to tell. It's important to get at the real issues. Don't worry, we won't take off for grammar."

Ha. Ha.

She wrote:

There isn't much I'd change about my mom. The problems mostly have to do with her not knowing how to deal with Doone.

"What are you doing?" Doone suddenly asked, startling Casey so much she practically squeaked. She stopped herself from slamming the book shut and tried to keep the guilt from her voice. "The Dr. Price assignment. Did you do it yet?"

Doone grunted and rubbed her hands across her face. Then let out a piercing yelp. "Ow! Get it off! Get it off!"

"What!" Casey asked shrilly. "Get what off?"

"I caught the pin on my bracelet!" Doone jumped up and moved quickly to the mirror above the desk; tried to pull back her wrist. The safety pin was dangling at a crazy angle. Casey felt like she might throw up. Blood made her nauseous. "I'll get Mom — "

"No! Just undo it! Undo it! I'll take it out the rest of the way. Please hurry!"

Casey forced herself towards her sister. She pried open the clasp and released it from the braided hemp. A cruddy paste of blood and yellow pus was on it.

Gross. "There."

"Thanks," Doone muttered, pulling the skin taut, unpinning her face. "Well, that sucks."

Casey went into the bathroom for some peroxide and was surprised by an aromatic cocktail of perfume and something fermented.

Doone must have already been up and gone back to bed.

Casey opened the drawer and grabbed a couple cotton balls. Little frown lines of concentration appeared on her forehead as she tried to identify the smell. The odor was elusive — an olfactory equivalent of an acquaintance's name. She reached under the sink for the peroxide that towered over cliques of lotions and oils — relics from middle school when bath products were exchanged like wampum — and then stood back up in a hurry.

She realized what the other scent was.

Doone got high in the house!

Casey's toes did a trio of clenches as disappointment and anger welled. Intellectually she knew that just going up to New York wouldn't change anything, but she'd unconsciously held onto her hope. She went back into the bedroom with the stuff, held it out stiffly. "Here."

"Thanks. It kills."

"I'm surprised you're feeling much of anything."

Doone got the dig. "You know what, Casey? Why don't you back off? You're as bad as Mom."

Casey's eyes filled without warning.

"Sorry," Doone said quietly. "Sometimes I just need to chill, you know? Don't you ever feel like that?"

Casey, whose toes were so tightly clenched she could have fallen over, nodded.

Doone offered a rare conversational follow-up. "Do you think Dad is going to keep doing the show?"

Casey ran her fingers over the words looking for the concealed barb, the swallowed sneer, found nothing. "I don't know. He seemed like he was on the fence. Do you really like Price, Doone?"

"I like how he says what he means."

"Really?"

"Why do you say it like that?"

"I kinda thought you mostly liked him because Dad didn't."

"There is that." The girls laughed together and Doone continued. "You should have seen the cow they made me go to here. I hated her. She made Dad seem laid back." Doone checked out the cotton puff to see what was on it then put it back on her face. "Did you know she's Alison's mother?"

"No way. Alison Greenly?"

"Yeah. How messed up is that? I didn't even know until the day I saw Dr. West's name on a parent-teacher sign-up sheet next to Alison's. They have different last names. Obviously. But you'd think there'd be like rules about things like that."

"I guess that's bound to happen in a small town. But it is kind of sketchy."

"After I found out I used to wonder if they like talked about me at dinner and stuff. It made me paranoid. I was going to bring it up but then thought I'd better not give her ideas. In case she didn't know. Sometimes the two of us just sat there and stared at each other for like an hour. I guess that's why I like Price. At least he talks. Shares his own stuff."

"That's weird that her mother was so snotty. Since Alison's supposed to have been ground zero for the herpes epidemic."

Doone's mouth dropped open and her hand drifted from her brow. "No way! Are you kidding me?"

"Word on the street," Casey smiled.

"Dude. I wish I knew that when I was still going to her mother. Of course she probably would have just said something like, 'What is the relevance of that to the work you need to be doing, Doone?' Wow. Dr. Judgemental's daughter, school skank."

Casey felt a twinge of guilt about gossiping. But for the first time in memory she felt close to her sister, so it was worth it. Doone, too, seemed to be enjoying the moment.

"Case, do you remember back when Uncle Terry was alive?"

"Sure. Of course. Why?"

"I woke up thinking about him."

"What about?"

"That time before he died when I went with him and Dad to the beach."

"When was that? Was I there?"

"No, you were sick. I remember you crying about not being able to go and at first I was like neny-neny-boo-boo. But as usual you were the lucky one."

Casey winced but asked what happened.

"It didn't start off all that bad. But it went downhill in a hurry. First I was pumped because Dad rented this van that could hold the wheelchair and I thought it was going to be really cool. *Not.* I got carsick like before we got on the highway. Plus, Uncle Terry smelled bad which made me feel even more like hurling. I was in the back with my eyes closed and Dad thought I was asleep. So he was talking to Uncle Terry like I wasn't there. And of course Terry couldn't answer so Dad was like on this roll the whole way there."

"What was he saying?"

"About what it was like growing up, which was actually kind of interesting because he never really talked about stuff like that to us. You know? Fake Hippie-Man's not all that in touch with his feelings."

Casey's smile tightened in concert with her shoulders. *How can sisters have such different opinions about the same parent?*

"He confessed to all these things he did when he and Terry

were kids. I guess things he always swore he didn't do."

"Like what?"

"Funny things like accidentally breaking Terry's pitching trophy and stealing his dirty magazines. But then he talked about Nana and how she was like in this constant battle with the universe. Do you remember her?"

Casey shook her head. "Not really."

"She was a clean-freak. And always telling these stories about people putting arsenic in candy and little blonde children getting snatched from amusement parks."

"Why blonde?"

"So the kidnappers could dye their hair black in the bathrooms on the way out. Nana was queen of stuff like that. Dad said that's why he wanted to be a scientist. To be able to prove things." Doone laughed. "Too bad *Snopes.com* wasn't around back then. He basically wasted all that time in grad school because of urban legends."

Casey smiled, realized she liked her sister high. "And you just lay there?"

"Yeah. I mean I guess I should have sat up or something. But it was pretty fascinating."

"It's funny that Dad would take Uncle Terry out like that. How did he do with all the tubes and everything?"

"That was part of the problem. Mom had been the one to organize the trip and this nurse was supposed to go, too. But then she backed out at the last minute because of bunions — which I thought was a hysterical word — and then you got strep or something, so Mom couldn't go either. She pushed Dad to go anyway, said he'd never forgive himself if he didn't. That it would make Terry happy to go back once more. So Dad caved."

"What happened?" Casey wasn't sure she wanted to know.

"At first he was kind of into it. But by the time we got to the bridge he was seriously stressing. And by the time we parked I finally realized it was not going to be like any other day at the beach." She paused and grinned a little. "I even wished you were there so I'd have someone to play with. Anyway, Mom had packed this fancy picnic lunch. She made chicken salad. You know the kind with tarragon?"

"Uh huh."

"Well, Terry was still sort of able to feed himself then. But I guess with Lou Gehrig's you lose different muscles at different times. Or something. I don't know. He couldn't swallow right anymore. He started gagging. Seriously choking."

"What happened?" Casey whispered.

"Dad panicked. Fell apart. But then this woman came running over. She unseatbelted Terry and grabbed him from behind and did the Heimlich. When the stuff came up, Dad was falling all over himself with appreciation. The lady said she was used to it because she worked at a nursing home."

"What'd you do then?"

"Packed up the van and came home. I think we were there for like half an hour, max. But the thing was, you would have thought that Dad would have stayed like all grateful and everything."

"He didn't?"

"No. He was seriously pissed."

"At what? Not at Uncle Terry?"

"No. At Mom."

"Because she talked him into going?"

"Yeah. And he just tore into her. Threw shade for miles. Totally forgot I was there again."

"What did he say?" Casey asked, blinking nervously.

"That he should have followed his instincts — that it was insane for him to take Terry on the trip, that it was standard Kik. Like she could have known that Terry was going to choke! And then he started going off on how he couldn't stand her mess. That nothing was ever where he left it. That the whole idea of him having an office at home was a joke because he could never even find the stapler. And if he ever had to search for something again he was going to kill himself."

"Wow." Casey laughed nervously. "That was a little insensitive."

"Ya think?"

Doone looked like she was going to say something else but shook her head, pitched the cotton ball into the trash, and went into the bathroom.

Chapter Eight

Their mom was at work and Casey was home with her sisters. She had come upon the website by accident and had been compulsively reading for almost an hour, refreshing the page every few minutes to check for new posts. Her breathing was strained and her eyes felt dry.

"Oh no," she muttered, scrolling down the online commentaries about her family. "No. No. No."

Homeschoolinmama: Is it just me or does Kick (what kind of a name is that anyway?!!) act a little above it all? She seems to think she's really something being a professor. And that little one is cute NOW — but they're going to have their hands full in a few years. They're looking at trouble with a capital T.

Texarkana65: I'm with you about the mother. No wonder that one girl is out of control. She talks to them like they're miniature adults. How does Dr. Price pick these families anyway? That last one was a train wreck, too!

Treyfun: I may be in a minority but I feel that the father has to take a lot of the blame here. Didn't he take a vow to be in the marriage? And also, doing the math, he left his wife WHILE SHE WAS PREGNANT! Come ON! (Unless the baby's not his?!!!)

Meowgal: How could those people let that Dune on TV looking like she just fell out of a dirty clothes hamper? I swear, every day, I get happier and happier that I have cats instead of children. I could barely look at that girl.

Theway: I hear what your saying, Treyfun. The unspoken Truth here is that this Family is in the Hot water that they are in because they have set aside the Bible. The Blueprint for Healthful living is right between those covers. If more Americans would Remember that, then Dr. Price wouldn't have to be Working so Hard!

Sally999: Hold the phone people! We only just met this family! I know a lot of decent parents whose kids have messed up. Let's give them a chance! I'm sure none of us would want our whole lives judged after only one appearance.

Theway: @Sally999 That makes me Wonder about your Family.

Meowgal: Sally999 — I don't know, I may not have much experience with children but I can't help but believe that good parents have good children. How on earth do these people think their girls aren't going to be doing drugs if they can't even control how they look?

ShenandoahSue: OMG! I know this family from my son's school! Doone has a reputation. OTOH, Casey is a dream child. ps. I volunteer frequently and haven't met their mother yet! Just sayin'.

SHOPPINGCHICA103: Bwaahaha! I thought my family was bad! LMAO!

CULTURE COP: I just love whiny, rich white people. Seriously do they not know what real problems are?

Sally999: What on earth does race have to do with anything??? Making light of other peoples' struggles is pretty petty. An out of control child is terrifying no matter what race you are.

The phone rang but Casey let it go. She thought if she opened her mouth she might throw up. She heard Doone answer in the hall. There was quiet for a moment and then Doone yelled something and slammed the phone back into the cradle. A minute later the bedroom door flung open and Doone stood on the threshold, her face contorted.

"What's the matter?" Casey asked, heart pounding.

"That ass-hat just quit!"

"Wait! What? Who quit?"

"Your perfect father, that's who!" Doone switched into a tight-lipped impersonation, "'I'm afraid I just can't do the show after all.' He said he and his stupid girlfriend talked, decided it wasn't right for him. Like I care what she thinks!"

"Did he say why?"

"Are you deaf?" Doone screamed. "I just told you what he said!" She slammed the door so hard that books levitated from their shelves and the mirror swayed drunkenly over the desk.

Casey closed her eyes. She wondered what her mother would say.

Across town, Kik had just gotten out of her last class and was hurrying to catch up with Parrish. Distracted, she brought a car to a screeching stop.

Parrish shook his head.

"Hey, Mr. Writer-Man," a student from a raucous group in front of the deli called out. "Sing us a song!"

Parrish, a campus celebrity because of the short-listing of *Peckerwood Swamp* for a National Book Award was also widely known for his music.

"Yeah," another yelled, flicking an imaginary lighter. "*Freebird!*"

"He can't," Kik said, grabbing her friend's arm. "We have an important meeting. Come along, Mr. Writer-Man."

The kids laughed as he shrugged sad defeat and allowed Kik to pull him towards their weekly happy hour.

"You're hopeless," Kik said.

"But that's what you love about me, right? My bad boy mystique?"

"Exactly how old are you?"

"Younger than you," he said, then inclined his head towards the disproportionately small monument of the school's founder that sat in front of the library. "Shrinkage."

"No points for recycled observational humor," Kik reprimanded. "In fact, I'm going to check the rules — you should probably be penalized."

"Penile-ized?"

"Ha."

"Hey, I tried calling last night, but the phone was busy for hours. And your cell phone rang forever. I almost got worried enough to come over."

"Why didn't you?"

"Figured if something really bad was going on I'd hear about it on TV."

"Not funny, Parrish."

"Sorry. Look. Here's the thing. I just feel like we need to talk. About the other night."

"If it's about that one stupid kiss, don't worry about it. I promise I won't make you marry me. If it makes you feel any better I haven't thought about it."

"Not even for a second?"

"No," she lied. "And in terms of truly important issues, I don't think you should be allowed to go out of town anymore on Drink Day. Your canceling our last one really messed me up."

"Clearly."

He smiled and held open the door and they climbed the steep stairs to the second floor restaurant. They were seated by the window.

"Hey, Parrish — I'm really cold. Can we move? It's like hanging out with Tess in the freezer aisle while she agonizes over ice cream flavors."

"At your service," he said obligingly. He picked up both coats and led her to a rear booth. "Satisfactory?"

"Still a tad nippy, but I'll survive."

"I'll warm you up."

"You talk the talk," she said, setting him up for a slam-dunk. "But can you walk the walk?"

"Woman, I can *sprint* the walk."

They laughed. It was an oldie but goodie from their treasury of student sayings. They kept a running compendium of quotes.

"Hey, I heard a great one the other day," Kik remembered. "This kid was trying to comfort a girl who just found out she was flunking a class."

"What'd he say?"

She lowered her voice and did her best frat-boy joviality. "'C'mon — graduating in four years would be like leaving a party at midnight!'"

"Good one," Parrish laughed. "Log it."

The waitress came with a bowl of salted nuts and their drinks. Kik ripped open a fat stack of sweetener packets and added them to her bourbon. Parrish shook his head. She ignored him. He grabbed a handful of cocktail mix and dropped them one by one deep into his mouth.

"Very appealing, Parrish. I think I can see your uvula."

"Are you insulting my manhood?"

"*U*-vula."

"Speaking of which, when I was back home Colette told me she thought she might be gay. I don't know why but the poor thing was scared to tell me."

"What'd you say?"

"That the only thing I wouldn't be able to cotton to would be her being Republican. Might just be a phase, though. Lots of young women experiment, I think."

Kik hoped he wouldn't ask if she ever partook. Because, frankly, the whole idea of lesbianism always kind of weirded her out. Anatomically, not politically, of course. It was terrain she had no interest in exploring. She could certainly understand the emotional inclination, though.

Just without the sex.

She started to ransack her mental file of Occasion Stories, trying to find one that not only fit but hadn't yet been utilized back when Parrish's wife came out. *That's the problem with topic-specific anecdotes,* Kik thought. *You run the risk of repeating yourself should circumstances recur.* Not for the first time she wished for some sort of cerebral rotation system like grocery stores had for restocking perishables.

They drank in comfortable silence for a few minutes then a naughty smile played on Kik's lips.

"What?" Parrish asked.

"I was just thinking that it's weird your dog is gay, too."

He laughed loudly and told her he was sure what she'd just said was reportable.

"Yeah, probably."

"So. How is everything, Kik? Really?"

The mirth vanished. "Pretty grim."

"What's going on?"

"You mean besides getting ready to go back up to New York to parade my parenting failures to the whole freaking world?"

"If it makes you feel any better I thought Owen came across like wilted lettuce."

"Yeah, well. The salad pulled out. "

"What?"

"He called a little while ago. And said he really wanted to do it for the girls — for Casey mostly, I think — but the reality was too jarring. He doesn't even like dinner parties, you know."

"Wasn't this whole thing his idea?"

"Not strictly speaking. It was really Casey's."

"So you're stuck holding the bag?"

"Kind of a familiar theme," Kik felt a dangerous pressure of tears.

"How are the girls doing?"

"I don't know how they're going to take Owen's decision. But how's this for sick — " she interrupted herself to take a sip, slow herself down. She enjoyed the paradoxical soothing burn of the alcohol. "Not only did Doone take the safety pin out of her face — she's been staying home a lot more."

"Wow. Extra points on the parental torture scale." He reached for another handful of nuts. "Why do you think that is?"

"I don't know," she shrugged. "I haven't been able to figure out why she does anything since she was two. Did you know there are message boards?"

He nodded, unfazed by the non sequitur.

"You do? How?"

"Bumped into a former student when I was getting my mail. Those Priceans are pretty brutal, huh?"

"I'm being crucified."

"Why do you care what they say?"

"What do you mean?" At Kik's very core was a deep concern for public opinion, a fundamental need to be liked.

"They're a bunch of trolls. Sock puppets. And the ones in the studio audience were like a herd of cattle going full-steam in one direction and then shifting course just as quick."

"Yeah. They respond to whatever cues Price puts out. It's weird, isn't it? I don't know if it's even conscious or not. They just adopt his reactions — exaggerated pleasure, hostility. Whatever. And they also mug when they know the cameras are on them. It's a little embarrassing actually."

Parrish drummed his fingers quietly on the table. "So if therapy in the real world is insurance-driven, is it ratings-driven on the airwaves?"

"I don't know. Per my usual lack of foresight I forgot to ask how we would know we were cured."

"Well, I hope it doesn't have anything to do with the show being renewed because I read this morning that it might not be."

"Seriously?"

He nodded once and then broke into a raspy rendition of *The Price You Pay.*

"Very funny."

"Just tell me you're not getting paid for this."

"Ummm."

All humor evaporated. "Come again?"

"Not for being on the show per se. But for something called licensing fees, for old pictures. I think it's just a slimy way that lets them say they don't pay guests for appearing. The thing is, I really needed the money. To pay back that stupid advance. So I'm not arguing."

"I wish you had just asked me for it."

"Can we please talk about something else? This has spiraled so out of control I'm about a minute and a half away from permanently losing it."

"Which, unfortunately, is as good a lead-in as any."

"To what?"

"I overheard Martin and Dorian this morning. Apparently both of them caught the show."

Kik groaned.

"I take it you didn't mention your family's participation to him beforehand?" Parrish asked.

Kik shook her head.

"Should I ask why not?"

"Honestly? I just didn't think about it."

"The dictator-ette ain't amused, Kik."

"Of course he's not. He was born without a sense of humor."

"And since you mine the obituaries for hilarity there's definitely room for misunderstanding."

Parrish was talking about the time in the faculty lounge when she was reading the newspaper and came across the death notice for a guy named Augie Sharpfinger. Kik asked her colleagues if they thought nose-picking was to blame. Everyone had laughed. Except for Martin.

"I'd ditch the TV therapy if I were you, chérie."

"I can't. I promised the girls. And unlike Owen, you know how I am about promises." Her fingers began to rub her temples, trying to ease the coming pain.

"Battalion on the move?" he asked.

"Yeah. The respite by the river is over."

"Sorry. Do you have your headache stuff?"

"Yeah, thanks. But I prefer to drink my relief at the moment." She looked into his eyes, smiled faintly. And then, because she'd run out of her own words, she quoted from *Horton Hatches the Egg* to explain her stubborn steadfastness.

"Oh honey," he said, taking her hand. "People can change their minds."

She waited for a quick squeeze of affection, then release. It didn't come. Instead he lifted her hand to his cheek. "What's going on, Parrish?"

He held her gaze. "Honestly? Unlike you apparently, I've thought about that kiss more than once."

"You're not one of those fetish men, are you?"

"What?"

"You know! The guys who only date 500 pounders. Or women who administer enemas or — "

He burst out laughing. "What are you talking about?"

"I mean, are you attracted to basket cases or something? And all of a sudden I fit the bill?"

"All of a sudden?"

"Oh, shut up," she felt light-headed. What was happening? She tried to take back her hand, but he still wouldn't relinquish it.

"Parrish, did I tell you about that cartoon I saw of a dog humping a woman's ankle while fantasizing about another leg?"

"I have no idea what made you think of that. Nor do I care to find out. What would you say if I were to tell you I wanted to give us a shot? That more and more I've been thinking what I've been looking for has been under my nose all this time."

"I'd tell you I couldn't stand to be deserted by you, Parrish. I need you too much. I love you too much."

The tears gathered quickly, started to spill. She pulled away from him and stood. "Will you get the check?"

Kik kept her head down against the biting wind, pondering one of her stand-by writing assignments. Her students had to come up with titles for their memoirs. She used to think that

Good Intentions would work for her own. Now, though, recycling Wally Lamb's *She's Come Undone* probably made more sense.

Chapter Nine

Horror music blared. Someone had scrawled Doone Marcheson is a Skank in black ink on the bathroom stall. Casey grabbed a paper towel, wet it, and tried to clean the words off, but the letters held firm. And with *Shh*, Ivy's underground blog, providing a link straight to the show's message board, no amount of scrubbing would ever erase the talk.

Even Tess was catching the fallout. The day after the show aired, a fifth grader had gone up to her on the playground and said the Marchesons were trashy. Which was a big mistake. Tess went ballistic, and grabbed a fistful of the girl's hair. Kik had to go to school to pick her up. Casey and Doone tried to make jokes about the kindergarten delinquent, but Kik was definitely freaked, saying it's not funny yet, and had gone to bed with one of her headaches.

Casey decided to go to the office and ask Mrs. Branch for help cleaning off the door before next period started. The only thing worse than the original declaration would be the comments it generated.

What have I done? What have I done? What have I done?

The secretary put up one finger signaling her to hang on while she finished a call. When she hung up she drawled, "I have to call that boy's parents so much I'm afraid I'm going to start dialing them in my sleep." She studied Casey for a second and said, "Honey, you look awful. Come on with me. I'll take a break."

The teen could only nod. Anything more than that and she

might lose it altogether. Mrs. Branch walked a fast clip down the hallway, long blond braid swinging between her shoulders.

She stopped by a window that looked out onto the Blue Ridge, glancing around to make sure no one was within earshot. "What is going on, Ms. Marcheson?"

"It's the show. It's my fault that we're on it."

"How's that?"

"Because I said something to him when I met him. About Doone. And now we're on a runaway train."

"What do you mean?"

"Everything feels so out of control. Everybody is talking about us and people are writing mean things about Doone in the bathroom."

"The one next to the cafeteria?"

"Yeah."

"Well, that's nothing! We'll take care of that. That kind of crap is normal wear and tear for a school."

"I just wish I never opened my mouth." And then to her surprise she burst into embarrassing sobs and Mrs. Branch hustled her into the bathroom. "I wish I could take it all back."

"Have you told your parents how you feel?"

"No."

"Why not?"

"Because Doone likes him. So maybe he *can* help. I don't know," Casey said quietly. "The other night I had this dream. I really wanted to go horseback riding and I guilted my mother into taking us up Ragged Mountain and then one of the horses slipped off. I woke up screaming. I couldn't tell whose horse it was."

"I guess you don't need Dr. Price for that one."

Casey shook her head and reached around Mrs. Branch

for some toilet paper to blow her nose.

"What do your parents think about the show?"

"My dad refused to do it anymore. And I don't think my mom's too crazy about it either. The thing is, any time we submit our journals, or go up there they get like hours of material. And that's not even including all the footage they got from when they put the cameras up in our house. He probably already has enough stuff on us to do like a whole season of shows! We're basically stuck."

"Come on, girly-girl. The only time anyone is ever stuck is in a casket."

"But I don't know how we can pull out. Or if we can. Like maybe even legally. My parents had to sign all these papers when we went up there."

"Well, they can get a lawyer. But you need to tell your parents what you're thinking. All you were trying to do was get Doone some help. And Little Miss Chip On Her Shoulder sorely needs some. Girl reminds me of a yellow jacket in a hot car."

Casey nodded.

"Do you want me to set up an appointment with Dr. Tim?"

"I think I'd rather chew my arm off. Thanks, though."

"Yeah, everybody says that," Mrs. Branch laughed. "Anyway, this seems like a group slip-up. You didn't hold a gun to your parents and make them participate, did you?"

"Not exactly."

"Oh come on, Casey-girl. Of course you didn't. And it's not like y'all are the only ones getting caught up in all this TV crap. I saw this show just the other night. These families let themselves get videotaped for like two years! And they seemed like pretty normal people. What would happen if you just told your mom you wanted to quit?"

"When I was in middle school I wanted to quit basketball and she made me finish out the season. But then there were other times when she let me pull out of stuff. But I think that was mostly so she didn't have to drive."

"Lord, I hear that! Sometimes I feel like I'm going to shoot myself driving all over kingdom come to my kids' extracurriculars. Look, honey — the best thing for you to do is tell your parents what you want. Or at least tell them that you're confused about what you want. People make mistakes all the time. Now, show me which stall needs the elbow grease and I'll get my special cleanser."

Casey was still very confused but felt calmer. "We're supposed to go back up tomorrow. Maybe I'll just give it one more chance."

"Sounds like a plan. Come on and give me a hug and promise you'll lighten up on yourself. You're a good girl, Casey Marcheson. People around here love you."

"Thanks Mrs. Branch."

On the way to class she saw Caroline's butt sticking out of her locker. Her friend was digging through piles of books, shoes and empty bags of Doritos. Casey pinched her. "Hey."

"Hey, yourself," Caroline answered, without jumping. As if people did that to her all the time. Her words echoed off the narrow metal walls. When she finally emerged she was smiling broadly. "Phew, I thought I left my report at home! Check this out. I was violated by one of those flying cockroaches. Right in the middle of French class! It jetted out of the vent and right up my skirt!"

"Okay, that's gross," Casey laughed. "What are you doing after school?"

"Jest chillaxin' with my peeps," she grinned. "What about you? Any plans?"

"I don't know. Doone's going to baby-sit."

Caroline tucked silky blonde hair behind an ear. "I can't believe your mother trusts her!"

"It's kind of a trial run. Dr. Price suggested giving her more responsibilities."

"Whew. Brave! Don't you think your mom could have just started with, like, getting her to feed the dog?"

Casey smiled.

"Seriously. Maybe y'all should invest in one of those panic buttons for Tess to wear around her neck. For back-up."

A little twinge of defensiveness fluttered inside Casey. Her toes clenched quickly to release it. Caroline shifted her book against her chest. "You all right, Case? You're looking kinda tragic."

"I'm doing okay."

"I wish we could hang, but I've got my stupid oral report to do and my teacher spazzes over the most random things."

"Like not showing up?"

"I know, right?" Caroline snorted.

"I'll call you, later, C-line. Watch out for cockroaches."

"Seriously. Seize ya later."

Casey rolled her eyes. Her friend had epilepsy.

Casey was still smiling when she pushed open the classroom door. Then Mr. Sanders rotated on his heels and said, "Well, if it isn't one of our most famous denizens!"

Her face felt microwaved. Denizens.

Occupants, residents, inhabitants.

Doone, too, had been hearing the same kind of stuff. Even though the Marchesons were prohibited from giving interviews, the newspaper had run a story the day before about the local family's brush with fame.

Afterwards they got a couple of crank calls. Doone hadn't thought she'd care, but she did. Even Mr. Gibbs had piled on that morning.

In front of the whole second period Latin for Losers!

"How'd y'all get suckered into being fodder for schadenfreude?" he'd asked.

"What's that?"

"Basically it's people getting enjoyment from the misfortunes of others."

For some reason, learning there was an actual word for it (even if it wasn't in English) flipped her out. So much so that she decided to blow off her afternoon classes to go to Dust's. To see if she might not find a little something to chill with. She'd heard he'd made bail.

But when she got over there all his stuff was on the sidewalk in front of the plumbing shop. The plaid couch, looking wasted, was standing up on two legs propped against a street lamp, ratty pillows down around its feet. A work shirt, with Dust's name sewn over the pocket in loopy blue script, was hugging a load of crap piled in front of the TV. The screen had been stomped in. Doone wondered who had done that.

The landlord? Cops? Some random walking down the street?

The wind kicked up, riffling the pages of a dictionary. Doone considered going to pick it up but didn't. She just stood there for a few minutes feeling sad and dislocated. She hoped Dust had taken off. Started over somewhere else. He wasn't a bad guy — just somebody who'd been born into a bad situation. Messed up parents. Ass-hat brother. She'd always felt sad for him about that.

Another gust of cold air slapped at her face and she decided to stop in at Country Kitchen and get a hot chocolate before heading back to Ivy. She waited in line while an old man counted out change to pay for his stuff.

"Hey, you," a voice said from behind Doone.

She turned. Her cheeks got hot.

"What are you doing here, Hank?" she asked, trying to be chill, walking over to his table.

"Hangin'. I had a root canal. A little trip to hell for my mouth. You getting lunch?"

"Yes. No! Just some cocoa."

"Want to sit with me while I eat? Solid food hasn't been an option for like a week. All I've been able to think about is cheese steak."

"Aren't you supposed to like not eat after the dentist?"

"Yeah. I'll just chew on the other side." He took a healthy mouthful, swallowed. "Everything copasetic?"

"Not really."

"Bite?"

"Vegetarian."

"You are? I didn't know that about you. It wasn't in the research I did." He smiled and Doone blushed again. "Is being on the show getting you down?"

"You know about that?" She started compulsively twisting the saltshaker's metal lid. On. Off. On.

"Of course I know about it. Everybody does. I don't spend all my time milking llamas. I guess it's not as bad as some of the other talk shows. But they all kind of remind me of crazy tabloids that print real news alongside the made-up crap. Know what I mean?"

"Uh — no?"

"So you don't know what's what. It's like a chocolate chip in a bowl of raw cookie dough."

"No offense, Hank," she laughed. "But I have no freakin' clue what you're talking about."

"The tasty morsels might be embedded in some serious salmonella." He took a bite, chewed slowly. "Did you see Dr. Price yesterday?"

Doone shook her head.

"I was home with this toothache — which, by the way, is why I haven't called you yet. It's been an unreal train wreck inside my face."

Her heart could have jumped right out of her sweater. "I'm sorry."

"Anyway, the good doctor had this woman on whose husband attacked her with a broken bottle. She didn't have any insurance. So Price got some surgeon to work on her for free."

"What's wrong with that?"

"Nothing. Except there are tons of people who need surgery and whatnot. He could have helped her *and* used his show to call for real national health insurance. Single-payer. He could make a difference to a lot of people."

She was quiet for a moment, contemplating.

"It's not a done deal, you know, Doone."

"What's not?"

"Who we are. We can still learn from our mistakes. Change. That's what my dad says anyway, when one of us screws up."

"Even if it's been going on for awhile?"

"Yep."

A strange couple rounded the corner by the assisted living

facility and inched down the sidewalk. The woman seemed to be wearing more than one winter coat although she had no stockings on under her dress. The man kept opening and closing his mouth like a guppy. Doone watched him, wondering if words were coming out or only air. They went over to Dust's things and began picking through the piles.

"Sad," Hank said. "I hope that couch doesn't fall over on them."

"Yeah." She thought about the things she'd done on that sofa and looked away.

"So. Since you're already playing hooky and I won't have to worry about being a bad influence, want to blow off the rest of the afternoon, come back and meet the llamas? I can drive you home later."

"Cool."

He lived way out in the country in an old farmhouse with a smattering of outbuildings and a windmill. His parents were outside doing some kind of yard work.

"Welcome to *American Gothic,*" Hank said. "Hippie style."

They're real hippies, Doone thought, after talking with them. *Not the fake kind like Owen.*

Doone and Hank hung out for a couple of hours. They looked through his portfolio of drawings, experimented with new oil sticks he'd gotten, and listened to a mix from when he DJ-ed on the alternative station over the summer. They played ping-pong and Hank shed his relaxed style, turning into a trash-talking Charles Barkley. Doone almost fell over from laughing so hard, which, she explained to him, was the only way he won.

As an afterthought they stopped in to look at the llamas.

On the way home Doone tried to remember the last time

she was with anyone for that long without being high. She asked Hank if he was straight edge.

"Not hardly. Actually, I even have a couple of my own plants. But I don't smoke that much anymore. Mostly I run or play the guitar when I want to be chill."

"I used to run, too."

When they pulled up in front of the house he didn't try to kiss her. She thanked him for the ride and he gave her his lopsided grin and said, "No worries. Maybe we can do it again? Or we could run together? When it's a little warmer, I mean."

She'd smiled all the way to the front door. He waited until she got in the house before driving off, which was the only time that had ever happened. Not long after she took her coat off, the phone rang.

"Doone?"

"Yeah?"

"It's Hank. Listen, Felix called me on my cell."

"Who?"

"The tall spotted llama?"

"You're insane!"

"Anyway, the poor beast was hemming and hawing all over the place. Finally asked me when you were going to be coming back. He wanted to know what you thought about trans-species love."

"That's a little gross," she laughed.

"Don't judge. Hey Doone — when we were together did I mention what a great smile you have?"

Which made her tumble deep into some unknown place, a place that bathed her in a soft and gentle light, a light in which she did not recognize herself.

They said good-bye. The phone rang again. She answered

laughing, but this time it was Kik.

"Hi, sweetie! I'm so glad you're home. Thank you for babysitting!"

That was close! Doone had gotten home before Tess but only by accident. She hadn't remembered she was supposed to be babysitting. She raced up to the bus stop just as the kindergartener was getting off.

"I did not see you!" Tess said accusingly, her face all red. "You are supposed to be standing right here when the bus comes!"

"The bus was early."

Tess gave a little shudder. When she exhaled snot bubbled on her nostril and she was scratching at her wrist above her mitten.

"Are you sick, junior?"

"No."

"What's the matter, then?"

"Malcolm told me his mother said we were putting our business on the street," she heaved once and snuffled.

"Is that all? Quit scratching, it's gross. Plus you'll get that impetigo again."

"But what does that mean! Putting our business on the street?"

"If you don't even know why are you crying?"

"Just tell me!"

Doone considered ignoring her but knew that could end in an ankle-kicking temper tantrum in the middle of the sidewalk. Definitely not worth the aggravation. *Or as Dr. Price might say, the aggro.* They eyed each other warily. "I guess Mrs. Malcolm was talking about us being on TV. Don't worry about it."

"Her name's not Mrs. Malcolm! It's Mrs. Lee."

"Whatever. Anyway why do you care what she thinks? She has a stick up her a — butt."

"What is an abutt?"

"Her butt, Tess! Her butt! She's always frowning. She walks around looking like she smells something. "

Tess's obsidian eyes got bigger. Then she giggled and wiped her nose on the back of her mitten. "I do not always like to go there. Lots of times she makes me and Malcolm stay in the den. And we can only take out one clay at a time. So the colors do not get mixed. And that is stupid and boring. And sometimes when Malcolm does misbehavior she says she is going to make him go live with his father!"

"Wow," Doone was startled. "That *is* mean."

"Yeah! And sometimes she forgets that I do not like butter on my peanut butter and jelly sandwiches."

"Gross. Come on. I'll make it right for you."

"Doone?"

"What?"

"Harperly told me that she might have to go away soon. It made me sad. I cried at school."

"That's stupid, junior. She's imaginary! You tell *her*, not the other way around."

Tess's bottom lip quivered again.

"Okay, my bad. I shouldn't have said that. I just meant that you should just tell her she's not going anywhere. You're in charge. Like Mom is. All right? And don't worry about what Mrs. Malcolm said. Anybody who uses butter with peanut butter doesn't know anything."

"Okay. Will you put it in a sandwich bag?"

Chapter Ten

They overslept and finished packing in a flurry, following last minute instructions to bring enough clothes for three tapings. The producer had called the night before to explain that the marathon sessions would be better for everyone's schedule.

"Even contestants on game shows do it, so they don't look like they have poor hygiene," he'd laughed heartily. "And with Dr. Price it means not having to break for a week right at critical points!"

Which made sense to Kik, even if felt somewhat dishonest. *Shouldn't the TV audience be informed? Isn't that deceptive?* Then she thought, *Why do I care what the audience thinks?*

The trip up was different without Owen. Even Tess felt it, yelling over the plane's engines that she thought it was rude. "Like when Malcolm did not come to my birthday party just because he was going to be the onliest boy."

"You'd think Tess would be used to it by now," Kik heard Doone say to Casey in the seats in front of her. "His middle name is no-show."

Tess pulled on her mother's sleeve. "Why does Doone hate Daddy so much?"

"She doesn't hate him, sweetie. She's just angry and sad."

When they got to the studio, Liza flapped into the dressing room with a blue silk scarf for Kik. "It'll bring out your eyes?"

"I don't normally do scarves," Kik protested. But the assistant looked so dejected Kik caved and let her drape it over her right shoulder in a wide triangle, stewardess-style.

"Like a bib for people with neck issues," Casey whispered on the way to the stage.

Doone's smile froze when they took their seats. The audience response to their arrival was Arctic. "Did we crash a party?" she murmured.

"Yikes," Casey whistled under her breath.

"So, I'm back today with the family I've been working with. The parents, Owen and Kik — who *is* here — are divorced but share the raising of their children. Somewhat, anyway. Owen, who was present last time, decided that this isn't his cup of Earl Grey. And that's fine. Problem solving is not for sissies," he paused for laughter. "No — I'm joshing, my friends. Owen decided that he'd rather do his work off-camera and I have to respect that. But his lovely ex-wife and their three beautiful daughters have decided to stick with the program. Hopefully he'll be able to piggyback off their hard work. We're going to be watching some tape that was recorded at Kik's house. We'll talk about it on the other side of the footage."

Dr. Price patted Tess's calf when she kept turning in her seat trying to match the video on the big screen behind them to the images on the smaller floor monitor.

The first clip was of the pajama fight. When it was over Price leaned forward.

"So, young lady how was wearing your PJs to kindergarten?"

"Fine! I got to talk about them at sharing circle! And Malcolm said he is going to wear his Redskins pajamas next time! But probably his mother will not let him. She has a stick up her abutt."

Price laughed, shook his head. "Well, that wasn't quite the response I was digging for. But all right. We'll come back to this one. Let's play another package."

Next up, Doone was stomping in the kitchen, scowling. "Mom! Mooom!" she screamed until Kik came running down the backstairs in a bathrobe, wet hair plastered against her head like a cheap wig. She was clutching the beltless terrycloth with two hands.

"What happened, honey?"

"Bean had diarrhea in here!"

The video showed Kik looking down around the refrigerator, confused.

"Doone. I jumped out of the shower because I thought something was wrong."

"Something is wrong! I stepped in it! Barefoot!"

The studio audience tittered nervously.

On stage, Doone was blushing amethyst. Dr. Price looked over at his production assistant. "Okay. Let's stop the tape here."

"Now, young lady. Why don't you talk us through what happened on that morning?"

All she could think about was Hank. She'd never realized what she looked like when she got really mad before.

So ugly.

"Doone? Do you see anything wrong with screaming at your mother that way?"

"Yes," she whispered. Tears welled in Doone's eyes. She felt a deep shame.

"So why do you do it?"

"I don't know," she said quietly.

"And you, Mum," Price swiveled in his seat for added punctuation. "You can't possibly believe you are doing her any favors letting her act like that?"

"Sometimes it's just easier — " Kik tried to explain.

"But you know as well as I, that being a mother isn't about *easier*." He paused, "Don't you?"

The audience thundered their approval.

Kik closed her mouth. She was feeling disoriented. The little wavy silver lines dancing on Price's tie in the light weren't helping either.

"Well?" he pressed.

"Sorry. I, uh, thought it was a rhetorical question."

His narrow right shoulder twitched like the broken wing of a bird. "I'm not in the habit of asking rhetorical questions. What's your answer?"

Kik's hand rose. "Whoa, wait a minute. Please! I didn't say it was okay! I mean that's why we're here! I'm trying to learn — "

Why is he being like this? Casey wailed silently. *How did this all go so horribly wrong? I just wanted him to help Doone! Why is he being so mean to Mom? He's never like this!*

"Let's watch some more tape, all right? We'll pick this up in a minute."

The video montage that followed was equally damning. Doone carried on. Tess spoke funny. Kik seemed overwhelmed. Casey over-compensated.

Kik tried to point out that the way things were edited was like freeze-framing someone on the way to making an expression. It was true — but not the whole truth.

"What are you suggesting?" Price enunciated carefully, his clipped indignation echoed by hostile shuffling in the audience.

"Nothing! It's just that I don't think what's being shown is representative of *all* that goes on. It's just that there were — are — some good times, too."

"I'm sure that's true. But unless I'm mistaken you're not here because of the good times. Are you?"

Suddenly, Kik felt as if she was trying to get a word in with a prosecutor whose career rode on every exchange. Price had turned pugnacious.

And I don't know why.

"This isn't a documentary, my dear. It's a compilation. You don't really expect us to play three days' worth of footage, do you?"

Again, clapping ripped through the studio.

"But it's not everything," Kik argued again, weakly.

"Let's move on, shall we? Who's in control at home, Kik?"

"I am. I try to be."

"Well, judging by how Doone here talks to you, and how little Miss Tess walks all over you, and how your middle girl is nothing if not shell-shocked, what kind of grade would you give yourself? And let me suggest it should start with D. Now. I'd like to turn to the journal entries from my new workbook, which I'm not too proud to admit is already a bestseller — "

The audience clapped maniacally.

"The first entries," he continued, "have to do with the girls' dad, who has decided not to be a part of this process."

How many times is he going to work that in? Casey wondered, her toes performing a trio of clenches. She'd already figured a good twenty percent of the program was recaps and product placement. *Add in the Owen-bashing and there might not be much time for anything else.*

She kept zoning out, nervously doing character sketches of the people in the front row.

The helmet-haired blonde is a teacher nobody likes. The smiley guy in the plaid sweater hangs out in chatrooms pretending to be a jock. The woman next to him is terribly sad. She has a big secret.

Price cleared his throat. "Little Tess had this to say about her dad — which somehow through the miracles of modern technology started off as a tape recording and then ended up on a computer screen."

The audience clapped.

"'My daddy is the best father in the whole world. And Virginia, too. I love him very, very, very, very, very much. Also he is silly and makes me laugh. I like Vivy too. She can french braid.'"

The audience smiled.

"Who's Vivy, Tess?" the doctor asked.

"My daddy's friend," she responded. "Duh."

"Well, pardon me!" Price said. "Isn't she something?"

Casey noted a couple of disapproving glances exchanged in front of her.

"Here's what Miss Tess said about her mom. 'She is quite a great deal of fun. A long time ago on my birthday when I woke up there was a long pink ribbon that went from my bed, all the way down the hall, and then the steps, and all the way into the kitchen. At the end of it was my very own Paige doll! Also, my mother is very beauteous'."

Price smiled at Tess. "Those are some mighty nice words you said about your mom."

"Yes," she agreed.

"Now," Price said. "Before we move on to some of the serious issues that the family is facing, I'd like you all to take a peek at this doodle that Miss Doone here did in her journal."

He tilted it for to the cameraman. The sketch was of Casey and Tess on the couch, the little one's hand with jagged nails resting on her sister's knee, realistic as a snapshot.

"Wow," mouthed a silver-haired woman.

Yoga doer, thought Casey. *Affirmations on the mirror. Scented candles in every room.*

"Here's Doone's entry: 'I lost a lot of respect for my dad when he left. He tries to see me but I don't want anything to do with him. His leaving really hurt my mom. She cried every night for a year.'"

Price looked into one of the cameras, held up his book.

"Read my book. You'll see how the parents handled their divorce in this situation is a prime example of what *not* to do." He turned back to Doone. "Be that as it may, even when people are justifiably angry, they can't go around blasting others, right?"

She nodded.

"I'm wondering, my dear, if you think there's a relationship between what you wrote and the dog poop clip?"

"No."

"Well, I'd like to propose there is. That missing the family you used to have comes out sideways in a million different ways. One of which is a short fuse.

"I would encourage you to read my chapter on relaxation techniques. Will you do that for me? Because even when there's a constant heat source you can release some of the steam. We'll be right back."

The director in front of the audience signaled them to clap by raising his arm like a conductor. A make-up woman with a powder puff walked across the stage to tamp down the rhinestone perspiration on Kik's forehead. The light was reflecting off it.

More clapping. Another recap.

"Should I assume, Doone, that it wasn't too long after your parents' split that you started to self-medicate, get high?"

She didn't answer.

"Let's not muck about. I have it on good authority that you've been doing Ecstasy, coke and illicit prescriptions since middle school."

Doone spun around and glared at Casey, whose heart immediately started banging to the point of nausea.

"Before you unfairly blame your sister, let me say my staff has done their research, Doone. They've interviewed people in your hometown."

Kik's fog lifted, her head jerked up. "Your staff did *what?*"

Right then Tess scooted off her seat and headed to the stage exit.

"Hang on, young lady," Price called after her. "Where are you going?"

"To play in that green room. I am not enjoying this today."

"They seem to be dropping like flies around here," Price mugged. When the laughing stopped he said, "We'll be right back, folks, to work with the Marchesons. Providing there are any left. I'll see if I can't convince the little one to hang around. Stay tuned."

"I think we better just let her rest, Dr. Price," Kik said. "And honestly, I don't know how much longer I can do this either. I'm getting one of my headaches."

"I guess you can tell this isn't scripted!" he said jovially to the studio audience. But his face was tight. And his eyes no longer looked kind. "We'll try and wrap this up as quickly as possible, Kik."

After the director orchestrated the clapping again, Price folded his hands and focused his gaze back on Doone. "So, my dear, let's get down to business. Talk about your risky behavior. The drugs you do."

"I..." Doone let her voice trail off. She might have told him if she hadn't all of a sudden begun to worry that maybe she could be arrested for admitting to doing something illegal.

"Honesty is of the essence."

"I've smoked weed before," Doone finally admitted.

"Let's be serious here, young lady. How about you take a polygraph? So we can at least agree on the facts."

Kik was so shocked she stood without even realizing it. "Whoa! Wait a minute! Did you say you wanted to *polygraph* my daughter?"

"That's right," Price glanced down at a card on his lap. "Thanks to a new partnership with Detection, Inc. — one of America's leading undercover detection firms — I'm now able to provide this service on the show. It will be instrumental in doing interventions in cases like this."

"Absolutely not!" Kik erupted. "You absolutely cannot do that! What are you thinking?"

"Let's not triangulate, here," Price said.

"She's not under arrest! Listen — you know what? I'm not sure this is right for us. I think we all feel a little attacked. *Ambushed.* Which is like the opposite of help. And honestly, the reason we agreed to doing the show was because you didn't seem to do things like that and — "

"I'll address your concerns in a moment. Please have a seat. This isn't *The Jerry Springer Show.* You came here because you wanted some help and that's what this is — help. We have to admit what the problems are before we address them. Do you have any idea how many people beg to come on my show?"

"Well, they can take our place. Come on guys. We're outta here."

"Just a minute!" Price commanded.

But Kik had already yanked the microphone pack from

beneath her sweater, inadvertently revealing her soft stomach and stretch marks in the process (an unfortunate occurrence as this would be the clip played on all the entertainment shows) and hustled the girls offstage. They went into the green room, collected Tess, and in their haste abandoned the clothes that still hung from metal racks in the dressing room. Kik didn't care. She had her purse and the girls had their coats. She'd replace everything else.

"C'mon, c'mon," she urged, ushering her daughters down the stairs and through the lobby, pulse pounding in her ears.

Kik hailed a cab, told the driver to get them to La Guardia as fast as he could.

Step on it, she wanted to scream. *Hurry!*

And the whole trip to the airport she kept turning her head to look out the rear window.

Meowgal: Well I've seen everything! I'd be so mad if I was Dr. Price. He offered right much help to them and they just spat in his face. I knew right from the minute that they came on that this wasn't going to end well.

Babycakes: I was in the audience (sixth time!) and lord was Dr. Price mad!!! He stood up on the stage and said they were going to put what happened at the top of the next show, cut their losses and move on. He said they're going to find a family that really wants to be there and is comited to truley changing. He was HOT under the collar.

Meowgal: I just wish he'd read them the Riot Act to begin with. Not wasted our time. I just can't believe that the mother didn't see that ever since they've been going on the show that the oldest girl doesn't look like a freak anymore! Where's their gratitude at? A woman who lets her child wear pajamas to school!

Social.worker: I don't know about terminating with them yet. It's usually the resistant client that needs the most help. It's possible that when they all calm down, they'll change their minds. When I was a caseworker I witnessed a lot of irrational decisions. But you just have to suck it up. From one professional to another, I'm sure you can handle it, Dr. Price! I'm very impressed that you went ahead and showed what happened.

Sandma7: I think it was very big of Dr. Price to run the show even after the family walked (ran!) off his stage. From what I understand he didn't have to. He could have just put another family on and said that one just didn't work out. That mother should have understood that doing a polygraph is in her best interest! My own daughter drug tests her son once a week.

Theway: They should serve as a Warning to all the sheep that are Straying from the path of The Righteous. Vengeance is mine, sayeth the Lord. Adultery. Fornication. Drugs. Divorce. You don't get to choose which of God's laws to Abide. That's why the Sins of the Parents are visited upon the Children. Satan is always trying to gather more Souls. He has hijacked this family. They have been hijacked! The End Time is around the Corner. Tornados and earthquakes Serve as warning. THE TIME TO REPENT IS NOW!

MOSTLYMOCHA: I wish there was a way to find out what happens to them — I'm dying to know! ICYMI, the mom from the last Price family is in rehab.

Shoppingchica103: Baahahahahaha

Deleted by Administrator

Francie: I love this family, says no one.

Chapter Eleven

The central heat pumped lassitude throughout the house. Under the doors and through the transoms lethargy drifted from room to room. By late afternoon all three girls were draped over the den furniture, logy and immobile. The TV smelled like it was melting.

"I am quite bored," Tess announced. Again.

"Tess!" Doone reprimanded. "If you complain once more, I'm going to . . ."

"What?" Tess demanded, stomping her foot against the side of the couch.

"Make you go live with Malcolm's father!" Doone exploded.

Tess's eyes got huge and then she burst out laughing. Casey, who was totally ready for her younger sister to lose it over a threat, was shocked. "What does that mean?"

"Tell you later," Doone answered.

There was a knock at the door and Tess went to get it. "Oldest sister, it's a boy for you!"

Doone got up slowly, wondering who it was. Hank was standing in the hallway.

"Hey," he grinned.

"Hi!"

"I just thought I'd stop by on my way into town. I wanted to check up on you after I read the newspaper."

"We're doing okay. Now. Way better than a couple days ago!"

"Good." They stood together in the hallway, smiled at each

other. "So what all happened?"

"Price said he wanted to polygraph me about drugs. My mother went nuclear."

"Good for her. My parents would have freaked over that, too. It's pretty police state when you think about it."

"The whole thing was insane. We jetted out of there so fast we left like half our stuff," Doone said, her body suddenly feeling unruly with nerves. She went and sat on the second step from the bottom, her stocking feet sliding from side to side like windshield wipers.

Casey appeared in the hallway, completely stunned to see the hottest guy at Ivy standing in her hallway talking to Doone.

"So, are you glad to be finished with Price, too?" Hank asked Casey.

"Yeah. It was kind of a like a slow-mo car wreck," she said, trying to take in the fact that he'd come to see Doone. Then she felt guilty and clenched her toes. "Your fam going to be doing anything fun over break?"

"We're just going to be doing some relative visitations," he grinned. "Some visitations will be longer than others."

"Who's the worst?" Doone asked.

"My Uncle Rob. Hands down. He's a Tea Partier who teaches at a fundamentalist college. And my dad's other brother is a serious hippie. Which makes for some interesting get-togethers."

"They get together?" Casey asked.

"Under duress. Mostly at funerals. But even those can be extreme. When Uncle Rob was eulogizing this cousin of ours, Uncle Jim provided an alternate commentary in the back pew."

"Heckling at a memorial service?" Doone giggled.

"Yeah. Good times, right? We used to stay with my Uncle

Rob's family for a couple of days over Christmas. Then we cut it to one night. Now it's just a dinner. I figure by the time I'm in college, it'll be down to a drive-by carol or something."

The girls laughed.

"I better go check on Tess," Casey said. "Make sure she's not doing anything bizarre like calling Mom to tell her we have company."

Doone smiled at him. "Tess — the gnome who opened the door — lives for telling on people."

"Are you doing anything for vacation?" he asked.

"Not really. We're supposed to split the time between here and my Dad's. I usually try and get out of that, though."

"Is he that bad?"

"Do you mean does he ever like beat us or make us watch porn?"

"Yeah."

"No. It's just that he swings between being non-existent to being like this control freak. Plus he's cheap." As an afterthought she added, "My sisters like him, though."

"So, a two thirds approval rating."

"Not if you factor in my mom."

He laughed. "Hey, any chance you could come with me while I do some errands for my 'rents?"

"I wish I could. But we're supposed to be going out for dinner in a few."

Hank gave her his mega-watt smile. "Maybe over vacation we can get together?"

"Sure," she grinned.

After he left, Doone went into the bathroom and studied herself, trying to see what he saw. She smiled. Her face transformed, her features softened. The scowl lines disappeared.

She looked surprisingly like Casey. Doone ran her finger over the scab from her ill-fated brow ring. There'd probably be a scar, but it definitely looked better.

Bean started to bark.

"Mommy's home!" Tess announced.

"Who's ready to eat?" Kik asked.

They passed little shops strung with twinkling lights and three country clubs right down the road from each other. As they approached the island of stores with Zeus Grille, Tess said she might prefer going there for dinner instead.

"I'd rather have pizza," Doone announced, throwing down the gauntlet.

Kik's shoulders launched involuntarily, but she said calmly, "Tess, sweetie, we already decided on pizza before. We'll get Zeus next time."

"Oh, bother."

Surprisingly, that was it. For about a minute.

"A boy came over to see Doone while you were at work," Tess sing-songed.

The atmosphere in the car grew heavy.

"Mom," Casey rushed in. "Hank Carlisle is like the nicest guy in school. Seriously. I'd donate a kidney to have him talk to me!"

"Thanks," Doone whispered, torn between resenting her sister's stamp of approval and gratitude for the backing.

Kik got the subtext — the kid was different. She knew they were wading in seriously snake-infested waters. The topic was loaded and they all knew it.

Do I not reprimand Doone just because Casey endorsed him?

She pulled into the side lot and decided to just give herself the night off from policing. She just wanted one night.

"All right. Let's just concentrate on caloric intake, okay? What toppings are we talking?"

Bundled in their winter coats, the Marchesons trudged into Pepperoni's across from campus. The restaurant was buzzing with boisterous students in finals mode. A lot of the family's stress was leached out amidst the good-natured shouts between tables. The waitress delivered a basket of pizza crust breadsticks.

"This will be perfect," Kik pronounced. "An all dough dinner! Exactly what I need."

"And look!" Tess commanded after dunking one of the long crusts in a plastic well of garlic butter until its head bowed. "I am making candy canes for dessert! Mother? Do you suppose Santa will be bringing anything to Harperly this year? He did not last time, you know."

"How do you know he didn't bring her something invisible?" Doone asked.

"Why would he bring her something she could not see?" Tess demanded, her brown eyes flashing.

"I don't think Harperly lived with us last Christmas," Casey intervened.

"Who did she live with, then?"

"Why are you asking us?" Doone responded.

"Hmph!" The little one crossed her arms, nearly upending her soda in the process.

"Hey, Ms. Marcheson!"

Kik turned, smiled in recognition. "Luke! Hi! Why aren't you at the library writing the short story for my class?"

"There was massive concern I was spending entirely too much time there doing just that. The librarians kicked me out for dinner."

"Right," she laughed.

"These your girls?"

"Doone, Casey, and Tess," she pointed to each. "Meet Luke, one of my favorite students. Also a lacrosse player, right?"

"Guilty," he grinned. The girls said hello.

"You're even cuter in person!" he said to Tess.

"What does that mean?" she asked.

"That you're even more adorable in real life than on TV." He looked at the older girls. Both of their hearts flipped. "There's a case of Snickers in it for you guys if you can get your mother to inflate her grades."

"Make it Bud," Doone countered. "And you've got a deal,"

"Doone!"

"Lighten up, Mom. I'm just kidding."

"Hey, it was nice meeting you all. I'm going to head on back, reassure the librarians."

As soon as he was out of hearing range, Casey leaned towards Doone. "How hot was he?"

"Seriously. Hashtag: TakeYourDaughterToWorkDay!"

"No fair!" Casey laughed. "You've got Hank!"

Which caused a hot flush to travel up Doone's neck.

Their pizza came and they concentrated on eating for a while. Then Kik decided to broach The Subject. Again. Her last three attempts had been rebuffed and she figured she had to give it two more shots before being able to lay the thing to rest without guilt. "You guys still doing okay after our brush with notoriety?"

"Yeah," Casey said, looking out the window. "But I'm hoping those flurries will turn into a two-week blizzard, which will take us straight into vacation. Hopefully things will die down by the time we go back."

"Hate to break it to you, little sister," Doone said. "But the only thing on *Shh* is our big adventure. It'll take more than bad weather to knock us off."

"*Shh*?" Kik asked. "What's that?"

"School blog," Doone answered. "I just wish there'd be another herpes outbreak."

Tess was suddenly interested again. "Who peed at school?"

"Nobody. Keep playing with your food," Doone passed the last breadstick and another little plastic specimen cup of liquid butter down the table. She looked back at her mother. "Herpes was a way hotter topic than us. There was even a section for sore sighting."

"Gross, Doone! We're eating," Casey complained.

"Wait!" Kik almost knocked over her own water tumbler. "Ivy has a blog and people are writing about us? Do you want me to call the principal?"

"No!" the older girls said together.

"It's not an official website or anything, Mom," Casey explained. "It's an underground thing. The school can't really control it."

"And only an STD would bump us?" Kik asked.

"Pretty much. Anyway, it doesn't really matter. I'm just glad to be done." Casey's eyes filled and she trained them on the table. "I'm really sorry about getting us into all that."

"Oh honey," Kik said.

"Hey, speaking of herpes," Doone offered. "Mom, guess who it started with at school!"

"Who?"

"Dr. West's daughter."

"No!"

On the way home Kik began to wonder if maybe it really

would be possible to start over. For the first time in recent memory she didn't feel like a desperate doctor rushing from bedside to bedside, secretly worrying that somehow she'd been the one spreading the infection all along.

"Hey, Mom," Doone said quietly.

"Hm?"

"Thanks for sticking up for me. You know, with Price. And the whole lie detector thing."

A million different responses flooded Kik's brain. She settled on a simple one. "I love you."

They spent the rest of the ride talking about vacation plans and play dates and Christmas-slash-Chanukah shopping. Casey asked if she could go sledding at Caroline's if school was cancelled. And Kik realized with a thrill that she could say yes.

When Kik got into bed that night (after pitching Price's workbook towards the trashcan in the corner), she allowed her thoughts to roam.

As they so often did, they sauntered right over to Parrish.

And this time she let them.

The first thing she thought of was his eyes. How in her whole life she'd never known anyone else who could melt her with a look. A flash lift of a brow somehow conveyed getting naked and staying in bed for hours and hours.

She remembered the time they slow-danced at a wedding. She'd been self-conscious and tense.

"Relax," he'd whispered.

And she had leaned into his long body while he hummed the words to the song. Their feet barely moved. She'd smelled his sweat that night and pretended not to feel him harden against her hip. But she had. And when the music was over Kik was breathless and couldn't meet his eye.

Parrish had always existed outside of possibility.

Lying in bed that night, Kik allowed herself to actually try on a relationship with him. It fit the way her favorite sweatpants did — like something she'd be happy to spend the rest of her life in. She imagined all of it. Having breakfast together, sharing their four daughters, laughing, and watching TV, gossiping about work, listening to music. Eventually her directed fantasy gave way to the disinhibition of sleep and in the morning Kik woke up disoriented and a little embarrassed. She dressed quickly.

The radio announced the school closings and Kik let the girls sleep in. She went downstairs, pushed Bean out into the snow on the deck, called him back in after he peed on the porch swing, and then ran-hopped to the car trying to avoid the divot puddles in the gravel. Halfway to campus she realized she'd left her cell phone charging on the counter and it was too late to go back.

She stopped in the office to call the girls and warn them she'd left her cell at home. She noticed her boss right as she was reaching for the phone. "Hi, Martin. How are you?"

"I think more to the point, Klara, is how you are."

He stared. Hard. She started paddling.

"Just fine! Fine! Getting ready for vacation? Are you all going anywhere? I can't believe school was canceled again. What'd we get, half an inch last night?"

He didn't respond and she clamped her lips. Her left eye began to twitch.

"I heard you've resigned from reality TV?"

"It wasn't so much reality TV as — "

"I'm glad to hear it. It was rather ill-advised, don't you think? And as far as that goes, I'd like to have a moment of your time later."

Her head started to pound. "Um. Now? Because I — "

"No, not now. *Later*," he repeated slowly. "Why don't you check with Joni and make an appointment?"

An appointment?

Her brain felt like it was diving against her skull, rebounding and doing it again.

Red Rover, Red Rover let Kik's gray matter come over.

"When?"

"After your last class would be fine," Martin said, dismissing her with a curt smile.

Was it her imagination or did he lean on *last?*

Although Parrish had warned her about Martin she hadn't been prepared for the degree of displeasure. A fluorescent buzz of anger hummed off of him.

What ever happened to the First Amendment?

But her self-righteousness quickly gave way to self-doubt, then nausea. Maybe there was something in her employment contract that prohibited her from going on TV?

Why didn't I think of that before?

Kik jammed her shaking hands into the pockets of her loose knit pants. Her thighs felt palsied inside the expensive fabric. She made her way to Joni's desk.

"Everything okay?" the secretary asked with an overly sympathetic moue. The woman could cull gossip from a Benedictine monk. Kik always had to put herself on high alert around her.

"Fine!" she responded too emphatically. Dialing it down, she said, "Just fine. Thanks."

On her way to class she thought of the high from the night before. How good she'd felt with the girls. And now, just a few short hours later, her job was on the line.

How I'm supposed to go teach all day like I'm not being called into the principal's office? Is he kidding?

She decided to just run exam preps, answer questions about good essay construction, bag the syllabus. Saroya was the first to raise her hand. "What was Dr. Price really like? Give us the dirt!"

Kik's teeth clenched. "I was thinking more in terms of class relevant topics."

Saroya's dark complexion deepened to a dangerous shade of eggplant and Kik immediately felt terrible for snapping at her.

"Oh, what the hell." She felt a surge of adrenalin. "Going on the show ranks right up there with the biggest mistakes of my life!"

Kik truly admired people who measured their words. But she'd never been able to figure out how to modulate without sounding like a paranoid schizophrenic worrying about hidden microphones. Much as she would change this about herself, sharing was an all or nothing proposition.

She let loose.

"He attacked my girls. He attacked me. He attacked my ex-husband," she paused for effect. "And everyone knows that's my job." The room laughed. Then she added, "And of course, our public humiliation was lucrative for him and the network."

"How?" Saroya asked.

"Through advertisers buying commercials. The better the ratings, the more valuable the ads. You know, like how they cost more during the Super Bowl?" Kik wasn't totally clear on the economics, but that sounded about right.

"So maybe Price was trying to pump up his ratings with the whole lie detector thing?" the student asked.

Kik shrugged.

"Why'd you do it then?" one of the ubiquitous blonde sorority girls challenged.

"I was trying to help my kids. But it was stupid. Really stupid. The fix just became another screw-up. I will say this. I didn't listen to my intuition when I should have. And that was really dumb."

"Well, at least your deafness was transient," Luke offered.

Kik flinched a little.

"Too soon?" he asked, innocently.

"It's not even over yet," she said, thinking of her upcoming meeting with Martin.

Throughout the day, Kik fantasized about a student boycott demanding not only her rehiring, but tenure too. Like a good stew she kept adding ingredients. She threw in Martin apologizing. Then going on sabbatical.

Permanently.

The final element in the recipe was a call from her agent saying a publisher wanted her to give up teaching and just write full-time. For the rest of her life.

Although maybe I'd teach a class or two. Like Dorian.

At the end of the last period, a kid she thought of as Haiku Hal, stuck around waiting to speak with her.

"Mrs. Marcheson?"

"What can I do for you?" Kik tried hard to be patient, encouraging. Hal could pass for a nerdy middle schooler. Everything about him was spare, hesitant, immature. "Is something wrong, Hal?"

"Uh . . ."

He reminded her of when Doone was little and had a reluctant bladder. Kik would have to turn on the spigot to persuade her to go. "Hal? I don't mean to rush you but I have a meeting."

To get fired.

"This is really awkward, Mrs. Marcheson, but I thought you'd want to know."

"Know what?"

"That when I was out a couple weekends ago, I saw your daughter in a bar. The younger one. The middle one, I mean. At the Ale Factory."

Kik's reaction to this news went as follows:

You go out?

Then: *Narc!*

Then: *Casey?*

And finally: *Perfect.*

"I thought you'd want to know. It wasn't like she was drunk or anything. I actually didn't even see her drinking. But the thing is the police are really cracking down on fake ID's. Because of terrorism."

"Thanks, Hal. I'll look into it."

Kik gathered her things and wondered how long it would take to de-deputize everyone. Then she wondered what Casey had been thinking and if Doone was passing the baton.

On her way to Martin's office she asked herself what was the worst that could happen and immediately wished she hadn't. The answer laid itself out like yards of stained carpet.

I get fired. We burn through our savings in two months. We lose the house. And insurance. She corrected herself: *Well, not the kids — but I will. The car breaks down. I come down with some serious disease that can only be treated with medicine I can't afford. Then I die. And the girls go live with Owen and Vivy. And they all end up liking her more than me.*

Kik tried to think of a job she'd be qualified for, one with benefits. Could she teach in the high schools without an education degree? She wasn't sure.

Maybe I could work in a bookstore. Do they have benefits?

Then she envisioned herself arranging a pyramid of Dorian's latest novel in the store window. And knew she'd become suicidal.

Breathe. Breathe. Breathe.

She told herself that no matter what she wouldn't cry in front of Martin.

I will not give the pompous ass the satisfaction!

She pulled open the office door and was surprised by a group of blue uniforms huddled in front of the secretary's desk. It was a startling scene and for a second she felt like she was in the audience and a curtain had just opened on frozen actors.

"There you are!" Joni exclaimed in a weird tone.

Kik's brain was trying to decode the emotional content.

Sympathy and something else. Fear? Excitement?

No one moved.

"Hi? What's going on?"

One of the cops shifted and she saw that the computer monitor had been rotated so the police standing opposite Joni could read it. Kik saw her own schedule on the screen. All of the saliva in her mouth immediately evaporated. She tried to ask what was going on again, but the words were sticking on the back of her tongue, little tufts of dandelion hair. She felt light-headed.

A policewoman and Martin started towards her. Her boss held out his hand. "Klara, Kik . . ."

"Oh. Oh!" she went weak with relief.

Oh, of course!

She'd heard of people being escorted out of offices after being let go.

Thank God! What was I thinking! He just wants to be sure I don't take anything that belongs to the department! But almost immediately doubts began clawing, scratching at her reasoning. *What does he think I'll take? The stapler? The faculty phone book?*

"You didn't need to do all this, Martin. I wouldn't have created a scene! I'll just grab some stuff, my own stuff, quickly, and then ..." her words petered out when he wouldn't look her in the eye. A stocky black woman in uniform approached. All vestiges of reprieve evaporated. Kik backed up, her hand rising to stop the words. "Don't," she whispered. "Please?"

But it was like trying to stop the wind.

"Mrs. Marcheson? I'm Detective Larraine Warner. From Child Crimes."

"What? Child what? Is this about Casey going to the bar? Hal just told me about it! I'm going to handle it right away. I promise! Right now as a matter of fact!" She backed away so fast she stumbled. "I'll just go home — "

"Ma'am," the policewoman reached out.

"Don't say it!" Kik fell into the wall.

"Come in here, please, ma'am." The woman clasped Kik's arm. "We need to speak. Can you hear me?"

A strange question but in fact Kik could barely hear anything. The sounds had grown distant. She remembered being little at the pool with Maddie and how they used to shout to each other below the surface, trying to make words come out before the water rushed in.

Kik was guided into Martin's office. Somebody closed the door.

"Ms. Marcheson? We need to talk to you now. Are you hearing me?"

"Yes."

"It seems that Tess has been taken."

"Taken?"

"Abducted, ma'am."

The scream of an oncoming train accompanied Kik's slide to the floor. When she resurfaced she was gagging on the smell of a cleaning supply. She opened her eyes. The detective was holding something under her nose.

"Hang on a moment, Mrs. Marcheson. Take some deep breaths if you can."

"Wait a minute, wait a minute!" Kik's brain was cloudy. Then it came back to her and she began wailing. "Where's Tess?"

"Ma'am, we're doing everything we can to find her. What we have so far is that a man, possibly dressed in a police uniform, got her into his car," Detective Warner said. Then she added gently, "You still with me, hon?"

"Yes," Kik whispered.

"Your other girls are at your home with your husband. Ex-husband. He just got there. They're waiting for you."

"Why didn't they call me?"

"Apparently the secretary here was out for part of the afternoon and the line was turned over to voice mail."

Kik remembered her cell phone charging on the kitchen counter. She moaned.

"We'll bring you to them, Mrs. Marcheson. We've already triggered the Amber Alert. Information is going to be flashed on highway signs. Everyone from the state police to utility workers will be on the lookout for your girl. The Center for Missing and Exploited Children and the National Crime Information Center. They've already been contacted. We were called right away, which is critical. The first hours are the most important."

A noise a wounded animal would make, a keening, started to well up in Kik. She couldn't stop it. Parrish came running in. "What's going on?"

"Tess . . ." Kik moaned.

"Are you a friend of Mrs. Marcheson?" Detective Warner asked.

"Yes."

"Would you accompany us to her house?"

"What's going on?"

"It appears that her daughter has been kidnapped."

Parrish blanched, put his arms around Kik. "I'm here, darlin. I won't leave you. Hold on to me."

Coatless, they made their way to patrol cars parked in front of the building. Flashing lights splashed pools of red on to the snow. A group of students stepped aside, silent, respectful, and obviously aware that something very, very bad had happened. One girl looked like she was crying.

Images of cars parting for the shrieking processional played on the dash-cam screen. Briefly set asunder, they would soon be back on course. Kik knew her own life would never be the same. She was moving from horror to shock, tears leaching from her eyes the way milk used to seep from her breasts whenever one of her babies cried. Parrish sat behind her on the edge of the seat, his hand pressing into her shoulder.

"Slow, deep breaths," he ordered again and again like a labor coach.

She thought of all the safety rules her former mother-in-law had passed down. No pitching tents in the yard (an advertisement to pedophiles your kids are sleeping outside!) No hitchhiking. No looking for lost puppies with strangers. Or helping people with crutches carry things to their cars.

But she never told me to warn the girls about not opening the door to the police!

Kik's whimpering began again, the sound lost beneath the siren's scream.

Cop cars and paddy wagons lined the street. The fat gravel of the driveway was covered by shallow snow and the tire tracks at its mouth were being photographed. Yellow crime scene tape enclosed the property. She stumbled out of the car, didn't close the door.

"Walk this way, Mrs. Marcheson," said the detective, pointing to a narrow path across the lawn. Kik's knees started to buckle.

"Pull yourself together," Parrish commanded behind her. "They're going to need you for information. And Doone and Casey need you, too. You can do this. We can do this."

"No, Parrish. I don't think I can," she begged, looking for dispensation, a hall-pass out of this.

"You've got no choice. You've got to pull yourself together, Kik. *Right now.*"

"Oh." She took another deep breath and stood up straighter. "Okay."

They went through the kitchen and into the family room. Tess's backpack was still next to her snow boots where she'd dropped it. Owen was in the leather chair, leaning forward, deathly pale. The girls were standing together, rocking like baby birds teetering on the edge of the nest, swaying above the hereafter. Kik shuddered.

"Mommy!" Doone cried.

Kik looked at her first-born blankly. Only Tess called her that any more.

"Mommy," she wailed again. "I'm sorry!"

"Tell me what happened, Doone!"

"I was in my room and Tess was down here watching a movie."

Doone couldn't bring herself to admit the rest.

It was a Shirley Temple and I refused to watch it with her and Tess called me the meanest big sister in the world and I just said whatever junior and —

"Doone!" Kik repeated sharply. "Tell me what happened!"

"The doorbell rang and she yelled she got it. I thought it was Malcolm! They talked on the phone and I thought maybe she'd invited him over. But after a minute I didn't hear anything and I called her and she didn't answer. I went downstairs — "

"Tell me!" screamed Kik.

Doone wiped her sleeve roughly across her eyes and took a deep breath. "The door was kind of open and there was a policeman getting in a blue car at the top of the driveway. I thought it was a policeman. I started yelling to him. Asking him to help me, to wait. I guess because the way the door was open I knew something was wrong. But he acted like he couldn't hear. He just hurried. And then I realized that he had her. He had Tess! She turned around and looked out of the window. Oh, God, Mom. She looked so scared!"

Kik wanted to cover her ears, scream at her daughter to shut up. "Where was Casey?"

Casey jerked forward. "I was with Caroline, sledding. Remember? You said it was okay!"

"Of course I didn't! I never would have." All memories of entrusting Tess to Doone had evaporated. Not even the slightest tinge of remembrance had been left behind. She shook her head in absolute denial.

Detective Warner stepped in. "We got a fairly good description of the vehicle, ma'am. It's out over the wire and we got some tire prints."

Casey bowed forward. Kik thought her daughter was reaching for her, but instead she pitched and vomited on the ottoman. Kik watched as a slow dark stain spread over the leather. Owen pulled Casey into his chest and stroked her head. Doone went to get a washcloth from the bathroom.

Kik was paralyzed.

Detective Warner called a cop in uniform over and asked him to carry the hassock outside. "If that's okay. Ma'am?"

Kik shrugged. She'd been gutted. It was likely that she might start screaming and never be able to stop.

"All right. We need to go over a couple things," Warner said. "The Emergency Alert System will be broadcasting information about Tess. The Amber Alert's in motion. BOLOs have been ordered.

"What are BOLOs?" Owen interrupted.

"Be On the Look Outs. The state criminal information network is on-board. The transportation guys will flash information up on the highway signs. The physical evidence techs are collecting samples. I'll go into everything in more detail later. Right now, I need a few things from you, starting with the most recent photograph you have."

"Wait," Kik was having trouble keeping up with the words; they were coming at her like bugs in headlights. "What?"

"She wants a picture, Mom." Casey said.

"Or a current phone movie. Or DVD," Warner said. "That would be very helpful."

"We have a recent one, Mom!" Casey interjected. "From the show!"

"What show is that?" Warner asked.

Casey answered when Kik didn't. "*Dr. Price.* We were on a couple of times. We quit. It was in the papers."

The cop hunched her right shoulder like she was trying to shrug an errant bra strap back in place. "You know, I thought you all looked familiar. Why were you on?"

Doone answered. "Because of me."

"Because of all of us," Kik corrected, auto-pilot triggered.

"And the little one was on? Tess was on?" Warner asked.

"Yeah. We only went up there — to New York — twice, but they filmed in the house, too," Casey said, dully.

"When was this, Ms. Marcheson?"

Kik forced herself to answer. "Over the past couple of weeks."

"Did you get any unwanted attention from strangers?"

"Just on the message boards," Kik answered.

"Come again?"

"The show has a website. People went on and talked about us."

The detective was leaning forward. "Did anyone try and contact you directly?"

"No — how could they?" Kik said defensively. "Our address was never given out!"

"We got some crank calls," Casey said.

"We did?" Kik spun around, her question an accusation. "When!"

"Hang on a minute, ma'am," Warner said to Kik, putting up a hand. "Do you remember what was said, Casey?"

"Dumb stuff. One guy said we were making all of Charlottesville look bad. Another one said to stay classy. Things were written about us on the school blog, too."

"Okay. We'll pull the phone records. What's that web address?" the cop's words came out efficiently and with authority. Casey gave it to her. Detective Warner wrote the information down and then repeated it back. "How about the clips from the show?"

"Doone, get it. Please," Kik said. "We only have one. They didn't give us anything when we walked off."

"It's probably on YouTube," Casey said flatly.

Doone reached into the armoire. A Shirley Temple case tumbled out. She pulled her hand back as if stung.

"Why did you quit the show?" the detective asked Kik.

"The whole thing was wrong. Going in the first place was wrong. It was insane talking about our problems on TV. I should never have said yes. But what's this have to do — "

"It was my fault," Casey whispered. "It was my idea."

"It absolutely wasn't your fault, Case," Owen said, forcefully.

"Has Tess mentioned anything out of the ordinary to you? About strangers?" Warner asked, gently. "Family acquaintances? Any subjects paying too much attention to her?"

"No," Kik said vehemently.

"How about to you, Mr. Marcheson? Has she mentioned anything to you?"

"Nothing."

"She told me that Harperly was perturbed about being famous," Casey whispered.

"Who, Cassie?" the detective asked.

Casey corrected the pronunciation of her name and then said, "Harperly is Tess's imaginary friend."

"Those were her words?" Larraine Warner asked dubiously. "Perturbed?"

"She's very precocious," Owen interjected, impatiently. "Why did she say that, Case?"

"I don't know. I didn't ask." And then she began weeping again. Owen put his arm around her.

The detective turned to a couple of officers. "Let the FBI know about the show. We'll want to look at the message boards. See if they had to take anyone off." She turned back to the family. "Now how about around here? Anybody make any of you nervous? A neighbor? Mailman? Teenager who shovels the walks? Anybody who seemed to pay too much attention to Tess?"

Everyone said no.

"Does she use the computer?"

"She can't read yet," Kik responded, guilt swamping her.

Why can't she read? Is it because I haven't played phonics games with her? Or does she have a learning disability and I've been too distracted to notice? Was I too burned out from dealing with Doone's school issues to investigate the possibility of her having them too?

Kik began to shake.

Detective Warner said something about putting in phone relay lines so the kidnapper could get through but Kik was having a hard time following. It was like trying to understand a Spanish conversation with the random vocabulary left over from high school.

"Whatever," she blurted, her hysteria rising again. "Do whatever! Just hurry! Hurry!"

"Okay. You need to calm down, ma'am. We're also going to announce a tip line. Do you want to offer a reward?"

"Anything!"

"How about ten thousand?" the detective asked, looking at

Owen.

"Is that enough?" Parrish interrupted. "I've got some stashed. And I'm sure we could ask friends, colleagues — "

He let his sentence die out when the detective shook her head. "Let's just get this out there. Sometimes too much offends people. It turns them off. They think the victim's family is trying to say that one missing kid is more valuable than another."

Detective Warner asked to see Tess's room. Kik walked her upstairs but they didn't actually go in, they just stood in the doorway. Still seated at the white wooden table were the guests of Tess's last tea party.

"Anything out of the ordinary, Ms. Marcheson?"

"No. She doesn't usually let all her toys come to the same party, but they're all there. She usually makes guest lists, has one of us write them for her. She didn't let Milly — "

"Who?"

Kik pointed at a doll. "Tess wouldn't let Milly come because she didn't grow her bangs back after Tess cut them. And she never invites Monsieur Raccoon because he doesn't have pants that fit over his tail and she says it's rude to go to a party without them."

Detective Warner smiled. "She sounds like quite a character. Anything else seem out of place?"

Kik began to sob.

"Ma'am?"

"No. It's nothing. It's just that she cut one of the other doll's bangs. She probably just didn't want Milly to feel different."

"Ms. Marcheson? I'm not following."

Kik pointed to the ridiculous fringe on the toy's forehead. It was such a little kid thing to do. "She's so precocious I'm always surprised by anything she does that seems immature. Not immature — just age appropriate."

Terror rocked the floor.

"You okay, ma'am?"

Kik nodded but the rug buckled and roiled. She crouched low, put her head down.

"That's it. Just breathe."

"Okay. I'm okay."

"Good. That's it. Take your time. I'm right here with you."

Kik noticed the acrid sweet smell of urine. "Did she wet the bed?"

"Yes, ma'am. We were going to ask you about that. Was that a regular occurrence?"

"No. Well, this would be the second time since New York," Kik whispered. "She didn't like being talked about at school. I think that's why."

Tess's scarlet kimono was in a heap on the floor, her famous pajamas next to it. Both were gifts from Aunt Maddie who, girl-deprived, indulged Tess's fru-fruness. A dirty dish with stale peanut butter and jelly crusts sat on the low bookshelf. Even from across the room Kik could see how old and tired the sandwich was. An evidence tech began pulling back the bedclothes.

"What are you doing?" Kik demanded. "I want those!"

"We're taking these into the lab, ma'am."

"Why? She just had an accident! All little kids do that!"

He looked down. "We want to be sure there's nothing else on them."

"That doesn't make sense!"

"We just want to be sure whoever took her hasn't been here before."

Kik began tearing at her own clothes. She saw herself from above and thought how much she resembled the Arab women whose worlds had been demolished by tanks and bombs. She'd never understood the desperate impulse to get everything off her skin before. Detective Warner put a restraining arm around Kik's heaving shoulders and when she calmed led her back to the rest of the family.

A bald man in a uniform came in, a gun hanging from his belt. "Okay. It's a few before five. The first 911 logged in at 3:50. We're actually in pretty good shape in terms of getting the information out quickly."

"Does that mean you're going to find her?" Doone whispered.

"We're going to do everything we can," the man said. 'Now if it's okay with you folks," he looked over at Kik and Owen. "We'd like to speak with each of you separately."

"Yes, yes!" Kik said. "Hurry!"

"Let's you and I go find a place to talk, Casey."

The fourteen-year-old nodded and he followed her upstairs. He sat on the edge of Doone's bed and she sat on her own.

"Casey, do you have any idea about who might have done this? Any friends of yours like your little sister in ways that made you uncomfortable?"

"What? No!"

He was writing in a small notebook, using a fancy pen.

An early Christmas present, Casey thought, her mental mechanisms removing her from the horror. *Maybe from a favorite niece. A niece who he takes out for lunch maybe. His brother's child. His brother who died of leukemia. And he's a little in love with his sister-in-law but thinks that might be too*

*weird. But he thinks about her all the time, making up reasons to
go and visit and to call —*

"Casey?"

"What?"

"I asked about parents of your friends. Anybody give off
weird signals around Tess?"

"No."

"I'd like a list of everyone who's been over recently. Maybe
they saw something, noticed somebody hanging around."

"Okay."

"How about your sister and Tess?"

"What?"

"Look, I had a kid brother. I know how aggravating they
can get. Maybe she pissed Doone off . . ."

"What?"

Does he think Doone did something to Tess?

Casey's heart started to pound. Her Juvenile Justice class
had watched a documentary about kids being tricked into
confessing to crimes they didn't commit. Or blaming innocent
people. She began twisting the long end of her plaid ribbon belt.

Maybe Mom or Dad should be in here?

Around and around she curled the accessory, corkscrewing
the belt the way Tess did the park swing, winding it tighter and
tighter until it uncoiled fast and furious, spinning her around in a
rush.

"Casey? You with me?"

"Yeah. Sorry."

"How 'bout it? What's Doone's relationship like with
Tess?"

"Doone loves Tess."

"That's not what I'm asking Casey."

"Stop it!" she screamed. "Doone wouldn't have hurt her!"

He waited as she pulled herself together, watched. "How about your dad?"

"What about him?"

"What is his relationship like with your sister?"

"He adores her."

"In what way?"

"What do you mean! Like a father does! Like he does me. And Doone. Why are you asking questions like that?"

"Casey, just bear with me. Okay? Has he ever said anything about having Tess go live with him?"

"No."

"What's his relationship like with your mom? Do they get along?"

"They're divorced."

He smiled a little. "Point taken. How about your mom? Does she have any boyfriends with any kind of relationship with Tess? Good or bad?"

"What? No. No boyfriend."

"What about that guy downstairs? Paris?"

"Parrish. He's just a friend of hers. His daughter used to be best friends with Doone."

"Used to be?"

"Before she moved to Louisiana with her mom."

"What about other friends of Doone's? Any buddies of hers that appeared on your radar screen?"

"She hardly ever has people over."

"Why is that?"

"She just doesn't."

"Y'all were on TV?"

"Yeah."

"Because of your sister's problems?"

She nodded. It felt as if the ceiling sank lower.

"What exactly are her problems?"

"She was just making dumb choices. Drugs," she whispered, eyes filling again. "Sneaking out. Lots of kids do it!"

"Do you know what kind of drugs she does?"

"No. Well, weed. Maybe ecstasy."

"Can you tell me who her friends are at school?"

"She used to hang out with this kid named Dust before he got kicked out."

"Why'd he get expelled?"

"Drugs."

The officer flipped through his little note pad. "Dust — the kid who was recently arrested for meth?"

"Yeah." She wondered how he knew all this already.

Maybe there's a central registry of information on everyone?

She kept having to reach for her thoughts. They were like the little mercury balls that raced all over the floor the time she dropped a thermometer.

"Does she have any other friends?"

"She's friends with this girl, Felicity Adere. And some sketchy people down on the Mall. I don't know any of their names. I think she's also friends with some kids in her art class. Oh! And a really nice guy named Hank. He came over yesterday."

"Last name?"

She told him and he wrote it down.

"It's interesting your sister has such a diverse peer group. Different entrees, same restaurant, though, huh?" he asked.

"Hank really is nice."

"No offense, but what's he doing with Doone?"

She flinched but said, "I think she's getting better."

"In what way?"

"She just doesn't blow up as much as she used to. She's not as mad."

"Do you know why? Could it be drugs?"

Casey thought of the other morning and the weed in the bathroom. "I — I don't know."

He studied her. "I need to talk about Tess a little. Bear with me again. Okay?"

"Yeah."

"I know she was wearing denim overalls and a blue shirt. What about shoes?"

"Moccasins, I think."

"What color?"

"Light pink. With embroidery on them. And beads."

"Any jewelry?"

"A hemp bracelet with little things hanging off it."

"Hemp?"

"It was from a kit!" Casey tried to reign in her defensiveness.

"What kind of things hanging off it? Charms?"

"No. More like silvery bangles. Beads. And she wore a necklace with a gold locket."

"With a picture inside?"

"No. It was just one of those cheap things that came with a book." Casey started crying again. "She asked me if I thought it would be something a princess would wear. I was going to get her a real one for Christmas. A sterling one. She's obsessed with things like that. Tiaras and jewels. She asked our old babysitter if she could have her rosary beads!"

"Who is this babysitter?"

"Marta."

"Is she married?"

"No."

"Boyfriend or kids who came around?"

Casey shook her head. "She's in a nursing home now. She's really old."

"Oh. So Tess likes jewelry?"

"She even likes it when those little balls of snow get stuck on her mittens. She calls them magic gems. A couple weeks ago we couldn't find her gloves anywhere and then she remembered that she'd put them in the freezer so the gems wouldn't melt."

He smiled. "How about underpants? Know what kind she was wearing?"

Casey shuddered. "No. But her favorite's a purple pair with crowns. We have to check and make sure she actually puts them in the hamper and doesn't just keep wearing them."

He smiled. "How 'bout socks?"

"I don't know."

"Can you think of anything else I should know?"

Casey shrugged, tears clouding her eyes.

"You've been very, very helpful, sweetheart. Hang in there. I know your folks are going to need you. Could you send Doone in for me?"

She wiped her face and made her way down the backstairs into the kitchen. It was teeming with people. Outside, a bunch of reporters and a satellite truck had appeared. A couple cops whose backs were to her were talking about the bulletins that had gone out.

"Well, I sure hope they're better than that one up north.

Did you hear about that? All it said was 'Boy missing!' Give me a
break."

"Yeah."

"No wonder the turkey buzzards found him first."

Don't listen, don't listen!

Casey's toes clenched. She forgot to release them.

Uncle Drew and the boys were huddled around the
television in the den. A picture of Tess flashed on the screen
with the hotline number for the Commonwealth Police running
below. Casey turned away and saw Vivy. She was holding onto
Owen, who was swaying. The presence of her father's girlfriend
in her mother's house didn't seem at all strange. Nothing did.

Casey told Doone the detective was waiting upstairs.

Doone swept the fringe of black bangs back from her face
and went up.

The cop was really familiar. At first she wondered if he was
someone's father from school. Then she realized she'd seen him
on the news when really bad things went down. Doone was trying
hard to think of something new. But there wasn't anything else.
She only saw the kidnapper for a second. And he'd been wearing
mirrored sunglasses and a cap that covered much of his profile.
"He never turned around when I yelled."

"I understand that, but let's walk through the whole
sequence together."

"Okay."

"How could you tell it was a man?"

"Instead of a woman?" she asked guilelessly.

He smiled. "Instead of a teenager."

"Oh. I don't know. I just assumed it was a man. His body
seemed more adult, you know? His shoulders were big, I guess.
At school, except for the football players you can pretty much tell

most of the guys are teenagers. But maybe he was just big. I don't know."

A young cop with a badge attached to his front pants pocket and an open leather jacket over a black pullover walked in and asked to speak to the detective in the hallway. He was talking in a low voice but Doone could hear them. He said a couple neighbors confirmed seeing her chasing after a car, barefoot and desperate. "Just didn't want you to waste time going down blind alleys."

Both cops came back into the bedroom.

"I'm going to join in, if that's all right," the young cop said without asking.

She shrugged and studied him. Where the other guy seemed like a serious dad, this one seemed like he was just angry. Standing next to the guy in uniform, he stared back at her, all concave angles and hollowed shadow. Poster boy for the Dust Bowl.

"Could you tell the perp's race, miss?" he asked.

"White."

"Light complected or dark?"

"I just saw a tiny piece of his profile!"

"Well, chances are both sides would match." The young cop's words were dipped in sarcasm.

"Not necessarily," Doone responded.

"Well, I was referring to his coloring. That's generally the same on both sides. Ya know? So was he light or dark complected?"

"Light, I guess."

"Facial hair?"

The phrase reminded her of playing *Guess Who* with Tess. Ever since Casey had explained that asking if the mystery person had facial hair eliminated two groups at once — some of the men and all of the women — that was always Tess's first question. "Does your mystery person have facial hair?" One night while high and bored, Doone had taken a charcoal pencil and shadowed a mustache on a couple of the chicks. Tess had thrown a monster fit and gotten her in trouble. Doone was supposed to buy a replacement game but had never gotten around to it. Regret splashed over her. And for the first time ever she understood that making things right wasn't always an option. Sometimes it was too late.

"No. No beard or anything," she whispered.

"Okay. When he was getting into the vehicle where did the door come to?" the older cop asked gently.

She closed her eyes and saw the man standing next to the car. "Mid-shoulder."

"Good. That will help us figure out height." He scribbled on the notepad. "What was he wearing?"

"A blue jacket. But so what? Don't you think he'll just take it off?"

"Maybe. But maybe someone else saw him in it, too. And maybe they can remember other details that we can add to yours."

"Oh."

"So how about his hair — how long beneath his cap did it come?"

"It didn't. It was short. A buzz."

"Could you tell the color?"

"Brown."

"Did he turn around at all when you called out to him?"

"No."

"When he opened the car could you see if he had any rings

on his hand?"

"No. He had on blue gloves." She thought for a moment. "Those gloves didn't look right. I mean they looked more like ski gloves than cop gloves."

"Good!" the older cop said, praising the new detail, writing notes. "Did you actually see Tess in the car?"

"For a second."

"Could you make out any of the license number?"

"No."

"And you couldn't tell if they were Virginia tags?"

"No. There're so many different styles of them now!" Her voice rose in agitation. "It might have been. But I don't know!"

"That's okay. I'll get a sheet for you to look at with all the specialized plates on it — so you can see if anything looks familiar. Now this is going to be rough question, but what made you think he had Tess in the car at first?"

Doone shuddered. "The way he was hurrying and pretending not to hear me. I was screaming! There was no way he didn't! For a second I thought the car was going to get stuck in the gravel at the top of the driveway and I started running up the hill. I couldn't go that fast because I was barefoot. It was like my feet wouldn't let me!" She was sobbing. "I tried, I really did! But the car rocked and peeled out before I got to the top. That's when I saw Tess."

"The guys outside said there are some deep grooves that don't match your mom's car. Unless anybody else was here since it started snowing this morning, parked at the top of the driveway?"

"I don't think so."

"Okay, so after he started to drive away what did you do?"

"I kept screaming. Mr. Bride from next door came out.

He's the one who called you."

"And when did your other sister come back?"

"Just a few minutes after. She got here about the same time as the cops did. She was sledding."

Doone shivered as she remembered Casey's howl when a policeman told her what was going on. The younger cop crossed his arms, put his foot on the metal frame under Casey's box spring and said, "So. What can you tell us about your friend? The one who's taken a tumble for meth."

"Dust? Nothing! He's never even been here! He doesn't have anything to do with this!"

"Well, instead of trying to figure out why someone *isn't* involved I like to take the opposite approach. See if they could be — then work back. Do you get my meaning?"

"Everyone starts off guilty?"

"Something like that."

His deep-set, too-close eyes drilled into her, evaluating. They made her feel gross. Beyond naked. Like when she went to get birth control and was worried the doctor would be able to tell how many guys she'd been with or what she'd let them do. She crossed her arms, squeezed her own shoulders.

"We know he's involved with meth. How about you?"

"No!"

"You go in more for hillbilly heroin? Snort a little? How about crack? You don't look the type but you never know."

The older cop moved away from the younger one, realigning his position so they formed more of a triangle than a firing line. It worked. Doone felt less attacked. He cleared his throat and spoke gently. "The reason why we need to ask these questions, Doone, is because the people who deal — particularly meth — are downright unsavory. Motorcycle gangs. Cartels."

"Not to mention backwoods trailer trash who cook the poison up, killing their own kids in the process," the younger guy threw in. "If you pissed one of them off they'd come for your little sister quicker than a New York minute. Payback time."

"I didn't! I didn't even know Dust was cooking until he got arrested!"

"See, that's one of the things that I'd be worrying about if I was you."

"What? What do you mean?"

"If he finds it interesting that you were at his place right before he got busted, you know? We need to be on the same page to be bringing back Tessa. A 10-year-old got shot in the head because she stumbled on a meth lab last year."

Doone gasped at the implication.

Could *Dust be involved in this? Please, God, please don't let this be happening. Don't let it be more my fault than it already is.* "I don't even think he knows I have a little sister."

Then she felt everything in the room — the bulletin board, the mirror, the computer, the chair — start whirling, spinning faster and faster. She thought she might faint. She opened her mouth, but nothing came out.

"Doone?" the older cop questioned.

"The last time I saw him he made a joke about Tess being hot."

"Nice." The younger cop whistled through his teeth. "Nice company you keep. We'll check and see if he's connected to any of the known sex offenders. Any other buddies we should interview? What about Hank Carlisle?"

"Hank? What about Hank? How do you know about him?"

"Time is of the essence, Doone. We're not screwing

around. We're lifting up every rock, seeing who comes out."

"What does that mean?"

"Don't the Carlisles live on some hippie commune?"

"It's not a commune! He lives with his family!"

"Well, we'll be chatting with him." The young man crossed his long arms, leaned against the wall, never breaking eye contact. "So why do you choose such sleazeballs to hang with? You got some issues?"

Fury at the misplaced focus rose like vomit. "You want to do therapy? Get in line." Doone stood tall. "I don't need this! Are we finished?"

"For now. If you feel like that's the best you can do."

She walked out. Behind her the men's voices rose in agitation at each other. The redneck called her a spoiled smart mouth. The other one asked where he'd learned his interview skills.

The first floor was crazy with cell phones and walkie-talkies going off; Bean's barking added to the chaos. Kik stood next to Parrish, framed by the triple window in the den, her eyes vacant, but her body ready to bolt. Doone thought of a photo she took once of a plastic bag caught on a branch right before it became airborne.

"Mom?"

Kik didn't seem to recognize her. Doone began to cry hysterically.

"I'm sorry! I'm sorry I let her open the door! Mom? Please say something! Mom? Please say you forgive me!"

Parrish grabbed Doone and hugged her tightly. She buckled against him and he rubbed her back, not disengaging until the undercover cop who interviewed her approached. "Mrs. Marcheson?"

"Yes?" Kik managed to whisper.

"When the camera crew who set up for Price's show came — were they local or from New York?"

"I don't know! It never occurred to me — "

"Okay. We can find out. Now, about this," he said, thrusting a photo forward. "Is this what your daughter wore on the show?"

Tess had on her school's sweatshirt, its name crawling up the sleeve.

"Oh, my God," Kik said, obviously understanding.

"What?" Doone asked.

"If it was a stranger abduction then whoever had their eye on her could have seen where she went to school. Followed the bus. She takes the bus, right?"

"But they didn't have school today!" Kik argued. "Because of the snow."

"Doesn't really matter. Whoever did it could have just been waiting for opportunity. And if it was somebody who saw you all on TV, it wouldn't take long for your address to be tracked down."

"We're not listed," Kik said.

"That might add all of a minute to the search. No offense, ma'am, but putting your family on TV is like inviting every pervert in the country into your world."

Stunned by the rebuke, Kik felt vagueness return full-force. Her repertoire of reactions had been reduced to inertia and screaming pain, running together like the Mobius strip Tess brought home from school.

"Hey, buddy," Parrish drawled. "Any time a kid wears a shirt with his school's name, or swim club, or little league team, it advertises where he can be found. Right?" he paused as if actually waiting for a response. Then continued, "And anytime a kid's picture is in the newspaper for winning a spelling bee, some sicko could think of it as an open invitation." He took a step closer to the policeman. "So, I'm not sure that hinting at blame is productive."

The room was suddenly charged with testosterone and challenge.

"Sir, what did you say?"

The ringing phone defused an all-out confrontation.

"Wait a moment and I'll pick up the extension," an FBI agent instructed Kik as he had each time someone called on the house phone.

"Hello! Yes? Oh," Kik's shoulders sagged. "Thank you," she muttered, dangling the phone for anyone who wanted it. "It's Bill somebody from Dr. Price's show. The producer."

The FBI agent introduced himself into the receiver. "Our New York office will be interviewing everyone who's been in contact with the family. Someone should be there shortly." He paused, listened. "That's all right; I'll talk to the doctor. We don't need his permission. This is a criminal case. Got it?"

Every time Kik glanced at her watch she was surprised. Time was passing the way it did in a hospital: by turns leadenly and at warp-speed. She looked across the room at her family and thought of skiers on a cable car plunging toward disaster. Her lifelong Nazi nightmare surfaced. It had always begun the same — hiding, boots stomping; then it wended its way through the particulars of her own life. School. Club. Home. And it always ended the same. In the gas chamber. When she was a little girl she realized the adults could offer no solace, give no protection.

After she became a mother herself, the terror was that much worse.

"What's going through Tess's head?" Owen asked her. "Is he touching her? Is she tied up? This must be how Terry felt! When he couldn't move and was just waiting for the end."

Casey and Doone both looked horrified at their father's outburst.

"Owen!" Kik's hands exploded into the air like birds from a bush. Bringing his dead brother into the current crisis was gratuitous.

"Sorry," he said. But then he kept talking. "When that cop showed up at the lab I thought maybe there'd been a chemical spill in another part of the building. Or a bomb threat. It never occurred to me that it was personal.

"Then it all became clear and they put me in the car and someone asked about child support. And my relationship with you. And Vivy's relationship with you. One of the cops asked if I'd be willing to take a polygraph. I wanted to kill him for even suggesting what he was suggesting."

Casey couldn't take any more and went into the bathroom. She was struck by how odd it was that biology moved forward in the face of torture.

How is it that I still have to pee?

Her cry started silently and then grew bigger than any sound she'd ever made. She crumpled loudly in the corner. Vivy pushed open the door.

"Shhh," she said over and over. Casey sobbed into her lap.

Control eventually returned. She made herself breathe deeply, focus. And then a lusterless barrette on the floor between the trash basket and the wall caught her eye.

She moaned. Tess had called her at Caroline's to ask if she

knew where it was.

"It is my most very favorite," she'd implored. "Mother found one for me but not the other one! They are a pair! They must be together!"

Casey picked up the barrette. Long curly dark strands were woven through the clip's dull stones.

"Oh," Vivy said as Casey slipped the clip into her shirt pocket. Casey lifted herself slowly, the way her Dad used to lift Uncle Terry. "I'm ready to go back out, I think."

But as soon as she made it into the den she began sobbing again. "It's all my fault. If it was someone from watching her on TV — it's my fault!"

"Listen to me," Owen's voice carried across the room. It was low and authoritative. "The monster who took her is responsible. Nobody else."

"One time Tess asked me if 'gone missing' was like 'gone fishing'. She thought it was a place to go for a field trip," Casey whispered.

The voices of a couple of cops filled a sudden lull. "Someone outside getting names? You never know if the pedophile is part of the crowd, getting his jollies visiting the crime scene."

Another voice carried in. "I just wish it wasn't so frickin' cold. Makes everything harder."

"Who's the old guy in the parka?" the first one asked.

"A John Bride. One of the neighbors."

"Kinda skeevy looking, isn't he? Any idea why he's taking all this so personal? I think he's fixin' to cry hisself to death."

"The mother says he and the little girl go get ice cream sometimes. He's sort of a surrogate grandfather."

"This family's like a walking what-not-to-do."

"I hear ya."

The front door opened and one of the cops drawled "Excuse me, sir? Mr. Bride? Can we speak with you for a minute? Can you step over here for a moment, please?"

Casey looked through the window and saw reporters whip toward the hapless old neighbor. There was a silver ribbon of spittle on his chin and he looked terrified.

"Stop," Casey pleaded to the cops on the porch. "Mr. Bride's not involved!"

"No one's out to hurt anyone, miss. We're just trying to find your sister.

Chapter Twelve

Kik wondered about the crowd outside. Why were they there? Not the reporters of course, but the others. What made them stand in the frigid air, staring? The hours were starting to race by, which everyone knew was not good. The magic minutes of safe return had come and gone. The house had gotten uncomfortably hot with so many occupants and the phone had not stopped ringing.

Maddie had dropped her family off and gotten fried chicken and biscuits on the way back. The meal came with red beans and rice and coleslaw.

Sides! Kik thought with disgust. *Picnic at the Marchesons!*

She surveyed the food on the dining room table, the paper plates and two liter bottles of soda. Maddie had transferred the food from the Styrofoam containers to serving dishes. Something Kik didn't even do when things were normal.

Only the cops really ate. The one thing she was able to put in her mouth was a flaky roll, which she pulled apart bit by bit, letting the pieces dissolve on her tongue like communion wafers. She went alone into the den, sat.

Parrish found her, handed her a tumbler full of Diet Coke. "There's a shot of bourbon in there, sugah."

"Do you think I should?"

"I do."

"What will everyone think?"

"That your child is missing."

Kik shuddered and took a sip of the slow burn. "I can't believe this is happening. I keep waiting to wake up."

"I know. Just sit, chérie. Close your eyes if you can."

"No!"

"Okay. That's fine." He put his hand on her neck, massaged it with strong fingers.

"What am I going to do?"

"We're just going to take this minute by minute, Kik. Don't think about anything but getting through each one."

"What if last night was the last time I'll ever get to see her? What if we never see her again? Never know what — "

"Hush, Kik."

But her thoughts were taking flight. "Does the phrase Amber Alert come from children being preserved in memory?"

"You're going to have to stop yourself, Kik. Stop thinking like this."

"How?"

Detective Warner walked over to them. Both Kik and Parrish stood. Kik's hand shook and her drink spilled a little.

"Nothing to report, Mrs. Marcheson. Sorry to have upset you. Just wanted to know if you have a calendar or one on your phone?"

"I've got both. I finally switched," Kik said, handing over her cell. "The old one's in the kitchen. I'll get it."

The two women walked together. Larraine Warner said, "We like to look at people's schedules with them. See if there's anything there."

"What do you mean?"

"To see if something jogs your memory about what you've done over the past few days. Who might have come into contact with Tess."

"Oh."

The drawer wouldn't open. Kik had to slip her hand in and

push everything down before it would slide out, scraping the skin off her knuckles. She didn't notice. She extracted the date book that excreted papers and expired coupons. Half of the pages were glued together, courtesy of Tess's sticker phase.

The detective smiled at the decorations. "The little one do this?"

"My sister gave her one of those kiddie calendars last year. It had these do-it-yourself stickers for special occasions. Birthdays and sleepovers, sharing circles. It was supposed to teach organizing skills or something."

"I've seen those."

"Tess decided to organize me, too. When she ran out of stickers she used my stamps. Forty dollars worth." Kik's eyes filled and she whispered, "I got mad at her."

"Who wouldn't?"

"What?"

"Listen, Mrs. Marcheson. I've worked enough cases like this to know that one of the things parents do is start beating themselves up. Over real mistakes and imagined ones. And you really don't need that right now. Actually, it's pretty much the last thing you ought to be directing your energy toward."

They flipped through the planner but found nothing out of the ordinary, just the occasional orthodontist appointment and PTA meeting.

"I never realized how little we do," Kik laughed mirthlessly.

The detective smiled again. She put her hand gently on Kik's arm and said, "What we should do now is appoint a family spokesperson to deal with the media."

"Why?"

"Things just run smoother when one person does the communicating. And that's really important. Is there anyone in the family who would be good? While it's up to you of course, I don't think I'd recommend either you or your ex-husband doing it."

"Why not?"

"It's just very hard. Draining. The media can act like junkyard dogs, pushy and really ugly. It's hard to fend them off in the best of circumstances, you know? Anybody come to mind who would be calm and is a good speaker?"

"Let me think about it for a few minutes."

"Sure. Why don't you go talk to the others? Let me know in a few."

They clustered in the den trying to decide.

"I'm happy to help," Vivy offered from the hardback chair she'd brought in from the dining room. "I mean I'm sure you want someone else to be the actual spokesperson. But as an advisor, maybe? My being a reporter might give us an advantage."

"An advantage?" Kik hissed.

"I'm sorry. I didn't mean it to . . . It's just . . ."

The awkwardness of the moment — and their history — descended over the group like a parachute. Even in the midst of catastrophe everyone grew uncomfortable.

"I'm sorry," Kik said half-heartedly. "Go ahead."

"I was just going to say that it's important to stay on the press's good side. I know these guys. Some of them are great. Some aren't. They're people, with deadlines and grudges and dreams of Pulitzers. And with newspapers on the ropes everyone's that much more desperate. If we piss them off they'll slip the knife in by the follow-up."

"What do you mean?" Owen asked.

"Let's say someone shouts a really tactless question at you.

And you respond angrily. Maybe even saying something appropriately cutting in response. Well, that reporter might then stick something in a story about your temper. Maybe call Child Protective to see if you've ever been reported, then include in the article that the agency doesn't comment on reports; plant the seed."

"It's all so cynical," Parrish said.

"That's why it's really important to stay in control, manage the spin by keeping Tess on the front page, not anybody else in the family."

"Spin?" Kik repeated hysterically, causing Bean to whimper loudly, then bark. "What are you talking about? What's to spin? Someone stole my baby!"

"Calm down, sugah," Parrish said, stepping behind Kik and putting his arms under her ribs as if she were choking. Kik initially tensed and then relaxed and leaned into him as Vivy continued to speak.

"All we want the press to focus on is finding Tess. Nothing else. They'll run with the story for as long as it has legs." Vivy paused and then added, "At least she's white. Middle class. That's a major media hurdle right there."

"Come on, Viv," Owen argued.

"It's a morally bankrupt, disgusting reality of corporate journalism," Vivy said quietly.

Parrish regrouped first. "What do we need to do?"

She turned toward him. "Put together a press kit, make fliers, then keep on-message whenever we have a press conference."

"Kik, can I speak with you a moment?" Owen asked.

They went upstairs, the only place that wasn't overrun, and stood together in the hallway outside their former room. It had been years since Owen had been up there. Kik noticed him noticing the wall of black and white photographs. The ones in which he had figured had been excised, replaced with shots of the girls. Kik saw he was looking at one in particular. It was of Parrish at Walnut Creek Park. Tess was on his shoulders, Bean and Orbison flanking them. It looked like a Gap ad.

"What?" Kik whispered.

"I think Vivy should be the spokesperson. She knows what she's doing. I think that's the most important thing."

"You want the woman who broke up our marriage to represent the family?"

The eternal rage that flickered between them flamed.

"Are you kidding me? That's what you really want to focus on now?"

"What?"

"You're going to let your jealousy get in the way of finding Tess? Is that what I'm hearing? You're going to nurse your petty grudges instead of finding our child?"

"How dare you say that to me? You self-righteous prig! You didn't even want her in the first place! And don't think no one noticed that it was Parrish who offered more money for the reward! You — " And then she was pounding him in the chest with both fists. Owen absorbed the pain and then grabbed hold of her and they sunk to the floor. Both remembered the last time they had touched, the night their baby had been conceived. They clung together.

"I'm sorry, Owen. I know how much you love Tess. And she knows, too. She worships you."

"I'd give my life for her," he whispered.

"I know."

He bent forward in order to get leverage to stand. Kik saw

neat rows of scalp peaking through the silver strands. He straightened up. He looked truly terrible, a cancer patient waiting for more bad news.

"Do you mind if I use the bathroom up here?" he asked. "I'm not feeling well."

"Of course not."

He took her hand. "I want you to know something, Kik. I'm sorry about how I behaved towards you, the way I left. It was wrong. And I know that."

She went down and quietly helped Vivy put together a press kit. Everyone scrolled through their phones for recent snapshots.

"That's a good one," Vivy said, about one Doone held out. "It shows her eyes. And she doesn't have her usual grin, which really changes her face. You know? How her eyes squint and her nose crinkles?"

Kik nodded. Tess's face completely transformed when she was laughing. She knew her baby wouldn't be laughing now. They sat down together at the laptop to compose the text for the poster. Kik turned it on and the computer barked. The sound startled Vivy.

"Sorry," Kik whispered. "I've had the thing for two years. I can't figure out how to make it shut up. It yelps and slams doors, too. Sometimes it shouts 'good-bye' for no reason."

"I had a parrot like that once," Vivy said, reaching for the computer. "Here, let me. I know how to silence it."

"You didn't kill the bird, did you?"

They laughed a little, shocking Kik.

I shouldn't be laughing!

Vivy pushed a button that displayed a control panel, pushed another key, and muted everything. The computer was silent for the first time ever. "Voilà."

"Wow," Kik said.

Vivy typed out the description of the car and the man, the hotline number, the reward money, Tess's height and weight. Detective Warner came in and asked who Tess's dentist was. Vivy gasped and Kik jumped up. "Why!"

"Nothing, Mrs. Marcheson. Nothing. It's just standard procedure is all. I should have asked when we were going through your calendar."

Kik told her the name then asked if they were forgetting anything from the poster. The detective looked it over, the vertical lines of a smoker forming above her lip.

"No. It looks good."

Before Vivy left for the copy store, Kik asked if she'd be the press person.

"I'm so sorry, Kik. So sorry for everything. I feel like is this my fault. If I hadn't done that asinine show. Or if Casey hadn't come — "

"I can't do this right now," Kik said.

Vivy nodded. "I'm going to grab my coat, get the copies made up."

Casey was sitting in the closet. The teen looked like she was praying but her clasped fingers were opening and closing.

One two three. One two three.

"Oh honey," Vivy said, squatting, taking Casey's hands in her own. "What are you doing?"

The girl shrugged her narrow shoulders.

Vivy looked at her appraisingly. "Can you stop doing that?"

Casey shook her head and Vivy knelt down. "Let me hold you a minute."

Casey collapsed into the soft chest and again let herself be cradled. Her fingers eventually relaxed.

"Do you know there's a theory that bacteria can cause people to have to do things like that?" Vivy asked.

"What?"

"Yeah. Rituals like counting and hand washing might be brought on by strep."

"Really?"

"Yeah. If that's something that bothers you — gets in your way — we can look into it, okay? Whatever the cause, we'll deal with it."

Casey nodded and Vivy stood.

"I'm going to get some posters made up. Do you want to come? Get away for a little bit?"

"Do you think it's all right?"

"Absolutely. Just tell your mom or dad."

Casey sat silently in the car while the fliers were being printed and she stayed mute while Vivy drove to the hardware to buy a heavy-duty stapler and packing tape to fasten the thick paper to telephone poles and shop windows.

When they returned to the house, Vivy got Parrish to go outside with her and collect the names of the people willing to leaflet. "Take paper. Make them show you identification," she instructed him. "Tell them it's standard procedure in this kind of thing."

"Won't that just slow everything down?"

"We have to do it, just in case."

"In case what?"

She lowered her voice. "In case the guy who took her is out there, getting off on volunteering."

"Mother of God," Parrish muttered.

Casey staggered up to her mother's empty room and lay down, unaware that Kik was locked in her bathroom just a few feet away.

Kik had opened the window and was leaning against the cold screen, the familiar smell of old dirt and alloy and tobacco filling her nostrils. Long after her public declaration of quitting cigarettes, she used to sit on the wide lip of the old tub and exhale secret Merits through the metal lattice.

Eventually she pulled herself together enough to leave the safety of the bathroom. She saw Casey and went and stroked her head for a moment. "Stay up here, sweetie. Try and rest."

"Yeah."

Downstairs Kik overheard a policeman asking Doone if she knew the address of any of Dust's relatives. She told him about the brother in jail.

Kik asked why the police wanted that information and Doone had to tell her what Dust said, the hottie comment. Kik started wailing. "Where is he? Where is he? How could you have done this to your sister?"

"Stop it, stop it!" begged Doone.

When Aunt Maddie appeared with a vial of tranquilizers, Kik dry swallowed a couple and eventually calmed down. Doone went up to her bedroom, shoulders heaving. She vowed that if Dust did have anything to do with Tess's disappearance she would kill him.

Then myself.

Doone rocked back and forth on her bed, clutching her knees into her breasts. The deep pain felt right.

Why didn't I answer the door? Why didn't I just go downstairs? I could have played a game with her or just watched the stupid movie!

A few minutes later the dustbowl cop found her, Bean at his heels. "So, Doone, we spoke with your friend, Hank."

She stared, not getting the point.

"He and his family were visiting relatives."

"And?"

"So he's off the hook."

She shrugged. "I told you."

"Yeah, but the thing is, Doone? While we were over there, we happened to catch sight of a greenhouse. Do you know anything about that?"

"About a greenhouse?"

"About the weed your friend grows in it?"

"No! What's the matter with you? My sister's missing! Get away from me! Leave me alone!" Mad tears came out of nowhere. Bean barked frenetically and Owen appeared in the doorway.

"What's going on?" he demanded.

"He thinks my friend Hank is involved."

"No, sir. That's not what I said." While no more than half a dozen years older than Doone, he was completely unintimidated by her father. She wondered if that came from the uniform or the gun. He looked the older man in the eye. "We need to investigate any and all leads, sir, as I'm sure you can appreciate. This Hank had an alibi, but we needed to check him out. And while we were there we discovered an illegal substance growing on the premises."

"But nothing ties this boy to Tess?"

"Not at this time. No, sir."

"What does that mean?" Doone screamed. "Not at this time! Why don't you just say no! You're wasting hours going down the wrong road! JUST FIND MY SISTER!"

"Doone," Owen hissed. He grabbed her arm above the elbow. "Go take a shower. We're doing a press conference in a little bit. We all need to pull ourselves together."

She went downstairs, found her aunt's bag and helped herself to two tranks, then went back up, grabbed a towel from the linen closet and stood under the punishing spray until Casey knocked on the door and told her it was time.

The family huddled together on the porch while Detective Warner spoke, going through the events of the afternoon, asking people to look for Tess, to think if they'd heard anyone say anything, anything at all, that might have raised red flags. Then Vivy spoke. She talked of the family's appearance on *Dr. Price*, explaining that someone from as far away as California might have targeted her. She looked directly into the cameras and said she was a member of the press, too, and she pleaded with her colleagues to treat this case as if Tess were their child.

After midnight the activity downshifted and a hush spread slowly through the house, stilling everything. It reminded Kik of a midnight plane full of passengers being put to bed by stewardesses. Someone dimmed the lights, turned the television way down. Even Bean had quieted. For hours he'd been bouncing so wildly a cop threatened to shoot him.

Kik stared outside. The continuing cycle of lights on the police cruisers was comforting, the monotony oddly reassuring. Every three seconds she knew what was coming next — a bright flash of red. She kept thinking about the lack of warning before this happened. Tess was present and then she was gone.

Parrish had been sitting next to Kik on the couch for most of the night. A few feet away the girls were asleep in the easy chair, pressed together like puppies. The police were moving around in the kitchen and dining room murmuring, a thrum of low pitch static. Parrish's arm was around her, the pressure on her shoulders constant and safe. She was in the channel between light and dark, too afraid to let go completely. Twice she drifted off and awoke, startled, thinking she heard Tess calling out.

In her hazy consciousness Kik realized she had nothing left to plea bargain with God. She'd already offered her life in exchange for Tess's. Her health. Her stunted writing career. Her looks. Limbs. A lingering death. In fact, she'd made so many promises that she suddenly jerked forward, wide-awake, terrified that she should be writing them down. She reached for the legal pad and began scrawling her pledges.

Register at a bone marrow clinic

Tithe to the Emergency Shelter

Rid myself of sarcasm

Stop being petty

"What else can I do, God? What?" She hadn't meant for the entreaty to be spoken aloud, but it slipped through the place in her mouth that Casey used to call the word-catcher, the internal censor that saved people from getting into trouble.

Parrish sat up straight. "What are you doing, darlin'?" he whispered. He took the paper from her. "Oh, chérie."

"What if God wants me to exchange myself for Tess? How will I know?"

"Hush, Kik. It's fear talking now, is all. Just try and rest. You've got to get some sleep. You'll be useless otherwise." He pulled her back under his arm and began humming. It took her a minute to recognize the tune.

You Can Close Your Eyes.

She leaned in to him and soon he was swaddling her the way she used to hold fussy babies, cocooning her in his arms until she finally let go and tumbled into a dreamless sleep.

Early morning sun was heating the room. Obscene visions kept forcing their way into Casey's head. Violent home invasions of the brain. Newscasters talking about registered sex offenders in the area triggered them.

Obviously.

But so did innocent stuff, and that was worse. Those thoughts were like intruders who entered from unexpected places — not the usual backdoor or unlatched window, but from skylights and heating ducts. Casey would be thinking about going into the bathroom and suddenly imagine a naked Tess climbing from the tub trying to cover herself. Boops, she called her pale pink nipples. Casey remembered how Tess had a rash once and kept saying her china hurt. That's what she called her private parts for the longest time. Her boops and her china.

She looked at her mother. Kik was awake. "Do you think Harperly is there, Mom? With her?"

"What?"

"I just — I don't want her to be alone."

Kik crossed the room and cradled Casey, holding her the way she'd been held by Parrish. She stared out of the window, seeing for the first time the yellow ribbons that had appeared on tree trunks and mailboxes. She wondered if there was a conversion chart somewhere like the one for birthstones at jewelry counters, a crisis color code so that no one had to stand in front of the spools of ribbon trying to choose the appropriate hue for a specific trauma.

Kik found herself being lulled by the rocking motion, too, halfway listening to the snatches of cop talk that floated in from the kitchen. They would have been humorous if unattached, just out for a good time. The cops slid between street lingo and the stilted patois of low-level bureaucrats on-the-record.

She gave an assignment in the beginning of the year for her students to go someplace and eavesdrop, then write dialogue.

The best was by Luke-the-Lacrosse-Player. He went to a law enforcement briefing and then wrote an exchange between two rookies. It started with "A couple of perps were conversating." Kik had laughed out loud when she read it.

She froze.

What about Luke? Could he have done this? Where was he yesterday?

Her heart began pounding. "I'll be back," she said to Casey. She half-ran into the kitchen to find Detective Warner.

Casey settled back into the chair, startling Doone awake. "What's going on, Case?"

"Nothing. No news."

"Do you think your brain knows the plots before you dream them?"

"What? I don't know!"

"Because otherwise how could they make sense? I mean they're not just like a collection of random drawings. They have direction." She paused then posited, "Or maybe it's like when you paint something — you only know where something is going as it starts happening?"

"I don't know, Doone," Casey said again, wondering if her sister was high. She found the new loquaciousness banal, unwelcome. After so many aborted attempts at connecting, the irony of Doone reaching out now filled Casey with bitterness. But her sister seemed oblivious and kept talking.

"All I can think about are the times I was ugly to her, all the things I said. I was reading them off a list. In my dream, I mean. I guess they were like stored somewhere in my brain."

Casey sat forward weighing different responses. They were all lame. She supposed she should offer her sister some sort of absolution. But it wasn't okay. Words hurt. Casey's toes knotted in her socks. "I don't know. I guess all we can do is change the present."

"I wasn't always mean to her!"

"I didn't say you were. I can't handle this, Doone. I'm going to take a shower."

She stood and the blanket their Nana crocheted dropped to the floor.

"Whoa, Case. Wait a minute!"

"What?"

"You got your period," Doone whispered. "The back of your pants are gross." She kicked the blanket up with her foot and then put it around her younger sister's shoulders.

"Thanks," Casey said numbly.

Doone noticed the seat cushion was sticky. In other circumstances she would have been grossed out, told Casey to come and handle her mess. But she just went to flip it over. And gasped at the sight of one of Tess's sandwich bags with twin slices of American cheese curled into elf shoes.

The whole freakin' house is completely booby-trapped!

She dropped the pillow back just as a deliveryman holding the biggest flower arrangement Doone had ever seen appeared on the porch. She opened the door before he knocked and took it from him, muttered thanks.

"I hope everything turns out okay," he said. "Y'all are on my church prayer list."

Instead of a sarcastic thought bubbling up and out, Doone had a sudden impulse to throw herself into the stranger's arms. She looked him in the eye and thanked him again.

The flowers dwarfed a stack of posters on the table. The card read, 'On tour, but thinking of you! Dorian.' Doone brought it to her mother who was sitting in the kitchen. Kik read he note then shook her head. "What did she send?"

"This insane arrangement that's bigger than — " Doone braked before saying *Tess*.

"Show the card to Parrish. He'll appreciate it," her mother said.

Owen approached carrying a legal pad, his careful block print on the top page. He'd turned into an old man. "Kik, could you look this over? Add to it?"

"What is it?"

"A list of things worth investigating. I keep thinking the answer is embedded in our daily lives, an equation holding its own solution. You know?"

Kik didn't. "What do the asterisks mean?"

"That they might have cameras. Maybe picked something up."

PLACES WE'VE BEEN RECENTLY

Gas station off Barracks*

Grocery*

Bank*

Library

Downtown Mall

PEOPLE TO BE QUESTIONED

Malcolm

Mailman

Teachers

PEOPLE WHO MIGHT HAVE SOMETHING AGAINST US

She stopped reading. In this scenario Tess wasn't the main goal but a weapon of retaliation. Kik found herself getting excited about the possibility. It seemed better than Tess being the ultimate target.

Because if it was a revenge thing then maybe we'll find her
Otherwise the whole country stays on the suspect list.

"Do you really think someone would go after Tess to get at
us?" she whispered.

"Who knows? Academia is full of pettiness! Remember
that fight over Steven Marks last year? He was furious I didn't
endorse his tenure petition. On his last day he came to my office,
told me he'd remember. Called me Judas."

"You didn't support him? Weren't you friends?"

Owen inhaled audibly and exhaled equally loud. "My
point, Kik, is that people carry grudges."

Detective Warner intervened. "Do you have his number?"

"I can get it." Owen looked at his ex-wife. "Except for that
Hargrew character I couldn't think of anyone connected to
Casey — "

"Oh! I'd forgotten about him!" Kik said.

"Who is this?" asked Warner.

"A kid who had a crush on Casey last year. It was pretty
obsessive," Kik answered. "He'd leave poems under the
windshield wipers. It bordered on creepy. He asked if she'd go
to prom like in September. Casey's so sweet she didn't know
what to do. She didn't want to hurt his feelings. But it definitely
flipped her out. He texted her all of the time. And when she'd
block him, he'd just change his screen name. I ended up calling
the guidance counselor."

"Did the behavior stop?"

"Yeah."

While she was being discussed, Casey was sitting on the
floor of her mother's shower. The water was coming out in
halting bursts. She'd been under the hot, erratic spray for a half
an hour. Everything was foggy, inside and out. There were no

clear edges anymore, just blurry boundaries. She felt as wasted as she ever had, worse than she had when she'd gotten so drunk at a Derby Party that Caroline's brother had to drive her home. Casey'd spent the whole ride staring at the pair of sunglasses perched atop his backwards baseball cap. Then she threw up on the floor mat.

Doone knocked on the door. "Case?"

"I'm okay," she replied, speaking into her knees as another surge of water splashed over her shoulders.

"Do you need anything?"

Like what? A time machine?

"No."

"How about tampons? Are there any in there?"

"I don't know."

"I'll grab some. Case — I think we have to go down soon."

"Why?"

"Mom might need us."

How ironic, Casey thought. Then: *At what point in the row of dominoes does responsibility for a chain reaction start? Doone's behavior? My trip to New York? Going sledding? Doone not watching Tess better?* A new thought intruded. *What if Doone was smoking weed in the bathroom and that was why she didn't hear Tess getting taken? Then I'm to blame because I never told Mom when I caught her before!*

"Doone?"

"Yeah?"

"Were you high?"

"What?"

"When she got taken?"

Doone's breath caught. "No! I wasn't — I *swear* it! I was just upstairs because I didn't want to watch that movie again!"

The only sound was the water sluicing down Casey's body "Okay. I just had to know. You understand, don't you?"

"I guess."

"I'll be down in a minute."

When she climbed out of the shower a towel and change of clothes were on the toilet seat, a tampon sitting atop the pile like a paperweight. Casey had volumes of questions and no one to ask.

Will the reporters lose interest all at once? Or will they fall away a few at a time?

When a girl from Alexandria was kidnapped from a school dance, the cable news shows devoted days to the story. One even had a clock tracking the time she'd been gone. And then it was over. All the chatter stopped. The clock simply disappeared. No one ever found her or the timepiece.

They just moved on.

The only thing that Casey was sure of was that none of them were strong enough to withstand this much longer. This would be the seminal event that would change them all.

Seminal, she thought. *Decisive. Determining. Shaping.*

Casey dressed and took the back steps to the kitchen, which Aunt Maddie had obviously scoured. According to Kik, Maddie had been cleaning non-stop since kindergarten. Kik said just watching her sister made her eyes tired. Maddie's motion was constant. She straightened books, plumped pillows, smoothed tablecloths; was never still. At that moment Maddie was moving the toaster over, to scrub an ancient splatter. She'd already wiped down the cupboard doors and the wood gleamed. Casey wanted to scream at her to stop erasing things of Tess's touch. Instead, she clenched her toes three times, kissed her aunt's cheek, and thanked her for being there.

Foreign crockery had appeared with a variety of breakfast foods. Styrofoam cups and a huge coffee urn were on the counter. Arty pottery, that Casey figured was probably from the hipster couple in the house behind theirs, held muffins and homemade jam. A glass bowl with a colorful fruit salad sat next to a big aluminum pan with sausage biscuits. Casey found that to be an interesting detail. Was the cook being generous not wanting them to have to worry about cleaning and returning a good dish? Or was she afraid they wouldn't? Two completely different origins of behavior, Casey thought, each telling.

She went for a spoon. The drawer had been organized. The silverware that used to scramble over the sticky little walls of their stalls were all lined up now in some military exercise, hands to themselves. The newspaper was on the counter with a big picture of Tess on the front page. Casey began to read.

Missing Child

The little girl who stole America's heart on a nationally televised talk show by insisting on wearing her pajamas to school was kidnapped from her Charlottesville area home late yesterday afternoon.

According to Detective Larraine Warner from the Child Crimes Division of the Commonwealth Police it appears that someone posing as a police officer put 5-year-old Tess Marcheson into a waiting vehicle and then sped off.

Tess was at home with her 16-year-old sister, Doone, who was upstairs when the doorbell rang. The older girl assumed it was a friend of Tess's and let her answer the door.

A few moments later Doone realized she didn't hear anything downstairs and went to check on the child. The front door was open and she saw a man dressed like a police officer acting suspiciously at the top of the steep driveway. He was getting into an either dark green or black, late model sedan.

Doone chased after the vehicle and neighbors called the police. She did not see the license plate.

The Marcheson family has recently gained fame as featured guests on *The Dr. Price Show*, receiving televised therapy on the nationally syndicated program. It is not known whether the child's abduction was related to their TV appearance. According to police, nothing is being ruled out.

The show played a clip of Tess demanding to wear her new pajamas to school so that "My friends can see me in them."

"She is a little girl full of spunk and heart," says Dr. David Price. "Our show will be doing everything we can to foster her quick return."

"All leads are being followed," says Detective Warner. She asks anyone with information about the disappearance or whereabouts of Tess to call the hotline at 434-555-0000. Tess is a little over three feet tall and weighs forty pounds. She has dark eyes and curly brown hair. She was last seen in blue denim overalls. She was wearing moccasins at the time of the abduction.

A $10,000 reward is being offered.

Tess is the daughter of Dr. Owen Marcheson, a scientist, and his former wife, Klara Marcheson, a writing instructor. Both are employed by the University at Charlottesville. Ms. Marcheson is the author of *Heading South*, a novel. The Marchesons also have another daughter, 15-year-old Carson. The older girls attend Ivy High School. Tess is a student at Post Elementary.

Chapter Thirteen

By mid-afternoon, Kik was back in the kitchen hiding from the casserole-bearing procession that had been parading to the front door, arriving one after the other like *The 500 Hats of Bartholomew Cubbins*. Not only food had been delivered, Kik was sure she had more potted plants and copies of *When Bad Things Happen To Good People* than any ICU waiting room in the country.

She leafed through Maddie's record of gifts for thank-you notes.

A baby shower in reverse!

Kik absently traced the circles engraved into the table-top, souvenirs from Tess's earliest homework efforts. She'd been doing a work sheet that called for rings around the pictures that didn't belong. Her frustration with the task was borne out in the deep etching beneath the paper.

"But *why* don't they belong, Mother?" she had demanded about the nest of birds that presumably were to be excluded from the row of animals — cows, sheep, pigs.

"Well. Because these other animals live on a farm."

"Well, maybe the birds do, too!" Tess had argued. "You do not know where they live! They could live in a tree on a farm! Or maybe they live in the same house the pigs do! The barm!"

"Barn," Kik had corrected.

But by the time she'd finished working with her youngest daughter that afternoon in September, she too, had grown soft on classifications.

Maddie approached with a warm washcloth. "The press conference is going to be soon, Kik. I think we should clean you up a little."

She accepted the warm rag and rubbed her face, then startled when the doorbell rang again. "I understand why friends come by, Maddie, but why acquaintances? What makes them think if we didn't have real relationships before — that I'd want to start one up now?"

"They're just trying to be kind."

"Well, I think what they really want is to be able to report face-time with us." The target of Kik's anger was shifting constantly, a moving shoreline. She was helpless against the raging emotions. "I think they're just looking to claim proximity. So they can trade observations at book club or something."

"Oh, sweetie. I don't think that's it. At church, we all take turns bringing food to people who are having hard times. It's a way of showing concern."

"Do you ever think it's strange how you ended up Christian, Maddie?"

"You mean and you didn't?"

"Yeah."

"No."

Kik burst out laughing. "That may be the funniest thing you've ever said."

Maddie put her arm around her. "I love you, Klara. So much. I would do anything to take away this pain."

"Just keep dealing with the Bless-Your-Heart Brigade for me."

"Of course."

Kik blew her nose. "I almost lost it when Tess's

kindergarten room-mother showed up to say how sorry she was."

"Why?"

"Because her wretched spawn didn't invite Tess to her skating party last month." Kik burst into wracking sobs again. "Tess cried the whole afternoon."

"Oh, sweetie."

"Hands down, the worst so far has been Ailene Shuster spewing religious platitudes."

"Who?"

"*Exactly!* My new chairman's wife. Or ex-new chairman's wife. I'm pretty sure I was about to be fired yesterday. Anyway, I guess it's in the first-lady of the department job description. Of course, I had no clue who she was. Parrish had to come and bail me out."

"Like, when God closes a door — "

"Yeah. And my personal favorite: 'He has a special plan for little Tess.' What the hell does that mean?"

Maddie rolled her eyes.

Kik lowered her voice. "How could she have let this happen?"

"Who, Kik?"

"Who?" Kik looked at her sister incredulously. "Doone! Why did she let her open the door?"

Maddie squeezed Kik's arm in a painful vise. "*Don't*," she warned. "Don't do that! I can't count the times Tess let me in the house. You always let her open the door. And I always let my kids do it when they were little. Look at me, Kik. And listen to me. Don't let the evil man who took her, take Doone from you, too. Don't do it, Kik. Don't blame her for anything. It'll ruin her life. Do you hear? She's always had a tough row. Don't make it worse!"

The words pierced. Shamed, Kik looked away and whispered, "You mean her learning disabilities?"

"That. And her prickliness. She's just got a low threshold for discomfort. She always has. You know that."

"Did I do it to her?" Kik whispered. "Damage her?"

"Did you intentionally harm her? Of course not! Do we always know the best ways of dealing with our children? No. They're the sum total of genetics and biology and environment and experience and siblings and the weather and who knows what all."

"That's why I agreed to do the show," Kik began to rub her eyes. "I couldn't figure out how to deal with — "

"I know. You're not alone. A lot of parenting is about forgiveness, of your children and yourself. Ask me how well I handled walking in on Drew, Jr. and his girlfriend taking a shower together."

This was such a startling revelation Kik didn't even notice the way Maddie had effectively led her from an emotional minefield, the very last place she needed to wander.

Their conversation was interrupted by a knock on the back door.

An unfamiliar teenager stood on the back porch, rubbing his hands, shifting from foot to foot. His breath lobbed against the glass in gray blasts.

Kik pulled open the door. "Yes?"

"Mrs. Marcheson? I'm Hank Carlisle, a friend of Doone's from school. I just wanted to stop by and say I'm really sorry about all that's happened — "

Doone suddenly materialized.

"Hi," Hank said.

Doone burst into huge sobs.

"Want to go for a walk or something?" he asked. Then to Kik, "If that's okay?"

"I better not leave," Doone answered before Kik did. "But we can go sit on the back porch. Let me grab a coat."

She went to the hall closet where the empty jackets hung like ghosts and briefly buried her face in Tess's bright green rain slicker with the frog pockets, trying to inhale her little kid smell. She grabbed her cammo and a ski cap.

Kik watched as Doone led Hank to the swing on the back porch. The cushion had been put away for the season and Kik knew the cold of the wooden slats rose through their pants. They weren't touching, but only barely.

Doone appeared to be apologizing about something. The boy waved his hands at whatever it was, brushing it away. Then he put his arm around Doone and pulled her into him and let her cry against his side. He stroked Doone's shoulder and lightly, so lightly Kik wasn't sure if her daughter even knew, he kissed her hair. Kik experienced a shimmering instant of happiness at the strange tableau.

And then the phone rang and she was jolted back to reality. *Please,* she prayed. *Please God. Let someone have found Tess! Unhurt!*

"Hello?"

"Hi, is this Klara Marcheson?" a woman with a flat Midwestern accent asked.

"Yes?" *Pound, pound, pound.*

"Hi Klara. My name is Ann O'Dell. I'm an editor at *Voices*, a new imprint of Carmelle and Rowe Publishing. We specialize in creative non-fiction. I wanted to chat with you for a moment. I promise I won't keep you long."

"I'm sorry — who is this?"

"Ann O'Dell. I wanted to talk with you about the possibility of writing a first person account of your ordeal."

"What?" Kik felt like she was on drugs.

"Once everything's been . . . resolved, of course. I have to tell you, I was such a fan of your novel. You've got such a great voice. It deserved much more push than it got." The woman kept talking. "This time out I can guarantee we're committed to a tour — morning shows, book signings. You'd work with the in-house publicist all the way! I still have to run it by the board, of course, but I'm thinking a very healthy advance. And a serious commitment in pre-pub marketing."

"Who knew the only thing I had to do to get a good book deal was have a child stolen?" Kik whispered.

"Oh, please don't take it like that! This would be such an important work, a real contribution. It could be so . . . instructive, illuminating. Documenting the plague against our children."

"What?"

"Perhaps we could even hash something out where we'd have refusal rights over your next fiction manuscript. I'd be delighted to fly down and — "

Kik slammed the phone down with such force it jumped right back out of the cradle.

"Whoa!" Parrish came up and caught the receiver dangling from its cord like a trout. "What's going on?"

She told him.

"Now, Klara," he deadpanned. "Don't be so judgmental. Can you imagine the difficulty of her work? The poor woman probably has to troll cancer wards and Red Cross shelters looking for people to pass out book contracts to. Have some compassion!"

They stared into each other's eyes and burst out laughing.

"Did you get her number?" he wheezed.

They rocked. Parrish went down on a knee. Kik crossed her legs. Tears ran down her cheeks at the absurdity. Then she realized she couldn't stop. She was hysterical, truly out of control. Catching her breath was impossible. Parrish grabbed hold of her and held on until she calmed, motioning to the various people who'd come to see what was going on, to leave them be.

"Are you all right?" he asked, when her breathing stilled.

She nodded into his chest. "I better take a shower or something."

"Come on. I'll take you up."

She went into the bathroom, left the door slightly open — *because, really what difference does any of that make?*

— turned on the hot water, pulled off her sweaty clothes and stepped into the tub, letting the water stutter over her head and shoulders.

After a while Parrish called in from his perch on the corner of the bed. "Kik? You all right?"

"Yeah."

"It sounds like you got some issues with your pipes. A blockage or something."

"I keep thinking about how I was disappointed in my life," she said. "How I always wanted more. A successful writing career. A relationship. What the hell is wrong with me? All I want is what I had! And what if it's too late?" She rubbed her eyes and her elbow knocked into the mammoth shampoo bottle on the shower shelf. It landed on her big toe. A hammer blow to the nail. The pain was incredible.

"You okay in there?"

She could have passed out.

"Kik?" he gently pushed the door open all the way. Repeated her name. "Honey? Answer me, okay?"

She couldn't.

"I'm coming in, Kik."

He pulled open the curtain, careful to look just at her face. "Are you hurt?"

She was crouching in the corner, clutching her foot. "My heart's broken."

"Hang on, sugah. I'll get you a towel."

He passed it to her and then extended his hand to help. Kik lifted her foot too high above the side of the tub and tripped, her breasts flattening against his chest. The physical contact was suddenly overpowering. He enclosed her in his arms, stroking the back of her head until his fingers got caught in the tangles. "Sorry," he whispered, starting to disengage, pull away.

"No! Don't let me go!" she said, panicked. "Just hold me! Please."

He did.

She began crying again. Not the crazy sobs from before but the steady weeping of the grief-stricken. Agony bled from every pore in her body until Parrish too, succumbed.

"Please don't," she pleaded. "I need you to be strong."

He nodded and reached around her and unrolled a length of toilet paper and blew his nose. "Last tears, sweet Klara, I promise. Come on. Let's get you dressed."

Her guilt began running rampant again.

"Parrish? Am I bad person? A bad mother? Is that why this happened?"

"Kik, the only way I can answer that is to say that many of the happiest moments of my life have been spent with you and the girls."

"Really?"

He nodded. "Colette used to say she wished you were her mom. I swear it just about drove Patsy insane. I always had a suspicion that her jealousy of you played into her decision to leave."

"Wait — you blame me for Patsy leaving?"

He made an appreciative sound but it was a shadow of his real laugh.

"Listen, I get that things have been hard, that Doone is hard. But she's a good kid. And she knows you love her. All of them do. Please cut yourself a break, Kik. You've got to try, okay?

She nodded, felt momentarily calmed.

Until another wave of desperation surged and raged again. "I'm so scared, I'm so scared!"

"I know sugah, I know."

They looked into each other's eyes and something fell away inside of her. "I need you," she whispered. "Stop me from disappearing."

He cupped her chin to look into her eyes, "Are you sure?"

"Please?"

He locked the door and laid her onto the fluffy bathroom rug.

And ever so gradually Kik inched away from the edge.

After, he kissed her forehead. "We're going to make it through this. Together. No matter what."

"I love you, Parrish."

"I love you and I'm here," he kissed the top of her head.

"But for how long?"

"For as long as you'll have me."

They walked together into the kitchen where Owen and Vivy were watching the TV by the microwave. It was tuned to cable news. The talking heads were going on about the Marchesons. Tess's picture flashed and then there was a split screen.

Anchor: Do you know, Dom, whether the parents have been asked to take lie detector tests?

Former FBI Agent: No, Russ. At this point I don't know whether they've been asked.

Anchor: Well, what do you think of that idea?

Former FBI Agent: If it was my daughter that was missing, Russ, you can bet the first thing I'd do, would be to go and offer to take a polygraph. Matter of fact, I'd demand it.

Anchor: So do you think it's strange that the parents haven't volunteered to do that? And how about the sisters? Would you want them to get polygraphed if you were leading the investigation?

Former FBI Agent: Without a doubt. Absolutely. And I'd want it done right away so stories couldn't be worked on. The one thing we do know is that drugs have been present in this household.

Owen grunted, his face darkened. He looked like he could reach through the screen and strangle the men. Kik, too, grew rigid. Parrish took her hand.

Anchor: Apparently the family will be holding another press conference down in Virginia soon. And we will of course cut to it live as soon as it begins. In the meantime, let's swing over to the weather desk, see if this cold front is going to snap any time soon."

Vivy spoke up. "Forget it! They're idiots. The agent was probably fired for stupidity. That's why he's *former*. Let's just get ready for the press conference. Okay? Don't get distracted."

Upstairs, Casey and Doone were sitting on their beds as if anchored in place.

"I can't take this anymore," Doone muttered. She pulled a lone Marlboro from her shirt pocket and lit it.

Kik knocked on their door. Saw the cigarette, ignored it. "Georgina Branch is here."

"Mrs. Branch from Ivy?" Casey asked.

"She just wants to say hello. Do you feel up to it?"

Doone dropped the half-smoked cigarette in the toilet and they followed her down into the buzzing kitchen where the secretary waited. Mrs. Branch was wearing her hair loose and it hung all the way down to the top of her pants, wavy from the braid it was usually kept in. She opened her arms to them. "Give me a hug, girls."

They both melted into her and didn't let go for a long time. "Y'all are to call me for anything. Anything at all." She used the back of her hand to wipe away her own tears. "Listen, the teachers didn't get the snow day off. They took up a collection to add to the reward money or however it can best be used. It's right much. I've put my numbers on the envelope if I can do anything at all."

The girls walked her to the door. Outside, the crowd had mushroomed.

"Who are these people?" Doone asked.

"I don't know," Casey said. "I guess they just want to help."

"By staring at the house?"

"The cops gave out some more posters for them to put up."

"And the other ones? How about the slime who aren't helping?" Doone asked rhetorically. "What are they doing here?"

The crowd parted again and Caroline and her mother walked down the path, carrying a tinfoil pan crowded with chicken. Caroline started crying as soon as she saw Casey.

Caroline's mom went to find Kik.

"I tried to tell Mother that food is probably the last thing y'all need. But she stayed up like half the night frying the stuff. Our house reeks. The walls were like bleeding grease," she laughed a nervous peal.

"That was really nice of her."

"How's everybody holding up, Case?"

"Not."

Caroline looked her in her face. "I just keep thinking about the time we talked about what's worse being stalked or — "

Casey gasped.

"Case," her girlfriend's face crumpled. "I'm so sorry! I don't know what made me say that. That was so stupid!"

"It's okay, Caroline. Nobody knows what to say."

Casey looked away though, wondering if she and her best friend would ever again be on the same ground. The moment Tess was taken it was as if the little plot of earth her family inhabited had been sawed off from everyone else and they were now drifting on some ice floe of otherness.

And the chasm kept growing.

Casey's eyes rested on the black and white photograph on the side table that her mom had taken right after Tess was born. It was of the three girls lying on the bed, their feet arranged like ie wedges. Tess's were teeny, the soles smooth. Casey told her friend about what Doone said when the psychic appeared at the door offering her services.

"What?" Caroline asked.

"She goes, 'If you're such a mind reader how come you don't know we're not interested?'"

Owen interrupted their forced laughter. He reminded Casey it was almost time for the press conference. "You want to be there, don't you?"

The decision seemed too big. Everything seemed too big.

"I'm going to go round up Doone," he said. "Think about what you want to do. Thank you for coming, Caroline."

"Is it strange — your dad being here?" Caroline asked after he disappeared up the stairs.

"It's like falling down the rabbit hole. I think I might be going crazy."

"Oh, Casey," Caroline hugged her. "You're not going crazy! You're in hell. I'll stand with you outside, if you want."

"I don't want to. But what if she watches? And she doesn't see me!"

Caroline understood what she meant. "Get your coat."

The first speaker was Detective Warner, who again urged people to come forward if they had any information. She also said all leads were being followed, many interviews had been conducted and with various donations the reward had grown to $15,000.

In other words, Casey translated. *They've got nothing.*

Chapter Fourteen

Another night passed. Again everyone crowded together on the couches and on the den floor. No one wanted to be alone. Doone woke thinking of *Relativity*, the Escher lithograph.

Am I coming or am I going?

She went into the kitchen, got a pear out of a fruit basket with a yellow satin bow around the handle, and sat down at the table. Her father was talking at Detective Warner, using an authoritative voice that bumped up against abuse as far as Doone was concerned.

"I'm saying we would like to be briefed!"

The detective blinked in rapid sequence. Doone felt bad for her. She seemed like she was trying really hard. She'd been there like the whole time.

"We understand that, sir. But we can't fill you in on every little thing we're looking into. When there's any kind of significant change — I assure you — you will be told."

Doone braced for the control-freak explosion. It came.

"Why don't you let me be the judge of what's significant?" Owen yelled, outraged. "What is this need-to-know crap? I want an accounting and I want it now!"

"All right," the beleaguered cop said. "We're investigating a variety of leads. We're doing some computer traces, tracking down IP addresses. But listen, Mr. Marcheson — "

"It's Doctor. Dr. Marcheson. Has anyone even talked to that meth addict? The one Doone exposed her to?"

Something broke loose and sunk heavily in Doone's chest, disturbing the nest of old hurts.

"What happened to 'the monster who took her is responsible'? Or does that only apply to Casey?"

Owen looked over at his eldest daughter, but only briefly. "I'm sorry. I didn't know you were there."

"What else is new? I've been invisible to you my whole life."

"That's a ridiculous thing to say. And this is hardly the time to be discuss — "

The anger that continually seeped through Doone's defenses suddenly swelled and splashed over the crumbling walls.

"It's never the time, is it?" she screamed. "How about the day you told Uncle Terry about how you were having an affair — would that have been a good time?"

"What are you talking about?"

"When you confessed all about you and Vivy, when the three of us were in the car together!"

"I'd never do such a thing! What are you saying!"

"It was the day he almost choked at the bay! You wouldn't shut up about how trapped you felt with Mom. You listed all of her faults! You said the only time you were happy was when you were over at Vivy's, that all you wanted was *out* and you were just waiting for the right time. Oh, and you said that you were mostly worried about Casey because she was so sensitive."

Owen's skin mottled with angry denial. And then paled with realization. His voice dropped to a near-whisper. "I must have thought you were sleeping, Doone. I can't believe I did such a stupid thing. I'm so — "

"Yeah, well. It's a little late. But just for the record — walking around knowing before your mother does that your father's cheating on her and is going to leave — *sucks*."

"Doone — "

"You know what else, Owen? It's not my fault I'm not great at school. I try! And just because you're all close with Casey and Tess doesn't mean you don't suck as a father to me. I count too, you know!"

Doone froze. Saying Tess's name was like slapping her own face. She threw the pear on the floor. It landed with a thud and busted into green-capped chunks between them. Owen reached out, "Come here, sweetheart."

"Don't touch me."

She brushed past him and made her way into the den where she folded herself onto the window seat and leaned her forehead against the cold glass. On the other side of the window Parrish was sitting next to Kik on the porch swing, his arm draped around her shoulders. It rose and fell with her sobs.

Doone was shocked by her mother's appearance. Kik's cheeks were sunken like some old apple doll and her eyebrows — which she once made the girls swear to pluck if she was ever in a coma — were already careless smudges.

One time Tess got hold of a shaver and ended up with two little boxes above each eye. Every morning before school Casey'd had to use her make-up pencil to fill in the gullies. It took weeks for the little hairs to grow back.

Oh, junior.

No matter what Doone did she couldn't stop thinking of her baby sister.

The memories sat right under the surface like early drafts of paintings showing through the topcoat. She'd learned from Ms. Lonnie that there was a word for that.

Pentimento.

Images of Tess kept filtering in. When Doone was in the

bathroom she remembered how when Tess got potty trained she'd made other people wipe her butt for like a year. Even Kik had grown sick of it and told Tess she was old enough to do it herself.

Tess had replied, "Yes, but I would rather not."

Doone shuddered.

How do people go on with their lives not knowing if someone is alive or dead?

Tears leaked through closed lashes. She'd always drawn the line at needles. The idea of injecting something into her veins was terrifying. But at that moment, given the opportunity, she'd do just about anything to dull the pain.

The backdoor opened and Parrish helped Kik into the room. He was practically holding her up. And right then Doone realized that she couldn't do that to her mother. She remembered the thing that Hank had said about being able to change. And she found herself repeating the phrase first silently and then out loud.

It's not a done deal.

"It's not a done deal."

There was a sudden commotion in the dining room. Detective Warner was standing with her back to the window, clutching a cell phone. Where before she seemed controlled and measured, nervous energy was lifting from her body in waves.

Casey was afraid she might pass out. "What's happening?" she whispered, panicked.

The detective lifted a hand for quiet. "What we know at this point is that one of the visitors to Dr. Price's website has been missing for two days. He hasn't been at work. And certain suspicious indicators were discovered in his apartment in Baltimore."

Indicators, thought Casey. *Clues, markers, signs.*

"What was discovered?" Owen demanded.

"A print-out of a map of the area."

"Who is he?" Kik whispered.

"We're putting that together right now. Interviewing neighbors and family members. One thing that is very positive is that he has no criminal record of any kind."

"Of any kind?" Kik repeated pointedly.

"Correct. No violence." She paused, glanced at the girls, went on. "No sexual deviancy. On the other hand, whoever took her isn't right in the head. Obviously. The plan is to proceed with the morning's press conference, since it's already been announced. But we won't say anything that could send him further underground. We don't want him to know we're onto him until we can release every piece of information we can from license plate to shoe size."

Owen started to argue, but Vivy clasped his arm.

Coats were buttoned in stunned silence. Hope seemed to have entered the house, but with it came the sensation that time was running out.

"It feels like *The Amazing Race*," Casey whispered.

"Yeah, but where's the freaking finish line?" Doone asked.

Detective Warner's breath came out in forceful puffs of gray, careening off the bouquet of tall microphones set up on the porch. She told the reporters there were no new leads. Again she read the hotline number and mentioned the reward. Then Vivy stepped forward and reintroduced herself as the Marchesons' spokesperson.

Right away a volley of accusations in the guise of questions were fired toward the house.

"Has Dr. Price contributed to the reward money?"

Vivy turned to Owen to ask if he knew. But before he could answer someone else shouted.

"Do you regret the decision to invite outsiders to witness your most personal moments?"

"What do you say to those who argue that showcasing your girls on television was a tragic decision?"

"Wait! What?" Kik was briefly sidetracked but then got hold of herself. "Look, all of you! Please! We are shattered. *Shattered.* Our baby girl is miss — "

The word lodged in her throat like she was choking on a piece of food.

Everyone fell silent. The running engine of a satellite truck revved. Bean barked inside the house. Snow crunched beneath boots as weight shifted.

"Mom?" Doone whispered.

Finally, Kik swallowed and soldiered on. "I know you could fill a book with mistakes I've made. I've never pretended to be anything more than someone muddling through. But — please, please don't waste time analyzing us. Not now." She paused and shoved her bangs off her face and said, "I'm *begging* you to use your papers and news reports to help us find our little girl. There will be time for blame later. You can come after me then."

Doone, sobbing, moved forward and put her hand in Kik's.

Chastened, the reporters' questions started again, but they were quieter and without the self-righteous anger of hypocrisy. Despite the change in tone Casey felt lightheaded. She ducked back inside, pulled off her coat and dropped it on the hall bookcase. She was on the way to the bathroom when she heard a muffled chirp coming from her backpack. Amazed her cell phone was still charged, she dug it out. The display said unknown caller.

"Hello?"

"Hi."

Casey's stomach plunged into her thighs. "Tess?"

"Yes."

"Tess, where are you?" She was trying to sound calm while stumbling blindly into the kitchen where some cops were drinking coffee.

"Tess!" she repeated again for the cops' benefit and everyone froze. She went over to the detective closest to her and leaned into him so they could share the receiver. His breath smelled like cinnamon, a detail Casey would remember her whole life. "We're all so worried about you. Can you tell me where you are so we can come get you?"

"I think a church."

"Okay. Do you know what it's near?"

"I think another church."

"Are you in Charlottesville?"

"He never told me! We went over the mountain with your favorite view."

"Afton Mountain! Are you with a grown-up, Tess?"

"Not anymore. He said he was going to go get me another snack item but he did not come back this time. It was still dark. He told me not to go anywhere. Or use the phone. But I am doing disobedience."

"Can you see anybody else that you can ask for help?"

"No!" Tess started to cry. "I just want to come home, Casey!"

"Okay, that's okay. We'll find you. We're coming for you. Don't hang up, all right?"

The cop was talking excitedly into the mic on his uniform collar. He asked Casey for her cell number. She was so flipped it took her a while to remember. He repeated it to whoever he was speaking with and motioned her to keep talking.

"Everybody is going to be so relieved you're all right, Tessamessa. We've all been so worried."

"Bean, too?"

"Yes! He won't eat. He won't even chase that stupid squirrel!"

Suddenly Casey started freaking and slapped her hand on the mouthpiece in flat-out panic. "What if my battery goes dead? I can't remember the last time I charged the phone!"

"Tell her if you get disconnected for her to call back on the house phone."

Casey did. "Do you remember our house's phone number?"

"Of course I do!"

Casey laughed at the indignation. "Well, if my phone stops working, call back on the house number."

"Okay."

"Did he hurt you?"

Why did I ask that? I don't want to know!

"No. But he kept reading from the good book. All night long. And talking about the acropolis. It was scary. He said I needed to be saved. He needed to save me. He said the streets were going to get full of blood and that Mommy and Daddy's and yours and Doone's would be in it, too. Is that true?"

"No! He's a liar, Tess. None of that is true."

"He said Dr. Price told him to save me. He said he looked at him right through the TV and told me to. He made me pray with him."

"He told you a lot of lies."

"He said now I will not burn in hell. He had scary eyes."

Casey shuddered. "Let's not talk about that now."

The cop tapped her on the shoulder. "Ask if there's a lock on the door."

"Tess?" Casey's heart was again pounding so hard she thought she might faint. "Is there a lock on the door where you are?"

"Just come get me, Casey! Hurry! Please! I want to come home!"

"We're coming Tess! We are! Just look around and see if there's a lock. Don't hang up though!"

Tess put the phone down, knocking something over. She was snuffling when she came back on the line. "Casey, I got so scared I peed in my pants again."

"Of course you did, Tess! Who wouldn't? We'll bring you new stuff, okay?"

"Is Mommy there?"

The policeman motioned to another cop who went out to the porch. Everybody came bounding into the kitchen, pale and frenzied. The reporters outside were jolted alive behind them, yelling questions, their voices conciliatory now. Someone slammed shut the door, muting the noise.

Casey handed the phone to her mother.

Kik's hand shook so badly the cell bounced into her cheek. "Hi sweetie. Are you all right, my love?"

"Got it!" A cop yelled. "She's only up in Staunton! Tell her that policemen in real police cars are on the way. Tell her they'll get there first, but we're on the way! Tell her there will be sirens on real police cars. Get a bus to meet us there," he said to another cop. "They'll want to check her out at the hospital."

Casey squeezed Doone's arm and released it when she remembered her promise to bring Tess clean clothes. She ran upstairs and grabbed an armload from Tess's dresser, raced back down.

The family hustled out to the driveway, the press shouting questions; the policemen acting like the front line of a football team, pushing back. Kik kept talking into the cell, hunched over so she could hear above the noise.

"We're leaving, honey. All of us. We're getting into the police car right now. We'll be there in less time than one of your baths. Okay? You just have to wait a little bit more. I'm taking the phone in the car. But if it shuts out we'll still be there to get you. And you can call back on my phone or Daddy's. He's coming. We're all coming, sweetie. Your big sisters. And Vivy. And Parrish. And a nice police lady. Aunt Madomine's at the house making us breakfast. Is that good, sweetheart? Do you want chocolate chip pancakes? Pizza? Okay!" she laughed. "How many pieces?"

They were speeding over Afton Mountain when Owen asked for the phone. Kik was reluctant to let Tess go, but she handed it to him.

"Oh, little bear," he said, weeping into the crook of his left arm. "We've been so worried."

Casey glanced past Doone. Through a gauze of tears she recognized a scene that had appeared like a woodcut on the glass. Her sister had finger-painted their house and yard in the window's condensation, drawing the path that wended its way between the live oaks all the way to the cozy cottage. Casey wondered how long the picture would remain, who would see it. She wondered what stories they would tell themselves about the family who lived inside.

Owen's speech grew paradoxically deeper and lighter. "Hey, guess what Casey found! Your barrette! The one you were looking for! Right, right! The one with the dimonts!" He listened to her response and laughed. "Yes, you can still get new ones anyway! What? Oh, okay, honey. Hold on."

Owen twisted as best he could in the crowded front seat.

"She wants you," he said, passing the cell back. Before releasing the phone he touched Doone's wrist, and smiled.

"Hi," her voice quivered like an old woman's. "Yes, I hear them, now. That means they'll be there in a minute. We're coming to get you, junior. You and Harperly. You'll be home soon."

Then Tess started chattering and Doone cradled closely the familiar patter. The phone caught her tears, one after the other.

Epilogue

"Where did I put that stupid thing?" Doone muttered, tearing through her bureau for the bathing suit she and Kik had shopped for, finally coming upon the black and white striped one-piece in the bottom of her underwear drawer. She pulled it out and held it up. Off, the suit looked fairly plain. On, you couldn't miss Doone's serious cleavage and tiny waist.

"This'll be the longest we've ever been apart," Casey observed.

"Will you miss me, Kappa Kappa?"

The old nickname. *Minus the venom.*

"Yes," Casey said. "I will. Hey, Doone? How do you think it will be with Hank all summer?" Casey had recently begun worrying that something bad could happen between them and then her sister would have a setback.

"I'm not stressing. I like Hank and I like art. I'm going to take it as it comes."

Wow, Casey thought, envying the equanimity. "Hey, did you see that article yesterday? *The Marcheson Effect?*"

"Why do you keep torturing yourself with that crap?"

"I don't know," Casey said honestly. "It was a good one, though."

"What'd it say?"

"That getting help shouldn't be a spectator sport. That what happened to us should mark the beginning of the end of televised family therapy. People are talking about passing laws."

"That's cool," Doone said, putting a sweatshirt into the large duffel bag.

"Do you ever wonder how things would have been if Lermon hadn't killed himself? Like if there had to have been a trial and everything?"

"No," Doone said emphatically. She turned to look at her sister. "And I really think you should try and stop obsessing so much. Let. It. Go."

"I'm trying!" Casey said defensively, clenching her toes.

Tess appeared in the doorway wearing overalls with no shirt. Her hair was still wrangled in the two braids that Vivy had managed during the girls' last visit. Concern was crinkling the six year-old's eyes. "I have a very important question."

"Yes?" Casey prompted.

"How do you know when fishes are really done being hungry? Uncle Parrish said to not give them too much food but what if I am not giving *enough*? They always just do the same things."

"Parrish read you the directions," Casey answered. "People who spend their whole lives studying the perfect number of flakes-per-fish wrote them."

"But how do they know that one fish is not taking the other one's?" Tess asked dubiously.

Doone changed the subject rather than getting sucked into a whole discussion in this vein. "Have you thought of names yet?"

"Yes. Harperly One and Harperly Two. Since the *real* Harperly moved to New York. This way I can remember her."

"Good plan," Casey said.

"Because weird," Doone added.

"What?" Tess demanded, dangerously.

"Joking, junior." Doone stepped inside the closet.

"Do you think Uncle Parrish lives here now, Casey?" Tess asked. "He is here most of the nights."

"Kind of. But it's good, right?"

"Well, of course it is good. I was just curious. It is like having two daddies."

"Just don't call him Uncle Daddy, please," Doone said, coming back into the room with an armload of smocks.

"Who will take your turn to sleep with me when you are away at camp?" Tess asked her.

"Everybody else," Doone answered. *For like the twentieth time.*

"But then, when you come home you will take your turn, right?"

"Yep. By then though, you may not want anybody in there anymore."

"Oh, I do not think so," Tess announced. "And anyway, the last time Mom and I went to see Dr. Max he said I could have company for as long as I want."

Bean and Orbison bounded into the room, immediately followed by Kik. She was still wearing her nightclothes, her dark hair in a loose bun on the top of her head. She'd been up writing for hours. "Hola, chickadees."

"How's the work going, Mom?" Casey asked.

"I'm getting there, I think. I can see the finish line anyway."

The book had taken shape one night while she was sleeping. It was a roman à clef about her and Maddie's growing-up years with Shelby called *Coming of Rage*. The editor, the guy who contacted her all the way back in the fall, had secured a healthy advance. And Kik wasn't too worried about having to pay it back this time.

She was under no illusion that the post-publication buzz would be amplified by the family's ordeal. Especially since that horrible woman called —

while Tess was missing!

— to offer a freaking book deal. But Kik also believed her work was good. Good enough, anyway, to tell Martin Shuster that she was going to be taking time off from teaching.

The wind blew suddenly and a leafy branch brushed the window, rousing last winter's terror from its nap. She inhaled sharply.

"Mom?" Casey said, alarmed.

"I'm fine! Just a twinge."

"Are you sure?" Doone asked.

"Totally."

Anything could trigger the panic. But Kik was coping. She took another deep breath and made her way around the room, hugging each of her girls as close as she could, one after the other.

Acknowledgements

…ly, Jason, Zack, Maggie Ryan and Asa. Up to the sky and …vn again. And all the sands on the beach. Baba and Lynn, …ie and Sarah, Heather and Noah. Eden and Brandon. …nnah, Tommy, Teetah, Mariah, Boman, Daisy. Jedd, Sarah. …m and Jonny. So much. And my mom, who left too soon. …na, Bobbie, Tammy, Gary, Emmet, Mary, Scott, Satzes, …alids and Helen. Alperovitzes. Barnets, Cynthia, Raskins and …iedmans, Wellses, Lopatins, Crumbs, Blooms and Maurers … …mily who are friends and friends who are family … Deborah, …mmie, Ginny, Richard, Debbie, Honour, Lynn, Paul, Kelly, …ate, Hal, Milams, Bob, Carol, Bill. Chens, Bruce, Norwoods, …oxanne, Wrights. Lora. Landa, Kizzie. O'Beirnes. Wanda, …ebdie and Debbie. Fulton Hill crew. The solace of shared …istory and enduring tenderness. Kee, from 9 on. Ann and all of …ny Kings, Clairebear and Jutay, surrogates. The others I've …watched grow — Sarahdoyle. KayKay, Dukes, Kate CM, …Carolann, Abbie, DPs, Iantoscas, Moviuses. The amazing wordsmiths in my world. Alice. Meg, LLL, Ginger and the OGFY group, the Little High Writers – Lisa, Patty, Patrice, Janice, Stephanie, Susan x 2, Jen. Martha. Cullens and Kathleen. The Virginia Center for the Creative Arts. Beryl. Christian. Brian, for other reasons. Larry, Sascha and Charlotte. Thank you.

…and to Keith, my love since I was eighteen. You are my forever home. I am so grateful.

PS The inherent danger of personalized shout-outs is leaving someone out. I'm already cringing. Forgive me.

More books from Harvard Square Editions:

CPSIA information can be obtained
at www.ICGtesting.com
Printed in the USA
FFOW02n1306081014
7872FF